U0165789

Chinese English

英漢 對譯
實務與習作

中英文讀、寫、譯的新視野

葉乃嘉　著

五南圖書出版公司 印行

推薦序

翻譯與創作哪個比較容易？
對於這個問題，魯迅說：[1]

　　極平常的豫想，也往往會給實驗打破。我向來總以爲翻譯比創作容易，因爲至少是無須構想。但到真的一譯，就會遇著難關，譬如一個名詞或動詞，寫不出，創作時候可以回避，翻譯上卻不成，也還得想，一直弄到頭昏眼花，好像在腦子裏面摸一個急於要開箱子的鑰匙，卻沒有。嚴又陵說：「一名之立，旬月躊躇。」是他的經驗之談，的的確確的。

而我則建議參考以下答案：
1.要是你兩種能力兼具，不妨自己比較一下。
2.要是你願意花時間朝兩方面之一發展，功夫花得多的一面自然熟能生巧，日見其易。
3.要是你缺了一方面的經驗，那你與其花時間來辯證，還不如花時間去體驗。

　　中英對譯是對翻譯工作者兩種語文綜合能力的考查，譯者應該具有兩種語文的堅實基礎，注意體會兩種語文之間的差異，掌握翻譯過程中常用的技巧，才可能具有較可觀的翻譯能力來譯出能保全原作價值的好作品，譯者必須對原文與譯入文都要有深入的了解，應該要求譯入文準確完整，符合譯入文的表達習慣，因此，譯者應該注意訓練自己的譯入文表達能力，還要樂於字斟句酌地推敲琢磨。

　　葉乃嘉教授長期受到美國文化的薰陶，對中英文字的經營有深入的探索，是真正在這兩種文字上均有創作功力的極少數學者

1　摘自魯迅，《且介亭雜文二集》「題未定」草一，《文學》月刊第五卷第一號，1930/10。

之一。對於英漢文字中涉及文化的部分，葉教授比一般的翻譯工作者更具有直覺性的了解，他鑑於兩岸都日漸國際化，遂依據多年的雙語工作經驗，寫出這本不可多得的《英漢雙向翻譯實務與習作》，歸納主要的翻譯原則，並且舉出很多條例，分別加以評述。書中舉出一些中英對譯的例子，具體說明作者的翻譯理念，即翻譯時，宜靠近譯入文，以譯入文的讀者為中心，並著重原文?容的翻譯。互譯特點不盡相同的兩種語言，正是翻譯工作者的困難所在，只有掌握了兩種文字的特點和異同，翻譯起來才會得心應手。

　　《英漢雙向翻譯實務與習作》的第一篇為翻譯工作的綜合講述，將從事翻譯工作應有的考量、翻譯的一般過程以及常見翻譯問題的處裡等，分章扼要敘述，第二篇是翻譯實務，提供了十餘篇演講、心靈、學術、文藝、科技、管理、法規、合約及企劃等類文章的中英雙向對譯實例，第三篇則是輔助翻譯的「幫手」，列了英文俗常贅詞的簡化實例、翻譯英文俗語和常用句的中譯、以及中文成語和俗常用句的英譯等一千八百餘條目。全書對僵硬的翻譯理論著墨不多，而其取材之廣泛，則為翻譯類工具書中所少見。

　　葉君十年來出版的近二十本專書中，風格大都不太傳統，他不太中意過於嚴肅的事情，故行文之間，時涉幽默，寫作的雖是專業書籍，卻也多充滿趣味，《英漢雙向翻譯實務與習作》內容豐富，結構完整，舉例清晰，邏輯分明，不論對於初涉翻譯者、或是在生涯上必須和翻譯工作結緣的人士，都可說是最佳的參考書。個人在學界多年，對書中學術論文類的英譯部分頗感興趣。有幸先讀為快，對於個人翻譯的能力大有裨益，特此向大家特別推薦。

明道大學通識中心主任

蕭雅柏　謹識

2012/9/15

目　錄

第一篇

基礎與方法

本篇大要

第一章
綜談翻譯工作

本章提綱

1.1 信達雅新談

自嚴復立論以來，翻譯的目標就是「信、達、雅」，即「忠實、通順、優雅」。然而，能做到對原文忠實、譯文明白順暢就已經很好了，要譯文的文字優雅，談何容易。

有人認為，要把原文的結構與字彙完全不漏地轉譯出來，才算忠實，但是，如果為了要遷就原文的結構與字彙，而把譯文搞得文理不通，以致看了彆扭到難以卒讀的程度，怎麼還稱得上是忠實？請看下例：

From any given point of your existence, however, you can glimpse other probable **realities**, and sense the reverberations of probable actions beneath those physical decisions that you make. Some people have done this spontaneously, often in the dream state. Here the rigid assumptions of normal waking consciousness often fade, and you can find yourself performing those physically rejected

activities, never realizing that you have peered into a probable existence of your own.[1]

譯文一：

　　……由你存在的任何一點上，你可以瞥見到這些其他的可
能實相[2]，而感覺到在你所做的那些實際決定之下，那些可能行
動的回響。有些人自發地這麼做，通常是在夢境裡，此處正常
醒時的死板假定常常會淡掉，而[3]你會發現自己正在做你實際上
排除了的那些行動，卻絕沒想到你已經窺探進自己的一個可能
的存在了。[4]（138字）

　　譯文一採用的是以原文（英文）為中心的譯法，譯者想把原文中的
每一字都照顧到，因此疊了一堆不太搭調的字詞，這些字詞在原文裡本
來配合得還算不失其所，但是轉成中文之後卻累累贅贅，彆扭得難以判
讀，翻譯的目的既然是在引介作品給不諳原文的讀者，這種被原文逼迫

1　摘自 Roberts, Jane, "Seth Speaks: The Eternal Validity of the Soul," Reprint Edition, New World Library,
　June 1994.

2　*Reality* 有個眾所周知的意思，就是「現實」，把 *reality* 譯成實相，該文譯者似是始作俑者。這種
　譯法有點難知所云，因為一般辭彙中並沒有「實相」一辭，佛經中的「實相」則另有所指，乃是
　「不變的狀態」之意，非如 *reality* 一般時時在變，可是如今許多失察者紛紛跟進，*reality* 因此竟
　成了「實相」，混淆了佛經中「實相」的原始意義，識者見狀，大嘆無力，此皆一盲引眾盲之過
　也，其實，直接把 *reality* 譯成「現實」，表示「現在是事實」，再也洽當不過，實在不用另闢蹊
　徑。又，*reality* 也有「現實世界」之意，再不然，將他譯成「境界」，也遠比譯成「實相」更為
　傳神而易解。

3　考察該文譯者的其他譯作，其習慣性地把 *and* 翻譯成「而」，許多別的譯者亦復如是，像這種套
　公式似的譯法固然方便，也不妨說是不用頭腦，其實 *and* 在此乃是虛字，大可不譯。

4　摘自《靈魂永生》，王季慶譯自 "Seth Speaks: The Eternal Validity of the Soul"，方智出版社，
　2002/4。

得無暇照顧讀者的翻譯方式，所要達到的目的，也就相當有限。

譯文二：

在你有生之年的任何時刻裏，你隨時都會與其他的或然世界有著各種程度的接觸，同時還能感覺到在自己實際行動背後的各種「可能性」的暗潮。這種事情發生在很多人身上，但這通常都在睡覺做夢的時候。人在睡夢中的時候，他那種固執的人間意識通常都會消淡下去，而在這個時候，你往往會發現自己正在走著原來已被自己排除了的路。可是，問題是你永遠不會想到其實你所看到的正是自己某一個或然的部分。[5]（183字）

譯文二是以譯入文（中文）為中心的譯法，比譯文一多了 45 個字，將近 30% 的篇幅，內容似乎加了些解說的味道。有人認為，要做到忠實原文，就應該掌握好適度的原則，既不改變和歪曲，也不增加或刪減，要把原文的內容準確完整地表達出來，根據這個標準，譯文二確實是稍稍踰越了翻譯的範圍。但是，毫無疑問的，它比譯文一要流暢易懂得多了，可以列入「達」之列。

譯文三：

你在陽世隨時都能窺入他方世界[6]，同時還能感受到隱伏在你實際行動後的各種隱性事件[7]的影響。有些人（通常在做夢的

5　摘自《時空之外》，胡英音與王育盛合譯自"Seth Speaks: The Eternal Validity of the Soul"。
6　除了人類在清醒時的意識所能感受到的這個世界之外，還有正常意識所偵測不到，但與此世界平行或共存的其他許多「異次元境界」，叫做 *probable reality, probable world* 或 *probable universe*，最貼近華人文化的譯名，就是「他方世界」。
7　人生充滿了抉擇，譬如，選擇了出國，就沒有留在國內，於是，我們所未採取的行動就沒有在物質世界裡具體化，它們成了「隱性事件」，存在於「他方世界」，由我們的分身去執行。

時候）自動就已經這樣做，人在睡夢中，強固的清醒意識通常
會減弱，這時，你會發現自己做著你實質上已經棄之不做的活
動，可卻絕沒想到，其實你所看的正是自己某個分身[8]的演出。
（135 字）

　　本文兼顧了原文和譯入文，字數與譯文一不相上下，而其可讀性卻
不輸譯文二，只是，對於原文主題不熟的讀者，可能需要先做點功課才
能體會到譯者的用心，因為他選用了幾個需要另加解釋的名詞，而這也
是無可厚非的，由於原文乃是節錄自一本數十萬字的厚書，怎麼可能期
望用短短的百來字就讓讀者進入狀況呢？因此，雖非「信達」兼備，亦
算是「信達」兼而有之。

　　其實，「信、達、雅」三個評量譯事的標準，都不應出以「是」或
「否」的二分法，而宜以程度來判別，即，評審者或讀者實在不應該只
說某譯文「忠實或不忠實」、「通順或不通順」、「優雅或不優雅」，
而應該用量表的方式來表述自己對該譯作的相對觀感。

　　量表形式所在多有，其中一個比較有名的，乃是李克特氏量表
（Likert Scale，或稱李氏量表），李氏量表廣泛應用在社會與行為研究
中，乃適用於態度測量和意見判定的一種測量格式，此量表有一個基本
假設，即數位與數位之間的距離是相同的，以五點等距量表來說，每個
問卷題目的答項從「極同意」到「極不同意」分為五個選項，依序給予
5 分到 1 分，在這一假設下，不同的題目可以加總，得到一個量表的總
分。此類量表之量度有奇偶數之分，奇數量度的目的在於提供一個中立
的選項，偶數量度則在使答卷者無法保持中立，非得選邊不可，而這兩

8　人除了自己在清醒時的意識所能感受到的存在狀態之外，還有非自己正常意識所能偵測得到的其
　他許多身份和狀態，這些另類的存在體就叫做 *probable existence* 或 *probable self*，最貼近華人文
　化的譯名，就是「分身」。

種方式各有適用的情況，應依問卷者的需要來選用。

　　茲仿照李氏量表的模式製出一個十點等距量表，供讀者用以評量自己對本書中出現的各個譯文的滿意度，當然亦不妨用以評量日後所見的任何譯事。

表 1-1　譯文滿意度量表

	極同意									極不同意
	10	9	8	7	6	5	4	3	2	1
1. 該譯文忠實（信）程度										
2. 該譯文通順（達）程度										
3. 該譯文優雅（雅）程度										

1.2 創作與翻譯

　　創作的確是不容易的，創作者要能寫出好作品，就必須有相當的生活體驗、能收集到足夠動人的寫作素材，還必須有水準以上的表達技巧。翻譯也同樣不簡單，翻譯者要具有較可觀的翻譯能力，要譯出能保全原作價值的好作品，就必須對原文（Source Language）與譯入文（Target Language）都要有深入的了解，還要樂於字斟句酌地推敲琢磨。

　　創作和翻譯各有要求，很難斷說孰難孰易。

　　余光中先生認為，創作是從抽象的感覺到具象的文字，翻譯也是一種創作，是一種有條件的創作，翻譯文學作品，譯者首先要熟悉文字語言、背景，加上自身的感受寫出譯文。

　　二十世紀初，很多西洋名詞進入中文世界的時候，都還停留在直接音譯的原始階段，但中文不是拼音文字，不能像日韓等文在轉譯西文時一樣，因陋就簡地在自己文字裡找不到對應詞時，就以類似*德謨克拉*

西、賽恩斯和煙士披裏純[9]的「外來語」方式處理。如果這樣，那麼今天的中譯文一定停留在像當年那樣慘不忍睹的階段。還好，因為中文的獨立性，「因特網」這種譯名終究敵不過「網際網路」[10]，「伊媚兒」也只好給「電子郵件」讓路。

翻譯就像這樣，是從一種具象的文字到另一種具象文字的過程，實際上也就是再創作（Re-creation）的過程。

一九九〇年代，筆者在美居住，兩個孩子在幼兒階段都還能用母語溝通，之後他們開始上學，受到大環境的影響，漸漸偏離華語，我們雖然也送他們到中文學校就讀，無奈，非正規學制的中文學校只在周末有兩個小時的課，絕難擋得住「番邦」正規教育的優勢，我們於是眼見孩子們漸漸失去以母語交流的能力。先別說在英美等國，即使是身在華人世界的孩子們，也深受歐美文化及卡通影片的影響。由於西方文化長久處於優勢，至少有三個世代以來的國人從小就有機會浸潤在西方的兒童故事中，在灰姑娘、白雪公主、睡美人、米老鼠等的薰陶下成長，我們的古典故事對新一代華人青年的影響，根本不敵西方神話和卡通的衝擊，直到 1998 年，花木蘭的故事才經由狄斯耐（Disney）的引介，進入西方世界。

可是，我們的英雄又豈只是木蘭而已，魏晉的搜神、誌怪，唐的傳奇和明清以來類似聊齋誌異的小說等，全都充滿了想像與神異的空間，值得分享給西方讀者。對於那些古典小故事的偏愛，促使我集合了其中一些精采的內容，一方面希望給自己的孩子們介紹點自家文化的東西，一方面也想在東來的西潮中注入一道西向的回流，我就是基於這樣的心意，著手將這些故事的主人翁們以移花接木的方式，把故事發生的時代

---

9 *Democracy, science, and inspiration*，前兩字還有戲翻成「德先生」與「賽先生」者。

10 比較起來，「萬維網」才算是 World Wide Web 的信達雅中譯，而說到了涵蓋 WWW 的 Internet，「互聯網」這個譯名要比「網際網路」要中文化得多了。

用乾坤大挪移的手法，「再創作」了一部英文小說 *The Legend of Two Heros*[11]。

　　以下所錄的故事——*The Adventure of Lee*，就是節錄自該小說中的一章。如今，我以原作者的身分，把它翻成中文，來交代一下自己翻譯與再創作的歷史背景。

原文	中譯
... Quickly the third day arrived. Everything was as quiet as usual. Nothing had taken place during the day. And soon it was about midnight. As a well-trained martial artist, Lee was very alert. He locked the door, bolted the window, put off the candle, and went to bed with his sword. Just when he was about to fall asleep, Lee heard a scratchy noise coming from the window. He opened his eyes quietly. In the moonlight, a small, maple leaf leaf shaped thing slipped through the slit of the window. The thing tumbled down slowly like a falling leaf. Upon reaching the floor it started to grow. Quickly the thing was at its full size. It looked like a man wearing a white robe and carrying a long spear. 　　Without giving a chance for the thing to	……第三天很快就到了，一切平靜如常，白天沒有事故發生，不久到了半夜，李生武藝精熟，極為警覺，他鎖上門，閂緊窗戶，把蠟燭吹熄，帶著劍上床睡覺，就在將睡未睡的時候，聽到窗外傳來一陣窸窣聲，他靜靜睜開雙眼，月光下，一片小小的、楓樹葉子形狀的東西從窗縫裡穿進來，像落葉一樣，搖搖蕩蕩地往下飄，一落地就開始長大，很快就完全長成，模樣好像一個穿著白袍、帶著一把長矛的

---

11 原文曾在美國 Asian Gazette 上連載，中文暫譯「趙李傳奇」。

get ready, Lee jumped out of his bed and lunged at it with his sword. The thing rolled over and avoided the contact. It jumped high in the air and started to contract. Soon, it shrank down to a size no bigger than Lee's hand. As the thing was trying to slip out through the window slit, Lee leapt forward to strike another blow. The intruder was struck and wobbled down to the floor. Lee lit the candle and lean forward to examine the thing. It was a paper dummy cut in two pieces.

Just as Lee walked back to his bed, there came a loud crash. A fearsome man broke through the window. The man landed and spun around. Lee lunged at the man with his sword. The man parried Lee's stroke. They thrust at each other, seeking an advantage. All at once, Lee found an opening. He jumped forward and chopped the intruder with his sword. The intruder fell on the floor. Lee approached his enemy carefully to take a good look. It turned out to be a clay figure broken into pieces.

Right then a shriek came in from the courtyard. The house started to shake violently as if it would lose its foundation very soon. Lee

人。

　　不待那東西準備好，李生就從床上跳起來，拔劍向它戳去，那東西滾身避開這一擊，高高跳到空中，開始縮小，不一會兒，就縮得不比李生的巴掌大，正當它要打窗縫溜出去，李生跳前去又是一劍，那個不速之客中劍，搖搖晃晃，倒在地上，李生點亮蠟燭，屈身向前細看那東西，原來是個被砍成兩半的紙人。

　　正當李生走回床去，一聲巨響，一個長相可怕的傢伙穿破窗而入，落地之後就打起轉來，李生提劍朝他刺去，那人擋開李生一劍，兩人互擊，乘隙爭先，忽然，李生虛空縱向前去，一劍砍向來犯者，來犯者跌倒在地，李生小心翼翼接近來敵細看，原來是個破成一塊塊

kicked the door open and jumped out of the room. In the courtyard, there stood a monstrous creature as tall as the house. The creature carried a bow. Its huge face was colorfully painted. Its eyes gleamed with yellow light. Upon Lee's appearing, the giant uttered a bloodcurdling roar, then whipped an arrow out of his quiver and fitted it to the bow. It took aim and shot the arrow toward Lee. Lee briskly fended it off with his sword. The second arrow came Lee's way quickly. Lee dodged the shot and the arrow hissed into the wall behind him.

The monster missed Lee twice and became very mad. It unsheathed a huge cutlass and rushed at Lee with a bellow that shook the rooftop. As a proven mas ter of fencing art, Lee dodged and swung back at the monster with his sword. The monster, compared to Lee, was slow and awkward with such a giant body. Every time it missed Lee, the blade hit the bricks on the ground and broke them into pieces, which scattered far apart with sparkles. Lee leapt between the giant's legs and drove his sword into the giant's ankle. The giant was hurt and became so furious that it shrieked fiercely

的泥人。

那當兒，中庭又傳來一聲尖叫，房子劇烈搖動，好像房基馬上就快要垮掉似的，李生踢開門，跳出房，中庭裡站著一個跟房子一樣高的巨怪，這怪帶著弓，巨臉上塗得五顏六色，眼閃黃光，李生一出現，巨怪就發出令人血為之凝的巨吼，從箭壺裡抽出一隻箭搭上弓，瞄準李生就是一箭，李生輕巧用劍擋開來箭，第二箭又很快朝李生射來，李生矮身閃過，那箭嘶一聲射中了牆壁。

那怪兩次不中，惱怒之下，拔出一把大刀，聲震屋瓦地大叫一聲，衝向李生，李生劍術精熟，閃躲還擊，那怪跟李生比起來，身形巨大，動作笨拙緩慢，每次沒有砍中李生，刀口就撞在地上，把

and swung its cutlass madly. Lee jumped left and right, up and down to avoid those powerful blows. Finally Lee managed to spring and cling to the giant's back. Time and again, he plunged in his sword. The monster fell down, twisted a few times, then moved no more. Lee stroked the monster with the sword again and again until finally he himself was exhausted and collapsed on the ground.

Moments later, as Lee pulled himself up wearily, he found that the monster had shrunk. Not bigger then Lee himself, it was just a wooden puppet full of cuts.

Lee stepped back to his room. Though exhausted, he held onto his sword and tried to get ready for another fight. Knowing that one more attack like this would be fatal, he started to suspect there was someone behind these assaults.

Luckily, the rest of the night was quiet. The full moon shone high above in the sky. Wind breezed in through the broken window. Lee was not able to keep himself awake any more. He dozed in. With a few harmless nightmares, he finally survived the night.

石磚打得碎片紛飛，火花四散，李生跳到巨怪兩腿之間，把劍刺進巨怪的腳踝，巨怪受傷，暴怒狂叫，發瘋似的揮舞著大刀，李左跳右跳上跳下跳，閃避那些猛擊，最後飛身纏附在巨怪背上，一次又一次把劍刺進怪物身體，怪物倒下，抽了幾下就不動了，李生一劍又一劍砍在怪物身上，直到最後耗盡體力，倒在地上。

過了一會，李生虛弱地起身，發現怪物已經縮小成不比李生自己大，原來只是個全身刀痕的木偶。

李生走回房間，雖然疲倦，還是握著劍準備應付下一場戰鬥，心知要是再來一場像這樣的激戰，自己就沒命了，他開始懷疑有人在幕後主使這些暗算。

還好，下半夜總算平靜，滿月高掛天空，風透過破窗吹進來，李生再也沒法保持清醒，也就睡著了，他做了幾個惡夢，終算是平安熬過了這晚。

上面這段摘自 *The Adventure of Lee* 的片段，其原文和譯文都與翻譯和再創作有關。即令兼有了中英雙向互譯及中英文分別的創作經驗，我也很難斷說創作和翻譯孰難孰易。但是我的確有個肯定的答案，那就是，只要你樂在其中，再難的事，也會因其難而見其巧。

1.3 中英文表達力

互譯特點不盡相同的兩種語言時，只有掌握了兩種文字的特點和異同，翻譯起來才會得心應手。

英譯中時，應該要求中文準確完整，符合中文的表達習慣，因此，譯者應該注意訓練自己的中文表達能力。

中文在文字排列的次序方面，是比較自由的，但過於自由的結果，就不免鬆散，看看這個例子：

我們來討論四十個學校沒有教的寫作技巧。

這個句子翻成英文，可能有兩種相當不同的意思，其中第一種是：

Let's discuss the writing techniques not taught by 40 schools.

　　誰會這麼有心去調查，沒有教某某寫作技巧的，到底是哪四十個學校呢？依直覺判斷，數詞「四十個」所描述的，應該是「寫作技巧」，而不是「學校」。

　　在英文裡，任何修飾詞（Modifier）都得連著該詞所要修飾的對象，因此，上句中文例句比較合理的意思應該是：

> Let's discuss the 40 writing techniques not taught in schools.

　　所以，如果要表達得比較精確些，就應該把上面的句子改寫如下，才比較沒有語意上的困擾：

　　我們來討論學校沒有教的四十個寫作技巧。

　　但是，第一個中文例句的表達方式也屬常見，不全算是有錯，它在語意上雖然有點含混，我們還是可以判別其真正的涵義。而下面這個例子可能就比較費解了：

　　以下要宣佈三個同學沒有注意的原則。

　　不知到底說的是「三個同學」呢還是「三個規定」？在前後文中雖然可能釐清，但是，為免造成不必要的混淆，文字畢竟是精確些才好。

　　在英文中似乎沒有同樣的問題，因為英文裡根本就沒有「以下要宣佈三個同學沒有注意的原則」這種句法。

We will announce the three rules that students did not follow.

We will announce the three students who did not follow the rule.

分別譯成中文，就是：

1. 以下要宣佈同學沒有注意的三個原則
2. 以下要宣佈的原則，有三個同學沒有注意

除了在翻譯小說、劇本等類文字時，必須把其中人物說話時遣詞用語的習慣表現出來以外，高明的翻譯者應該有能力判別原文作者以原文表達的能力。

如果一意以為老美、老英等英語系國家的人寫出來的英文一定沒什麼毛病可挑，那就太過天真了。文字能力不足不光是本地的專利，更是國際性的問題，這種情形在網路上最為多見，中英文皆然，

我們且從身邊一些鬆散的句子中，找出某些作者無法使用精確中文來表達的例證，先看第一個例子：

　　當你將壓縮檔存放路徑設定為軟碟（如 A 磁碟機）時，便能啟動多重磁片之功能，讓一個數 MB 的大檔能夠分割成數片低容量的磁片，方便檔案的轉移。（64 字）

注意下文中*粗斜體*的部份。

首先，「當」是中文西化的產物[12]，在中文裡有不如無。其次，像「*讓一個*數 MB 的大檔*能夠*……」這個句子，除了多堆疊幾個字，讓句子更長而無當之外，把文字搞成這樣實在沒有特別的道理。

最後這個問題比較小，「檔案的轉移」只是多了一個贅字。

綜上所述，我們可以把上例修改成短了將近 15% 的：

---

12 參見第 3.6 節「關係代名詞與疑問代名詞的處理」中對 when 的解說。

　　將壓縮檔存放路徑設定爲軟碟（如 A 磁碟機），便能啓動多重磁片的功能，把數 MB 大的檔分割至數片低容量的磁片，方便檔案轉移。（56字）

　　說話的時候，話似乎自然出口，仔細想時，竟不知這些話是怎樣組合而成，甚至連如何開始，如何結束都不太覺察。像這樣說話不打草稿，沒有多餘的時間可以潤飾，因此它結構儘管鬆散些，也無可厚非。但是，寫作就必須比說話精確得多，因為，任何端上檯面見人的作品，事前都已經有機會加以修飾，如果品質還是像不經心就脫口而出的話一樣，就有點不負責任了。

　　再看幾個累贅或不精確的句子：

3. 將此選項圈選
4. 這對於現代的知識人而言，已經不能作爲藉口
5. 也對它的用處和用法不十分明瞭
6. 就一定要對市場上的商品進行全方位瞭解
7. 假使你有需要阻擋過大容量的信件的話
8. 可以在知識管理的訓練中，將自己各該方面的技能加以累積
9. 有時候我們經常的會收到一些沒有寄件者名稱或沒有收信者名稱的廣告垃圾信

——簡化之後就成了：

10. 圈選此項
11. 現代的知識人已經不能把這作爲藉口

12. 也不十分明瞭它的用處和用法
13. 就一定要全方位地瞭解市場上的商品
14. 假使你需要阻擋容量過大的信件
15. 可藉知識管理的訓練，累積自己各該方面的技能
16. 我們經常會收到些沒有寄件者或收信者名稱的垃圾信，
    或有時我們會收到些沒有寄件者或收信者名稱的垃圾信

最後且來討論一個日漸氾濫的語病，那就是「做……的動作」這種句型，如今已經到了成災地步，連寫作也受到牽連，例如：

我吃過飯第一件事就是進入書房開始做寫作的動作。
你要注意，最近上面隨時會來做查帳的動作。

至此，我倒要問問常常使用這種句型的朋友，「做吃飯的動作」到底有沒有吃飯？而「做跳樓的動作」又真的跳樓了沒有呢？

下面句子中的 wish to extend our wishes 就像「做……的動作」一樣累贅而無力：

We wish to extend our wishes for your success in the attainment of your career goals.

用行動動詞 attaining 代替 in the attainment of 之後，語勢就短小結實得多了：

We wish you success in attaining your career goals.

因此，何妨剷除「做……的動作」句型，把前述的例句改成：

我吃過早飯第一件事，就是進書房開始寫作。
你要注意，最近上面隨時會來查帳。

再看兩個英文表達方式不精確的例子：

The result of the experiment turned out to be quite a disappoint-ment.

I am giving authorization for you to release all my medical re-cords to ……

它們所表達的不外是：

1. The result of the experiment is disappointing.
2. I authorize you to release my medical records to ...

說了這麼多，我們的主題是：從事翻譯工作，難免會碰上一些原文本身就不太高明的例子，像下面那種出現在商務書信裡的贅句，你要怎麼翻呢？

I am grateful for the business you have seen fit to give our firm and am proud to have you as one of our customers.

怎麼樣？很頭痛吧！即使真的依原文逐字把上句翻譯出來，也不會有中文的味道。翻譯者應該有權利、也有能力照顧自己譯文的品質，所

以，我們不妨先理清該句的頭緒：

> I am grateful for your business and am proud to have you as our customer.

再把它翻成：

感激您的惠顧，也高興有您做我們的客戶。

回頭看看中翻英的情況，請看下面這段中文研究論文的摘要：

「品質成本制」強調藉由[13]「成本揭露與報告」的模式，可使「品管相關作業」獲得有效的績效評估與稽核管理，並促成品質經濟化與效率化的目標[14]，一舉解決企業多年來品質與成本無法兼顧的困擾，而備受歐、美產業界所重視，同時也引起國內[15]部分廠商對品質成本制（Costs of Quality）的注意與引進實施。本研究採實證研究的方式，針對國內前五百大製造業，首先進行「品質成本實施程度」之狀況調查，再繼之探討國內企業的品質成本實施模式。依本研究對國內製造業實施品質成本模式，以及品質成本實施程度，調查結果有[16]：國內五百大製造業品質成本制度之推行現況、品質成本資料之蒐集與彙整模式與品質成本管理體系之執行現狀。（276字）

---

13 把相同詞性的詞堆疊起來而未使用適當的標點符號。

14 遣詞累贅，語意纏夾。

15 在論文中提及所屬國家或單位時，宜使用其所屬國名或單位的名稱，不然，像「國內」一詞翻譯成英文的 domestic 時，就不知所指的是哪個國家了。

16 句子不完整（incomplete sentence）。

　　短短的文章裡，出現了句子不完整和主詞不明的問題，還有些無助於文意的、堆疊起來的名詞或動詞。很多以中文寫的論文都有這類的毛病，文字不中不西，沒有掌握到西方文字的優點，卻又失去了中文的原味，所謂的「邯鄲學步」，就是這種情形的寫照。

　　如果你是翻譯者，你要怎麼翻這一段呢？

　　照著原文硬譯嗎？

　　那你的譯文會好到哪裡去？

　　其實，應該先理清原文的準確意義：

　　　品質成本制（Costs of Quality, COQ）強調，藉由成本揭露與報告的模式，可以有效稽核管理品管相關作業並評估其績效，從而促成品質的經濟化與效率化，解決企業無法兼顧品質與成本的困擾，因此，COQ 備受歐美產業界所重視，台灣部分廠商對其亦加以注意，並且開始引進實施。本研究採實證研究的方式，調查了台灣五百大製造業品質成本實施的模式及程度，得出其品質成本之 1)制度推行現況，2)資料蒐集與彙整模式，與 3)管理體系執行現狀等調查結果，並分項探討之。（196字）

　　原文的毛病清除之後，只剩下約三分之二的篇幅，而且文意清楚得多了，翻譯起來不再那麼費力，譯文的品質也比較容易掌握：

　　"Cost of Quality Reporting" emphasizes that through "Cost Relevance Reporting" the quality management related operations are more suitable for the effective performance evaluation and audit management. This, in turn, helps to improve business efficiency while at the same time taking care of both the quality and the cost issues in business. The Costs of Quality system (COQ) has long been recognized by the industries in Europe and the United States. Some Taiwan enterprises have also started to pay attention to COQ and its implementation.

This research uses the Empirical Study method to survey COQ implementation status in 500 local manufacturers. The study reveals the surveyed objects' COQ implementation status, COQ information collection and compilation as well as their COQ management system execution.

　　上面那段中文摘要在修正以前，雖然小有瑕疵，但是還不算離譜，請看看下面這個真正難以解讀的句子：

　　作為主體性的最高級形態，類主體性的基本特性是以主體間性核心所形成的整體性。

　　光是看到就足以使人望之卻步了，遑論將它翻譯出來？又，或許這句話就是從哪個外國文字裡翻譯出來的吧？！總之，我可以確定它不是中文。

　　下面這篇文字也是疊床架屋，難以解碼：

　　自然語言理解研究本質上應當是獨立於具體的語言的。筆者不太相信脫離自然語言理解研究的全局而能夠單獨或超前取得漢語理解研究的突破。但以漢語為母語的學者又有責任也有優勢以漢語為主要物件對自然語言理解的一般規律進行研究，

從而為解決人類共同的科學難題做出貢獻。當研究漢語理解時，首先著力於指稱概念的實詞是理所當然的，但也不能輕視虛詞在漢語句子、談話、篇章中表達意義的作用。本文探討虛詞在漢語理解研究中的價值及其研究方法，倡議建設與北大其他語言知識庫可以有機結合的廣義虛詞知識庫，提出了構建這個知識庫的一些想法。

舉出這個例子的意思，是要提醒翻譯人員，在把英文翻譯成中文時，也該有能力辨認出原文品質的良窳，因為，不是所有英語國家人士所寫出來的英文都是通得過文筆檢驗的，當然，其文字結構也不見得經得起常態的分析。君不見上文這種「外星式」的中文就是老中所寫的嗎？

所以大家要是碰上實在太難解讀的英文，也可以不用一個勁兒地照常理去解析其中的句構，我們只要對自己的英文程度有信心，也不妨朝「原文本身文理不通」的方向去找出路，免得多費功夫做無益的掙扎。

另外，還有一個如鯁在喉的議題在此一併提出。

台灣、中國大陸、乃至於整個華人地區，語文不分的問題普遍存在，到處都是「說中文、說英文、說日文」的說法，網路上充斥的、大學裡開課的課名都像「英語應用文、商用英語寫作、英語閱讀能力」那樣語文不分，使得內行人既氣惱又無可奈何，因此海外也免不了有教講華語的「中文學校」，大眾傳播裡不乏「OO 中文廣播電台、OO 視中文台」。

其實，出之於口的叫作「語」，筆之於書的才是「文」，本來是再清楚不過的，但是因為大家以訛傳訛，結果，連中文系所的師生中，搞不懂「語」和「文」分別者也所在多有。

原來，這個「語、文」混淆的來源，可能是 *English*，英文或英語，

原文都是 *English*，本來就沒有像「中文、華文」和「漢語、華語」的分別，始作俑者也許是一時不察，又也許是覺得無所謂，因此也就說起「英文」、寫起「英語」來，*Chinese* 也漸漸受影響，說「中文」的就越來越多了。

　　每次聽到人家開口「說中文」，都有好心更正，但是耳聞眼見，在在都是這種「語病」和「文病」的氾濫，也只好默默祈禱，希望以後不會變本加厲，出現說「廣東文、上海文或閩南文」的情形發生，大家不說「華語、日語、英語」，也只好由他去也。

　　不過話說回來，從事文字工作的人，也許不見得個個都有能力促進文字的進化，那麼，盡點心力稍稍阻擋文字的退化，也是事所當為，所以，奉請大家師以授徒，長以教幼，嘗試說華語、說英語、說國語，改學英文應用文、商用英文寫作，促進英語聽力和英文閱讀能力，讓教講中國話的學校變成華語學校，大眾傳播界增設華語電（視）台，加播華語節目，千萬別再出現華語雜誌了。

　　這點「正名」的要求，實在不是吹毛求疵，想想看，譯事之難，千百倍於是，既然要從事翻譯，做的就是文字推敲的工作，宜有別於懶得判別、或無法分別到底是語還是文者。

　　嚴復[17]先生說到「定名之難」[18]，有謂：「一名之立，旬月踟躕，我罪我知，是存明哲。」

　　旨哉斯教。

---

17 嚴復（1853-1921），字又陵，又字幾道，福建閩侯人，清末啟蒙思想家、翻譯家，「譯事三難，曰信、曰達、曰雅。」即是他的名句。
18 嚴復，《天演論》「譯例言」。

1.4 本章習作

譯事信達雅評量習作

　　以下的原文是一篇學生論文計畫書的中文摘要，既然信達雅三個評量譯事的標準都應以程度來判別，而不宜用是／否的二分法，請用表 1-1 譯文滿意度量表，來表述你對此摘要英譯文的評量。

原文	英譯
本研究的目的在於： ‧探討各類型休閒農場資源應用現況。 ‧比較各類型休閒農場之消費者偏好之差異。 ‧探討休閒農場資源應用與消費者偏好之關聯。 ‧依照研究發現，提出供經營者在休閒農場資源規劃經營上之參考。 　　本研究擬將 B. Joseph Pine II 與 James H Gilmore (2003)對經濟形態所作的分類應用在休閒農場上，將農場分成農作生產休閒農場、農物販售加工休閒農場、客製服務休閒農場及主題體驗休閒農場，研究者將往訪所選定之休閒農場與負責	The purpose of this research is to: ‧Discuss how different types of leisure farms use their resources differently ‧Compare the preferences of the customers who visit each type of farms ‧Study the relationship between the way a leisure farm uses its resource and the preferences of its customers. ‧Provide the result of this research to the farm management as a reference for better business planning 　　This study will apply the economic conditions classified by B.

人，進行田野調查與深度訪談，以了解農場資源內涵，進而做現地觀察記錄，蒐集各農場資源項目、分佈、狀態、使用方式等第一手資料。並將訪談結果歸納分析，以作為問卷設計參考之依據。

　　本研究預期證明：

・農場資源的完善與否，會是吸引消費者之主因。

・消費者前往休閒農場後，結果若不如預期，會降低重遊意願。

　　研究結果可供消費者參考，裨其能依個人偏好，選擇適合農場從事休閒。

Joseph Pine II and James H Gilmore (2003) to categorize the leisure farms as 1) Agricultural Production Farms, 2) Agricultural Processing and Vending Farms, 3) Customer Service Oriented Farms, and 4) Theme Park Farms. The researcher will visit the chosen farms and their management for field investigation and indepth interview so as to explore the insight of each farm's resource planning. Further, the researcher will gather the first hand information by recording on-site observations, collecting resource items as well as their distributions and utilizations in each farm. The findings will be concluded and analyzed to serve as the guidelines for questionair design.

　　The research should be able to prove that:

・A well planned resource shall be the farms' major attraction to the leisure farm goers

	・A customer's desire to revisit a farms will reduce when the farms fails his/her expectation. The result of this research is suitable for the leisure farm goers as a reference for better vocation planning.
關鍵字：休閒農場、消費者偏好、農作生產	Keywords: agricultural production, customer preferences, leisure farms

創作與翻譯表達力習作

　　第 1.2 節中所譯之李生打退妖人的故事，取材自《聊齋誌異》中的「妖術」一篇，茲寫出其白話版的故事大要，請參照 *The Adventure of Lee*，將此文英譯。為了能英譯得更順利，你可以稍稍更動原文的文字，但是不要改變了故事的內容。

　　有個姓于的讀書人，從小喜歡練武，力氣很大，幾十斤重的香爐都能一舉過頂。有一年，他隨身帶了一個僕人和朋友們到京城去應考，哪知到了京師，僕人突然生了重病，于生聽說有個算命的很靈，就去問一問吉凶，不想算命的說僕人的病不要緊，于生自己卻不出三天就要死，要于生付十兩銀子，方才為他降妖捉怪。于生說生死有命，不用求助於法術，算命的很不高興，說他一定會後悔。朋友們都勸于生去求求算命先生，于生不肯，照常練武讀書，準備考試，

　　到了第三天，于生在屋裡讀書，身邊還放著一把劍防身，從早到晚什麼事也沒發生。到了深夜，窗外突然有窸窣的聲

音，接著，一個小人兒拿著一隻矛從窗縫鑽進來，飄然落地，轉眼之間就變成真人一樣大小，于生心知有異，不等那怪起身，一劍砍去，那怪一縮脖子，閃開劍擊，飛到空中，縮成原來那麼大，找窗縫正要溜出去，于生對準那怪又是一劍，那怪斷成兩半跌到地上，于生取來蠟燭一照，見是個紙人，這時他不敢大意，手提寶劍對門而坐，不多時，一個模樣嚇人的怪物從窗戶闖進來，于生不待怪物站穩，揮劍把它砍成兩半，那兩半倒在地上，不住扭動，于生怕它再作怪，又連砍了幾下，把它砍成碎塊，仔細一看，原來是個泥塑的偶像。

就在這時候，于生聽到窗子外有很大的喘氣聲，接著房子開始搖晃起來，于生怕房子倒了要壓下來，想想不如出去跟它鬥一鬥，就打開大門，跳進庭院，只見在月光底下有個比屋頂還高的黑臉大鬼站在院裡，鬼的手拿弓箭，眼睛閃著黃光，上身沒穿衣，腳下也沒穿鞋，見了于生，拉開弓一箭射來，于生趕緊用寶劍擋開，巨人再射一箭，于生一跳躲開。那箭竟然射穿牆壁，巨人見兩射不中，拔出鋼刀砍來，于生躲開鋼刀，那刀砍在石階上，石階碎成幾塊飛了開去。

于生鑽到巨人兩腿之間，對準巨人的腳跟狠狠一劍，巨人受傷，發瘋一樣吼叫。于生又跳到巨人脅下，一劍向它胸口刺去，巨人倒地不動，縮成真人一樣大小，于生又砍了十幾劍，劍像砍在木頭上一樣，發出咚咚的聲音，再細看時，原來是個木偶，中刀處還在流血，于生在屋裡點著蠟燭，一個晚上沒敢合眼，才領悟到是算命的在搞鬼。

第二天，于生把昨夜的事告訴朋友們，大家一起去找算命的。算命的遠遠看到于生，就突然不見了。一位朋友認出這是種叫做隱身術的妖法，用狗血一噴就破了。

　　于生回家備好狗血，又去找算命的。算命的重施故技，于生用狗血一噴，算命的滿頭狗血，無所遁形。于生把妖人解送到官府定罪正法。

第二章
翻譯的過程和考量

本章提綱

中英對譯是對翻譯工作者兩種語文綜合能力的考查，譯者應該具有兩種語文的堅實基礎，注意體會兩種語文之間的差異，掌握翻譯過程中常用的技巧，才可能具有較可觀的翻譯能力。本章舉出幾個中英雙向對譯的例子，具體說明作者的翻譯理念。

2.1 翻譯的過程

熟練的翻譯者拿起原文，隨讀隨譯，倒也不太講究什麼翻譯的過程，但是大多數譯者應該都會受惠於系統化的翻譯步驟，這些步驟可大分為三：

17. 理解原文，
18. 以譯文妥貼表達譯意，及

19. 以原文核校譯文

三者之中，理解與表達通常並不分立，因為在表達的時候，可以進一步理解原文，因此，兩者是往返推敲的過程，在翻譯當中，有時需要從原文到譯文，再從譯文到原文來回數次，以求盡善。到了全文譯完，還少不了最後的核對工作，把譯文從頭到尾順過一遍，在發現疑問地方，還要回頭參考原文，以求盡美。

2.1.1 理解與表達

熟習中文者在讀中文時多半可以一讀就懂，不需要分析句子的結構，除非文章實在寫得太差，或者我們對主題了解太少，又或者句子實在太長。

同樣的，熟習英文的讀者讀起原文，自然也是流暢易懂，懂了之後，即可寫下譯意，也不太需要分析句子結構。

可惜的是，有些英翻中的譯者，他們的英文程度仍然不夠流暢，句子稍一複雜，翻譯就發生了障礙，只好停工，先搞清楚句法結構再說。

分析句子結構時，又要把以前學的文法搬出來，以便明瞭句子的骨幹結構，句中所有實詞和虛詞的意義、句子本身的整體意義、還有該句子所處的上下文環境，並且看看句子是否有省略的地方，主句和子句的關係是否明確等等。

本書的著眼點與文法書大大不同，所以也不會找些句子來徹底分析其文法，只會舉出篇幅比較大的文字，以翻譯者的角度來解析該文的要義。

Art in Latin America has always been a vehicle for social and political commentary. This translates into straight-out propaganda in a full-length portrait of the independence leader Simŏn Bo-lĭvar, his heroism trumpeted in a scarlet banderole, by the Peruvian painter Josĕ Gil de Castro, ***an art-ist to remember***. Elsewhere the politics of class and race are more obliquely evoked, as in a mag-nificent mid-19th-century portrait of an Afro-Brazilian woman from Bahia, *who wears a scoop-neck dress, white gloves and gold necklaces that could be straight from Ghana*. (88 words)

在翻譯上文之前，要讀通全文。把握文章整體的內容。英文句子中不乏像這段文字那樣，摻入*補語*（黑斜體部分）或*子句*（斜體加底線部分）來描述未盡事宜的寫作方式，這些外加的補語和子句通常有形容詞或副詞的作用。若是把第一句譯成下面這樣就是誤譯了：

拉丁美洲的藝術始終是社會、政治評論的媒介。

理解原文階段的目的正在於弄清原文的意思，原文指的「藝術」是泛指所有的藝術，若僅僅是指拉丁美洲藝術，則其原文應寫成 ***The art of Latin America*** 或 ***Latin American art*** 才是。這段文字似乎可以翻成：

在拉丁美洲，藝術一向是作為社會和政治評論的載具。這種現象，可以在值得懷念的祕魯畫家－荷西修德卡斯特羅，所畫的革命領袖西蒙・玻利亞的全身畫像中完全表現出來，他的英雄事蹟不遺餘力地宣揚在深紅色的旗幟上。其他地方在階級和種族上，表現得就沒有那麼直接了。就好像十九世紀中那一

幅壯麗的畫像，畫中那位來自巴哈亞城鎮的非裔巴西婦女，穿著一襲圓領洋裝、戴著白手套、脖子配著可能來自迦納的金項鍊。（188 字）

　　現在再看看，原文只不過包含了三個句子，其中第二句就長達 34 個字，第三句更高達 39 字之多，這種句法在英文中雖不罕見，但是，對於一般母語非英語的人士而言，光是閱讀原文，就得要稍費功夫。其實，不論哪一種文字，長的句子都容易使文章過於冗長，要完整了解整篇文章需花較多時間，因此並不可取。

　　在英文中描述未盡事宜時，常常使用形容詞或副詞補語或子句，若照其固有的句型譯成中文，難免變成四不像的西化文字，此時最好依據其前後文，確定關係代名詞所指代的內容，把句子從該關係代名詞處斷開，分句譯出。

　　以上文為例，為了透徹理解原文，不妨依原文的前後文意，確定其中關係代名詞 *who* 所指代的內容，把長句從該關係代名詞處斷開，改寫成不傷原意的五個較短的句子：

Art in Latin America has always been a **vehicle**[1] for social and political commentary. This translates into straight-out propaganda in a full-length portrait of the independence leader Simŏn Bo-lĭvar, his heroism trumpeted in a scarlet banderole. The portrait was done by the Peruvian painter Josĕ Gil de Castro, *an artist to remember*[2].

---

[1]　Vehicle 除了交通工具，還有媒體、工具、管道等等意義，只要查查字典，就可擇優而用，不要一意只在「交通工具、載具」這類的意思上下功夫。

[2]　Remember 確實有記憶、記得、想到之意，但離「懷念」就比較遠了，它還有 consider、take into account 的意思，因此翻成「值得一提」反而比較貼切。

Elsewhere the politics of class and race are more obliquely evoked, as in a magnificent mid-19th-century portrait of an Afro-Brazilian woman from Ba-hia. The woman in that painting wears a scoop-neck dress, white gloves and gold necklaces that could be straight from Ghana. (96 words)

　　這樣一來，原文雖然變長，但是卻也變得容易用譯文表達得多了，譯文也因此而縮短了些：

　　藝術在拉丁美洲一向是社會和政治評論的工具，這種情形表現在一幅革命領袖——西蒙‧玻利瓦——的全身畫像裡，此畫宣傳意味十足，玻利瓦的英雄氣概大吹大擂地彰顯在深紅的旗幟上，該畫是由值得一提的祕魯畫家——卡斯特羅所作。在階級和種族的政治意味上比較收斂些的例子，則如某幅華麗的十九世紀畫像上的巴哈亞非裔巴西婦女，畫中人穿著圓領洋裝、戴著白手套、掛著大約是來自迦納的金項鍊。（181字）

　　另外，如果原文中的代名詞（如：*it, they, them, this, that, these, those* 等）特別多[3]，也要弄清楚它們所指代的詞或片語。這些詞和片語有時要到前面相關的句子中去找。
　　接上例，看看以下這些句子中是否含有代名詞和其他具有指代意義的詞：

3　參見第 3.5 節「人稱代名詞的處理」。

Even with its culturally specific content, this painting fits effortlessly into the international styles of its day. So did Latin American modernism in the early 20th century. Far from being out of the loop, it helped to create the loop. Diego Rivera developed a bravura brand of Cubism in Paris before switching to descriptive realism for his mural art. And he later applied that realism to portraits of New World socialites like Elisa Saldvar de Gutirrez Roldn, *whom he depicted, surely with irony, in lace-up sandals and a flounced "peasant" skirt, self-conscious[4] signs of Mexicanidad.*

　　此文的末句竟然長達 40 字，過長的句子與不分段的文章一樣，帶給讀者「文字過度緊密」的壓迫感，當然有改進的必要，要記住，文字的目的在達意，不是要考驗讀者分析文句的能力[5]。所以，不用羨慕人家有能力把句子拉得特長，而是應該同情他們不懂得體諒讀者的辛苦。

　　下面的譯文中，除了最後兩句需要討論之外，整體上算是頗為流暢：

　　縱然這幅畫有特定的文化內容，它還是輕易地融入當時的國際風格。在二十世紀早期，拉丁美洲現代主義的風格也是如此。這種風格不但沒有脫離主流，反而有助於創造潮流。狄亞哥・里維拉（Diego Rivera）在轉往用寫實畫風創作壁畫之前，發展過一種華麗的巴西畫風。然後他把寫實畫風運用在美洲新世界一些社會名流當中，像艾利莎・羅爾丹（Elisa Saldvar de

---

4　一些片語和的字詞常常具有多種含義和用法，這裡譯者面臨了「一文多義」的難局，參看第 3.3 節「一字多義的處理」。

5　葉乃嘉，《英文書信與履歷的藝術》，五南圖書出版公司，2005/9。

Gutirrez Roldn）的畫像裡，運用諷刺的方式反應出墨西哥精神－自我覺醒的象徵。如畫中，他呈現女子穿著繫帶涼鞋和飾有荷葉邊的「農婦」裙子。

想要把前文譯成較流暢無誤的中文，不妨確定其中關係代名詞 *he* 與 *whom* 各自指代的人物，再把最後那個長達 40 字的句子從 *whom* 處斷開：

······ And he later applied that realism to portraits of New World socialites like Elisa Saldvar de Gutirrez Roldn. Elisa was *depicted, surely with irony, in lace-up sandals and a flounced "peasant" skirt, self-conscious signs of Mexicanidad.*

另外，上文中的 *self-conscious* 有「自我覺醒的」和「因為受到注意而感到不安或不自然的」兩種截然不同的意思，此處所要表達的意思到底是哪一個呢？

這時就要按照自己的理解，看該部分的譯意是否與前後譯文的內容一致。在我看來，時髦的涼鞋（*lace-up sandals*）配上「土氣」的裙子（*"peasant" skirt*）是有點不搭調（*irony*），依此分析，*self-conscious* 在本文中的意義應該比較接近「不安或不自然」，畫家要諷刺的就是新舊過渡時期那種「土洋雜陳」、「進退失據」的味道。

最後，把原文重譯如下：

雖然這幅畫有它文化方面的意義，但還是輕易地融入當時的國際風格。二十世紀早期拉丁美洲現代主義的風格也是如此。這種風格不但沒有脫離主流，反而有助於創造潮流。Diego

Rivera 在轉型以寫實畫風創作壁畫之前，發展過一種華麗的巴西畫風。其後，他把寫實畫風運用在像 Elisa Saldvar de Gutirrez Roldn 的一些社會名流的畫像裡，畫中的 Elisa 穿著繫帶涼鞋和飾有荷葉邊的「農婦」裙子。頗有諷刺意味地反應出失措的墨西哥精神。

　　這兩段文章涉及了一些我們所不了解的文化背景，翻譯起來不太容易，如果沒有閱讀一些相關的資訊，真的是難以下手，好在今天的網路資訊無所不包，以文章中所提到的 **Diego Rivera** 為例：

　　我們可以從網路資料上得知 Diego Rivera 是墨西哥現代藝術之父，在畫畫上表現了獨特的形式與風格，使墨西哥在世界藝術史上取得一席之地。此外，我們也從網路上的墨西哥近代史資料瞭解到，一個藝術家的生活與歷史背景如何深深影響其藝術創作，藝術如何反映社會現狀，民族價值如何與國際藝術潮流相關。知道 Diego Rivera 壁畫運動以復興民族藝術為宗旨，以壁畫藝術為手段，以本土民俗、風景、歷史、現實生活為主要描繪對象，反映社會矛盾、現實鬥爭，不但具有強烈的時代性，也無礙 Rivera 保持自己個人的鮮明特性。在這段期間，壁畫在美洲藝術史上成就空前，衰落近四百年的印地安藝術也獲得新生。

　　這些資訊使原本困難重重的譯事迎刃而解。

　　總之，要先讀懂原文，不要急於動手翻譯，而要讀懂原文，不一定得死鑽在原文中，只要懂得好好運用網路這種前人所沒有的幸運，它就會提供很多原本無法迅速取得的資料，使我們在從事翻譯工作時，不致

於重蹈嚴復先生「一名之立，旬月踟躕」的痛苦。

　　且再談如何把原文精確地以中文傳達出來，中文和英文間文法不同，文句結構亦有差異，譯者把自己理解的原文內容用譯文表達出來，表達得好不好，取決於他理解的程度以及中文的修養。

　　下面是一段十九世紀英國作家王爾德的文字：

I do not think that even I could produce any effect on a character that according to his own brother's admission is irretrievably weak and vacillating. Indeed I am not sure that I would desire to reclaim him. I am not in favor of this modern mania for turning bad people into good people at a moment's notice. As a man sows so let him reap.[6]

　　名家余光中先生，把它精譯如下[7]：

　　他自己的哥哥都承認他性格懦弱，意志動搖，到了不可救藥的地步；對這種人，我看連我也起不了什麼作用。老實說，我也不怎麼想要挽救他。一聲通知，就要把壞蛋變成好人，現代人的這種狂熱我也不贊成。惡嘛當然該有惡報。

　　英文句子中有許多類似上例的形容詞或副詞子句，翻譯時要避免製造西式中文，就不宜逐字硬譯，不妨以原文的句子做單位，細心體會該句的意義，然後以中文固有的方式表達出來，有時候用直譯，有時候用意譯，兩種方式交互運用。

6　Oscar Wilde, "The Importance of Being Earnest."
7　余光中，〈創作與翻譯〉演講詞，中國中央電視臺，2006/9/15 取自網站 http://www.cctv.com/special/131/61/73133.html。

2.1.2 譯文的核校

　　翻譯工作的最後一關，就是把譯文從頭到尾順過一遍，做最後的潤飾，在發現疑問地方，還要回頭核對原文，以求無誤。本節中所示範的譯文中，「譯文一」是未經核校的，它們全都來自網路[8]，這些譯文在網上大量轉載，極易取得，但是品質也不是盡如人意。這些譯文經過筆者一一檢視後，就產生了品管後的「譯文二」。這樣做的目的，在於示範「盡信網路不如無網路」，讀者要有高出水準以上很多的判斷能力，才不至於受誤導。這些譯文大多譯自比較難以用中文直接傳達的原文，頗具挑戰性，不過話說回來，作者正希望藉此分享「因其難而見其巧」的樂趣。

　　以下且看看幾個譯文核校的範例。

As Dr. Samuel Johnson said in different era about ladies preaching, the surprising thing about computers is not that they think less well than a man, but that they think at all.	
譯文一	譯文二
正如在不同時代，撒母耳詹森博士所談論的女士佈道一樣，電腦的驚人之處不是它們的思考能力不如人類，而是它們居然會思考。	以詹森博士當年對女子佈道所下的評論為例：事情的離奇之處，不在電腦的思考能力不如人，而在電腦竟能思考。

　　譯文一雖然按照字面把原文翻譯出來，但是卻還是未能表達原文真

8　http://www.7kao.com/pro/441/96223825310.htm

正的涵義，那就是，在從前那個女子受到歧視的時代裡，Johnson 這位老兄對女人傳教所下的評語是，女人傳教像狗用後腳走路，走得並不好，但狗會用後腳走路就夠讓人驚奇了[9]。言下之意是「女人傳教傳得不好不足為奇，奇的是女人竟然能夠傳教。」[10]。

　　譯文二雖然也非完美，但是稍稍解決了這種文意不足的問題。其實，要能翻譯成這樣，是要對其中的文化背景有所了解的，光看原文實在不能體會這麼多。在此顯示了很重要的一點，即：翻譯之難不見得全是文字結構的差異所造成，在一些比較深入的主題裡，文化間的鴻溝才是真正的考驗。還好，從網路上尋找許多不同主題的資料有時並不太難[11]，從事翻譯者要是能熟習搜尋技巧，定然對工作大有裨益。

If food already contains natural carcinogens, it does not make sense to add dozens of new man-made ones.	
譯文一	譯文二
儘管食品中已經含有了天然的致癌物質，但是，再人為地增加一些有毒物質也是很不應該的。	食品裡都已經有天然致癌物了，那還再加進幾十種新的人工致癌物簡直是沒天理。

　　若將原文直譯，應該是：「如果食品中已經含有天然致癌物，就沒道理再加進人工致癌物。」

　　這種譯法好像漏掉了什麼，因為直譯文的語意好像和「東西已經夠

9　Samuel Johnson 是十八世紀美國作家兼評論家，他曾這樣評述女人傳教"A woman's preaching is like a dog walking on his hindlegs. It is not done well, but you are surprised to find it done at all."

10　此論不代表本書作者立場，如受冒犯，請找 Samuel Johnson 理論。

11　參見第 1.4.1 節「理解與表達」。

好了，再花工夫改進豈非多餘」有點像，而我們所要表達的卻是：「東西都已經夠糟了，難道還要把它搞得更糟？」

譯文一並非出於直譯，業已比直譯更能表達原文的意義，而譯文二則更能表達出原文的語氣。

其實，就本例而言，直譯文所傳達的意義之所以模糊，並不完全是因為翻譯得不高明，而是因為原文本身就表達得不清楚，此時我所選擇的補救方法是直擊原文，把它改進成：

> It's already bad enough for food to contain natural carcinogens. It does not make sense to make it worse by adding dozens of new man-made ones.

翻譯既然是「再創作」，把不怎麼樣的原文稍加修理，以利譯事，應該不是罪過。

> The electronic economy made possible by information technology allows the haves to increase their control on global market, --with destructive impact on the have-nots.
>
> Yet for all the talk of a forthcoming technological utopia little attention has been given to the implications of these developments for the poor.

譯文一	譯文二
資訊技術使電子經濟成為可能，而電子經濟將進一步加強富國對全球市場的控	電子經濟因資訊技術而成為可行，它讓具有資訊技術者加強控制全球市場，從

制，從而給窮國家帶來毀滅性的影響。 　　然而，儘管人們正在大談特談即將到來的令人神往的科技王國，卻很少有人意識到這些技術對發展中國家意味著什麼。	而帶給不具資訊技術者不利的影響。 　　然而，在大談即將來臨的科技理想世界之餘，很少有人注意到，這些技術發展對於貧窮階級意味了些什麼。

　　說到「再創作」，譯者的權利也該有個局限，譯文一把 *destructive* 譯成「毀滅性的」，就是僭越過度了。*Destructive* 雖然可做「毀滅性」用，但是鮮有人做此解。此外，因為不具備資訊技術而遭致毀滅性的傷害，實在並無此理，就像說「沒有手機的人活不下去」一樣誇張。*Destructive* 還有「破壞性、負面、嚴重、有害、不利」等等許多意思，任何一個都比「毀滅性」要適用於此。

　　另外，把 *the haves* 譯做富國，*the have-nots* 譯做窮國，也局限了原文，*the haves* 可以是任何具備資訊技術的單位、企業、國家或跨國經濟體，*the have-nots* 則反是。譯文二將上述的缺失一一修正。

　　譯者在詮釋原文時，豈可任意拿捏？

　　Not content with its doubtful claim to produce cheap food for our own population, the factory farming industry also argues that "hungry nations are benefiting from advances made by the poultry industry."

譯文一	譯文二
工廠養殖業已不滿足於為我國人口提供廉價食物的可疑說法，進一步提出了「讓貧困國家從家禽養殖業的發展中受益」的論調。	工廠養殖業用了「為國人提供廉價食物」這種可疑論點仍嫌不足，還提出了「貧困國家有自家禽養殖業所做的改進中受益」的論調。

　　原文意味的是：企業在用優勢技術來獲取大量利潤之餘，還用一個又一個的不實說法，來規避一些它們該面對的企業道德議題，譯文一涵義模糊，沒有充分傳達原文的意思，而譯文二則讓人一讀就能領會原文中所要表達的主旨。

Home schoolers have few **kind words** for public schools, charging **shortcomings** that range from lack of religious perspective in the curriculum to a herd-like approach to teaching children.

譯文一	譯文二
家庭教育的宣導對學校教育鮮有褒獎，他們指責學校教育的種種弊端，從課程表上沒有宗教課到放牧的教育方法，不一而足。	在家就學者對公立學校教育少有好話，他們所指責的缺點從課程缺乏宗教觀，到群體統一的教學方式等，不一而足。

　　除了把子女送到傳統的公私立學校受教育之外，美國的家長們還

有另外一種選擇，那就是 *homeschooling*（居家教學或在家就學），*Homeschool* 有點像以前公私立學校不普遍時的私塾教育，但不同的是並非請位家庭老師來家任教，而是由家長們加入一些 *homeschool* 的團體，議定應該修習的課程，然後在家中循自己孩子的步調施教。

「家庭教育」一詞有其傳統的定義，譯文一把 *home schoolers* 譯成家庭教育，顯然是譯者的誤解。另外，*kind words* 只是好話，與褒獎還有段距離；*shortcomings* 只是缺點，與弊端大有差別，譯者似乎有意放大形容，比無法翻出原意還要大違「信」道。還有，把 *herd-like approach* 譯成「放牧式的方法」，也讓人搞不清楚，到底是「放牛吃草的放任式」還是「不因才施教的集體式」教學？譯文二一一修正了這些缺失。

In promotions of a biography, the "unauthorized" characterization usually suggests the prospect of juicy gossip that the subject of the biography had hoped to suppress.	
譯文一	譯文二
推銷傳記時，未經授權的傳記往往意味著讀者有可能從中讀到傳主不希望公之於眾的，繪聲繪色的內幕故事。	促銷傳記類書時，使用「未經授權」字樣往往意味著其中有傳主想隱藏的、繪聲繪色的內幕。

Juicy 除了成熟、多汁之外，還有有趣、刺激、火辣、甚至醜聞性的意思，譯成「繪聲繪色」也相當得體，至於 *promotion* 在此文中的譯意，「促銷」要比「推銷」達意，此外，譯文二中「使用未經授權字樣」，要比譯文一中的「未經授權的傳記」精確得多了。

By studying mineral grains found in material ranging from rocks to clay articles, previous researchers have already been able to identify reversals dating back 170 million years, including the most recent switch 730,000 years ago. Several theories link polarity flips to external disasters such as meteor impacts.

譯文一	譯文二
通過研究岩石、陶器等一系列材料中含有的礦物顆粒，先前的研究人員已能夠確認早在 1.7 億年發生的磁場兩極轉化現象，以及發生在 73 萬年以前的最新一次兩極轉化現象。一些理論將兩極轉化現象歸因於諸如隕星撞擊等外部因素。	先前的研究者藉研究土石等等材料中的礦物顆粒，已能確認早在 1.7 億年前的磁極反轉現象，其中包括了在 73 萬年前的最近一次反轉。有些理論將磁極反轉歸因於外來災變——如隕星撞擊等。

　　譯文一採取靠近原文的譯法，第一句的主詞直到第二句才出現，譯文二則採取以主詞引導句子的中式表達法，應該更適合做為翻譯的典範。又，像「通過試驗……」「通過研究……」等等「通過……」的句型，是大陸地區發展出來的西化中文，在台灣則是使用「經由……」或「透過……」，殊不知中文裡早就有「藉……」或「藉著……」的句法，比較有助於避免中西失調。

Where is industry's and our recognition that protecting mankind's great treasure is the single most important responsibility?

譯文一	譯文二
企業和我們個人什麼時候才能意識到保護人類的資源寶藏是最最重要的責任呢？	「保護人類的資源寶藏是最最重要的責任」，企業和我們個人把這種認知置於何地呢？

原文中並沒有任何涉及「時間」之處，倒是有個疑問代名詞 **where**，而譯文一中竟出現了「什麼時候」一詞，這不是個很體貼原文的譯法，譯文二把 **where is...** 譯成「置於何地」，應可算是神來之筆，至少要比「什麼時候」更能貼切地反映原意。

Bottom retail prices-anywhere from 30% to 70% lower than those in Europe and Asia-have attracted some 47 million visitors, who are expected to leave behind $79 billion in 2005.

譯文一	譯文二
比歐洲和亞洲低 30%～70%的零售價價格吸引了約四千七百萬的遊客於 2005 年湧入美國，而這些遊客為美國留下了 790 億美元的收入。	特低的零售物價（比歐洲和亞洲低 30%～70%）吸引了約四千七百萬的遊客，指望這些遊客會在 2005 年給美國留下 790 億美元。

英文裡的破折號使用在文章中語氣有所轉折的地方，翻成中文時可以像在譯文二裡一樣，以括號代之。

Expect 有「預期、指望」的意味，在原文發表時所「預期」的事件，我們不能因為在翻譯時成了歷史，就任意改變譯意。譯文一中的

「留下了⋯⋯」反映了該事件已經過去，譯文二以「指望⋯⋯會⋯⋯」來賦予譯文一個未來的意味。

It is said that the public and Congressional **concern** about **deceptive packaging rumpus** started because a senator discovered that the boxes of cereals consumed by his family were becoming higher and narrower, with a decline of net weight **from 12 to 10.5 ounces**, without any reduction in price. The producers of packaged products argue strongly against changing sizes of packages to contain even weights and volumes, but no one in the trade comments unfavorably on the huge costs incurred by endless changes of package sizes, materials, shape, art work, and net weights that are used for improving a product's market position.

譯文一	譯文二
某參議員一家在購買盒裝麥片時發現，包裝盒變高了，變窄了，食品的分量也減少了，然而價格卻分文未降。據說，由此在公眾和議會中引發了一場關於欺騙性商品包裝的軒然大波[12]。	據說，公眾和議會關切商品欺騙性包裝的風波，始於某參議員一家在吃盒裝穀片時發現，包裝盒變高變窄，食品分量從 12 英兩減到 10.5 英兩，而價格卻分文未降。

---

12 「關於欺騙性商品包裝的軒然大波」乃是 rampus concerning deceptive packaging，而 concern about deceptive packaging rumpus 應是「對欺騙性商品包裝風波的關切」，兩者大有不同。

生產包裝產品的商家極力反對在改變了的包裝內裝上原有分量的商品，但他們卻絲毫不反對為了擴大產品的市場優勢，用於不斷改變包裝的大小、用料、形狀、製作工藝以及商品的淨重的大筆花費。（167字）	包裝產品的生產商家極力反對改變包裝來容納原有分量的商品，但卻無人對促銷產品時不斷改變包裝大小、用料、形狀、美工以及商品淨重的大筆花費持反對意見。（140字）

原文有兩段文字，每段竟然只有一個句子，分別為 49 字與 53 字，即使以「英文比較能容受長句」的標準來衡量，也嫌稍長了點，我們不妨直擊原文，把長句切割成短一些的句子，讓它們比較容易轉成中文。

A senator discovered that the boxes of cereals consumed by his family were becoming higher and narrower, with a decline of net weight from 12 to 10.5 ounces, without any reduction in price. This, as it is said, has caused the deceptive packaging rumpus that public and Congressional concern.

The producers of packaged products argue strongly against changing sizes of packages to contain even weights and volumes. No one in the trade, however, comments unfavorably on the huge costs incurred by endless changes of package sizes, materials, shape, art work, and net weights that are used for improving a product's market position.

　　注意，原文在從兩句變成四句之後，字數毫無增加，但卻變得易讀得多，至少對翻譯者是有利的。

　　譯文一的譯者把原文第一句細細解剖之後，才好不容易把原來在句首的「據說……」移到段末譯出，這還算是可行，但是，該譯者失察之處是，在公眾和議會中引發的，不是「軒然大波」，而是「關切」；又，「他們絲毫不反對」和「無人持反對意見」也有段距離，此外，譯者還漏譯了商品減少的量，不免失信於讀者。相較之下，譯文二以四分之三的字數，把原文譯得更精準、更貼切。

> Unlike other lawbreakers, who must leave the country, commit suicide, or go to jail, computer criminals sometimes escape punishment, demanding not only that they not be charged but that they be given good recommendations and perhaps other benefits.

譯文一	譯文二
其他的違法者或者逃亡國外，或者自殺，或者進監獄，電腦犯罪分子卻不同，他們可以逃避懲罰，並且要脅不要指控他們，甚至還要求為他們出具有利的推薦信或者為他們提供其他好處，他們的要求往往能夠得到滿足。（96 字）	電腦罪犯不用像別種罪犯那樣自殺、坐牢或亡命他國，這些人有時避過了懲罰，除了開出條件要求不受起訴外，還要求有利的舉薦或其他種種利益。（65 字）

　　譯文一的意思大致得體，但是在修辭方面還可以精簡，至於最後那句「他們的要求往往能夠得到滿足」並不見於原文，應是該譯者隨興之

筆，稍嫌翻譯過度[13]（或過度翻譯）。譯文二只用了三分之二的篇幅，就更得體地達成了任務。

　　有些譯者喜歡在譯文上加碼，原本可以簡單表達之處，他在不至於過度妨礙原意的情況下，加上一些枝節的字詞，這與其個人風格有關，本書則持精簡立場，不鼓勵節外生枝。

He concludes that **excellent job performance** is so common these days that while doing your **work well** may win you pay increases, it won't secure you the big promotion. Most women and blacks are so frightened that people will think they've gotten ahead because of their sex or color that they **play down their visibility**.

譯文一	譯文二
他得出的結論如下：如今出色的工作表現十分普遍，雖說工作出色你可以加薪，但你未必能夠高升。大多數女職員和黑人職員害怕人家說自己是因為性別或種族才得到提拔的，因此，他們儘量不去拋頭露面。	他結論：如今出色的工作表現這麼普遍，你做得好也許可能加薪，卻未必有望高升。 　　多數女性和黑人怕人家認為自己得到提拔是因為性別或種族的緣故[14]，因此，他們儘量低調。

　　把 *excellent job performance* 譯成「出色的工作表現」可說是貼切，

---

13 英文中稱這種情形為 *overkill*，表示任何過當的作為，不獨以翻譯為然。
14 美國聯邦法保障就業機會均等（Equal Opportunity Employment），雇主不得在僱用條件中限定受雇者之年齡、性別、種族或婚姻狀態等，另外，法律也保障婦女和少數族裔的就業機會，此舉稱為 Affirmative Action，它鼓勵雇主在任用或晉升人員時，優先考慮婦女和少數族裔者。

但是 **work well** 和 **excellent job performance** 之間有段距離，不應譯做同級的「工作出色」，這樣才能把僅僅是「好」和更高級的「出色」分開，給「好」只能加薪而不能升等這句話找個邏輯的台階。

　　Most 可以確定的意思是「多數」，能否譯成「大多數」則尚有可議的空間，因為超過 50% 即是多數，語義上可以涵蓋大多數，有人則可能不同意 51% 是「大多數」。把 play down their visibility 應該可以譯做「不多露臉」或「少露鋒芒」，把它譯成「不去拋頭露面」可以說是貪圖方便加上濫用成語，甚為不宜。

理解與表達之習作

　　說到表達，下面這篇原文就表達得非常有趣，現在就輪到你來理解其中的真意了，請加以翻譯，並表達你對作者寫此文的態度有何看法。

　　Like the other day, I was at school for most of the day (9:00 - 4:30) for brass band stuff, and just before we breaked for lunch, four girls came up to me and said "You eat lunch with us today! We go to ＿＿ restaurant together! Ok?" It's as if people assume that just because of my skin color I have to be treated like a movie star. Or when I meet extremely drunk strangers on the train and they try to make conversation, they attempt to speak in English! Just because I don't have slanty eyes does mean I can understand garbled English better than garbled Japanese. I got my hair cut the other day and they spent fifteen or twenty minutes longer on me than what appeared to be the average with other customers.

　　Do they think because I'm from another country that I need to have nicer hair? What Racism! And to add insult to injury, all of the other staff came over to admire my wavy hair. Or when I get discounts at stores or when girls scream when I come around a corner and then mumble something about Brad Pitt? Do they think that the fact that I am capable of growing facial hair means that they have to be nice to me? I mean I could understand it if I was attacked by gangs of young Japanese males or people pulled guns on me, or wouldn't sit near me on the train. But they act like I'm Mr. Charisma or something. At school teachers make a special effort to talk to me. How dare they! When I give presentations in classes about Canada, they pay attention. Such racism! Can't they just sleep like usual? They act like my skin color makes me more fun to listen to than their teachers.

Every day I have to put up with the friendly smiles, all of the helpful people, the shopkeepers that thank me for buying from them, everyone who wants to be my friend, people translating the bulletin for me at church, getting offered free lead for my pencil, and worst of all -- the way my homestay treats me like family. The JAPANESE ARE THE MOST RACIST PEOPLE EVER, JUST LIKE EVERYONE IN CANADA SEEMS TO THINK! I don't know why I bother to stay here at all.

2.2 翻譯的考量

在魚與熊掌不可兼得的情況下，翻譯者宜先考量自己的譯作到底要偏向以下三個選項的哪一端：

20. 靠近原文或靠近譯入文（Source-oriented vs. Target-oriented），

21. 以原作者爲中心或以譯文讀者爲中心（Author-orientd vs. Reader-oriented），

22. 重原文形式或重原文内容（Form-oriented vs. Content-oriented）。

　　這些細節若是深入討論起來，各方意見甚多，會把入門不久的翻譯新血們先唬一跳。其實，在真正拿起一篇文章來翻譯之前，全部的討論都是紙上談兵，固定的理論並不能一成不變地應用在所有的實況上。本書既然是以務實為主，也就不在理論上多花筆墨，以下舉出實例，將作者的翻譯理念和原則一一引出，以為譯事的參考。

2.2.1 讀者為中心重於作者為中心

　　所有的文字都應該以讀者為本位，即使是目的不在發表而只是寫給自己看的文字，也有一個讀者（即作者自己）需要照顧，讓自己能看得懂，才是上策。

　　在此，且用《閱微草堂筆》記[15]裡一則有趣故事的翻譯為例，來支持翻譯應以譯文讀者導向（Reader Oriented）而非原作者導向（Author Orientd）的論點，首先錄出原文：

　　寧波吳生，好作北里遊，後暱一狐女，時相幽會，然仍出入青樓間，一日狐女請曰：「吾能幻化，凡君所眷，吾一見即

---

[15] 《閱微草堂筆記》是清季紀曉嵐（1724－1805）所著的筆記小說，書中　述的多是紀氏聞自鄉黨、親友、同事甚或下人的「真實」靈異故事，間或亦有他自己親身經歷的事件，各則記事的後面常有紀氏本人的評論，其評論有時頗為符合現代的科學邏輯。

可肖其貌，君一存想，應念而至，不逾於黃金買笑乎？」試之，果頃刻換形，與眞無二，遂不復外出，嘗語狐女曰：「眠花藉柳，實愜人心，惜是幻化，意中終隔一膜耳。」狐女曰：「不然，聲色之娛，本電光石火，豈特吾肖某某爲幻化，即彼某某亦幻化也，豈特某某爲幻化，即妾亦幻化也，即千百年來，名姬艷女，皆幻化也，白楊綠草，黃土青山，何一非古來歌舞之場，握雨攜雲，埋香葬玉，別鶴離鸞，一曲伸臂頃耳，中間兩美相合，或以時刻計，或以日計，或以月計，或以年計，終有訣別之期，及其訣別，則數十年而散，與片刻相遇而散者，同一懸崖撒手，轉瞬成空，倚翠偎紅，不皆恍如春夢乎，即夙契原深，終身聚首，而朱顏不駐，白髮已侵，一人之身，非復舊態，則當時黛眉粉頰，亦謂之幻化可矣，何獨以妾肖某某爲幻化也？」吳生憬然有悟，後數年，狐女辭去，吳竟絕跡於狎遊。[16]

　　紀曉嵐一代文豪，以文言文而言，他的寫作功力堪與歷史上其他任何文人抗衡而毫不遜色，問題是，怎樣才能貼切地把這不再時興的文字翻成與之相去甚遠的英文呢？

　　忽視了文化的考量，就不會有成功的譯文，這段文字裡充滿了屬於華人文化的東西，像狐女，像埋香葬玉，別鶴離鸞，像白楊綠草、黃土青山、黛眉粉頰、又像北里、青樓、買笑、眠花藉柳、握雨攜雲、倚翠偎紅等等，譯者當然不能對原文所提到的文化背景一無所知，不然真的會無從下手，而除此之外，又到底要怎麼翻才得體呢？

　　上面這些字詞所包含的典故與背景，即使是受中文教育的人也不見得能通通明瞭，又怎麼可能用簡單的翻譯模式來傳達給完全不懂中文的

---

16 《閱微草堂筆記》卷一「灤陽消夏錄一」，第十三則。

人士呢？只有在譯文中附加注釋，說明原典的本事，才能解決問題，那麼，譯者不但要把表面的文字翻譯過去，同時還連同語出何典也要加以研究，一併譯出，這豈不是大大增加了翻譯的量和困難度？

其實，翻譯的要求應該沒有這麼嚴格，因為，即使是只把文言翻成白話，也都不可能顧到這麼深刻的層面了，遑論英譯。依我之見，英譯者的責任，應該僅止於把故事的內容如實而完整地表達給英文讀者，而不是教育他們那些用字遣詞後面的繁雜出典。

那麼，只要知道「埋香葬玉，別鶴離鸞，白楊綠草、黃土青山」跟人事景物的代謝有關，「北里、青樓、買笑、眠花藉柳、握雨攜雲、倚翠偎紅」跟狎妓冶遊、男女歡愛有關，也就不用 *white poplars, green grasses, yellow soils and dark green mountains* 地亂忙一通，更不用考慮「黛眉粉頰、倚翠偎紅」裡的「黛」和「翠」這兩種顏色到底深淺如何了。

最好的變通方法應是先免去那些文縐縐的成語典故，把原文轉成白話，這樣雖然頗費周折，但是為了幫忙那些不諳文言的譯界人士譯出以讀者為中心的譯文，也不得不爾。

白話原文	英譯
甯波有位姓吳的書生喜歡狎妓，他和一個狐精相好，不時幽會，又常常出入青樓，有一天狐女說：「我能夠變化，凡是你所喜歡的女子，我一見就可以變化成她的形貌，你只要想一想，	Wu, a Ningbo resident, indulged in dallying with prostitutes. At that time, he was dating a female fox spirit while lingering in brothels regularly. One day, the fox spirit claimed: "I am able to transform. I can transform into any girl you desire. All I need is a glance of her. She will appear

那人就出現了，這不是比花錢買笑好嗎？」

whenever you think of her. Isn't it better than spending your money on prostitutes?"

吳生一試，果然狐女立刻就變形了，跟真人沒有兩樣，因此吳生就不再外出買笑了，有一次他對狐女說：「能夠這樣眠花宿柳實在很開心，可惜這一切都是幻化的，終是有層隔閡。」

Wu gave it a try, and the fox spirit transformed immediately. It was as good as real. From that time on, Wu stopped been a prostitute patron.

Once, Wu told the fox spirit: "It's really pleasurable making it with different girls. What a pity that they are only illusions. Something seems to be missing."

狐女說：「你說這樣就差了，聲色之娛本來就有如電光石火，不能長久，豈只我變成某人的形貌是幻化，就算是某人自己也是幻化，我本身是幻化，千百年來的美女也全都是幻化，草木山河大地全都是古來歌舞之場，相聚的時間或以時刻計，或以日、月甚至年計，都有分別的時候，分別的時候到了，對於相聚了數十年的和只相聚片刻的人而言都是一樣，轉眼成空，有如春

The fox spirit said: "You are so biased. Carnal pleasures are as short-lived as lightning and sparks. Not only is the girl I transformed into an illusion, but the girl herself. Not only is the girl an illusion, but I myself. Those celebrated beauties in history were also illusions. Those places covered with dirt and vegetations today could have been glitzy places of amusement in ancient time. For a moment you are together, for the next you are not. Eventually you will die. All of these happen in a short while. Be it hours, days, months, or even years, the parting moment will finally come. Whether the

夢。即使是因緣很深，終身相聚，相貌也不可能一世不變，年輕時的形貌跟老年時的形貌不可能相同，年輕時的美貌還不就是幻化一樣？為什麼光把我變化成某某的樣子才是幻化而已呢？」	party lasts for decades or just momentary, at the time of departure, you will have to let go just the same. All is vanity. Everything becomes no more than a Spring-night dream. Even if you can be together throughout your life time, you will not stay young all the way. Your young look will not maintain as you get old. Isn't the youthful complexion of yesteryears but illusion? Then why is that you think only the girl I transformed into as illusive?"
吳生若有所悟，過了幾年，狐女離開他之後，他竟然再也不到花街柳巷去尋花問柳了。	Wu seemed to have been stricken by these words. The fox spirit left him a few years later. He had never resumed his brothel lingering habit.

　　林語堂先生在《英譯重編傳奇小說》[17]的前言裡說，他用英文寫那些故事並沒有依循翻譯的原則，因為他有時發現翻譯是不可能的事，首先是文字上的差異；其次，有的風俗和習慣上的不同固然可以理解，但也有的需要解釋一番；再者，讀者對於書中人物會有不同的感受；而最重要的是，現代小說敘事的節奏和技巧與古代有異，這些因素都讓故事有需要重述（Retold）。這段話可以為「讀者導向重於原作者導向」背書。

　　但是，偏重讀者導向有個缺點，那就是：同一譯者在翻譯不同作家的作品時，總是免不了陷入同一個筆調。既然譯者有自己的文字風格，

---

17 Lin, Yu-Tang "Famous Chinese Short Stories," 1952.

那麼他在翻譯不同作家的作品時，就很難克服自己的風格，這在文藝創作（如詩、散文、小說等）的翻譯上，不免是個缺憾。

　　還好，在以敘事說理為重的「非文藝作品」中，這個缺點不會造成太嚴重的問題。

2.2.2 原文內容重於原文形式

　　翻譯之道，乃是運用譯文準確而完整地表達原文的內容和思想（也就是意義），而不是把兩種語言結構做簡單的轉換。中英文形式差異之大，有如不可跨越的鴻溝，因此如果不是詩詞、韻文等特殊文體，就不需要特別講究其中的形式（或稱結構，如句法、對仗和押韻等）。譯文所要表達的，是原文的內容，而不是句子的結構。過於強調形式的譯法有時會使譯文缺乏可讀性，因此，翻譯時應以內容導向（Content Oriented），譯文所表達的意義應與原文保持一致，至於其形式和結構，則只是為這一目的服務，屬於末節，故不應形式導向（Form Oriented）。請看下面的例子：

> How far do you think a flower would get if in the morning it turned its face toward the sky and said, I demand the sun. And now I need rain. So I demand it. And I demand bees to come and take my pollen. I demand, therefore that the sun shall shine for a certain number of hours, and that the rain shall pour for a certain number of hours... and that the bees come - bees A, B, C, D, and E, for I shall accept no other bees to come. I demand that discipline operate, and that the soil shall follow my command. But I do not allow the soil any spontaneity of its own. And I do not allow the sun any

spontaneity of its own. And I do not agree that the sun knows what it is doing. I demand that all these things follow my ideas of discipline.

譯文一	譯文二
一朵花會得到什？如果它在早上把臉對著太陽說：我需要太陽。而現在我要雨。所以我要求。我還要求蜜蜂來取我的花粉……蜜蜂來的話要蜜蜂 A、B、C、D 和 E，因為我不接受其他的蜜蜂。我要求那原則運作，而土壤要聽從我的指揮。但我不允許土壤有它自己的任何自發性。我也不允許太陽有它自己的任何自發性。我不同意太陽知道所發生的事情。我要求所有這些都聽從我原則的理念。（168 字）	你想一朵花能夠如願多久？要是它一早就對著天說：「我要太陽，我要雨，你給我下雨。我要蜜蜂來採蜜，太陽得照幾個小時，雨得下幾個小時，蜜蜂也得來——還只許蜜蜂甲、乙、丙、丁、戊來，別的蜜蜂我都不要。照那個規矩來，土壤得聽我的，不許自己做主，太陽也不許自己做主，太陽哪懂自己在做些什麼，我要這些東西全都依我。」（151 字）

　　譯文一就過度拘泥於原文的形式，以致讀來相當彆扭。譯文二則是在融會貫通了原文的內容之後的改善譯法，不但顯得通順，也更貼近中文。

　　直譯（Verbal Translation）與意譯（Free Translation）的差異其實也就是「原文形式」與「原文內容」之別。

　　所謂直譯，就是條件許可時，在譯文中既保持原文的內容，又保持原文的形式。梁實秋先生在〈漫談翻譯〉[18]中說：

　　有時候，洽當的文字得來全不費工夫，儼如天造地設……但是可遇而不可求。

　　言下之意，在不得已時還是得捨「直」取「意」。
　　中文和英文存在部分共同之處，有些英文句子完全可以直譯成中文，既保持了原文的結構，又正確表達了原文的內容，一舉兩得。例如莎士比亞劇中的 *a pissing while* 讓梁先生想到他們北方的一句粗話「撒泡尿的功夫」，莎翁劇中的另一句 *You three-inch fool*，也由梁氏取自水滸傳，譯為「你這三寸釘」。
　　有些中文的成語[19]可以直譯成英文而不礙其原意，可謂貼切，例如：

- 危如累卵　as precarious as a pile of eggs
- 如坐針氈　to be as if sitting on a bed of needles
- 大公無私　perfectly fair and impartial

　　另有一些中文的成語在直譯成英文後，還可以看出字面上的意思，但是要靠英譯來明白原始的典故，就使不上力了，例如：

- 一暴十寒　one day of sunlight followed by ten days of cold
- 天衣無縫　clothes in heaven have no stitches
- 小時了了　very intelligent in youth

18 梁實秋，《雅舍精品》，九歌出版社，2002。
19 本節所選之中文成語英譯部分均取自僑教雙週刊之成語故事 http://edu.ocac.gov.tw/culture。

　　直譯不成，變成硬譯的情形所在多有，以下這幾個成語中翻英的例子似乎把每個中文字都照顧到了，但是英文的譯文卻完全沒有表達出中文典故的原意，並無可取之處，例如：

> ・月下老人　the old man under the moon
> ・四面楚歌　songs of ch'u on all four sides
> ・名落孫山　to be behind Sun Shan

　　有時因為譯者的不用功，羞於問人，又懶得查字典，不知道有些詞早就有一定的譯法，把 *deja vu*（似曾相識，潛在印象）音譯成「得加無」；*Joan of Arc*（聖女貞德）音譯成「亞克的瓊安」，把 *sperm whale*（抹香鯨）譯成「精液鯨魚」等。

　　有些則是因原文中的詞句實在是本國文字之所欠缺，例如五四時期前後把 *democracy* 音譯成「德謨克拉西」，把 *science* 音譯成「賽恩斯」，*inspiration* 音譯成「煙士披裏純」。

　　直譯因在選詞和句法結構上和原文較接近，但相對之下，常使譯文讀起來比較吃力。意譯在翻譯過程中，或多或少會過濾掉一些由形式所附帶的意義，因此如何在直譯和意譯之間取得平衡，就考驗了譯者的翻譯功力。到底應直譯還是意譯，往往要考慮到上下文、語域、體裁、讀者等因素，沒有一成不變的道理。若能直譯和意譯交替使用，就可以相互截長補短。

　　但是，最基本的，任何文字都應該以「可讀性」為重心，因此，譯者絕對應該在原文的內容上多加琢磨，以意譯為主、直譯為輔的方式行之。

2.2.3 貼近譯入語文重於貼近原文

　　翻譯的目的既然是在引介作品給不諳原文的讀者，就要儘量貼近譯入文，儘量發揮譯入文的優勢，增加譯文的可讀性，而不宜堅持原文導向（Source Language Oriented），使翻譯的目的無法落實。

　　以下的原文中，數處以英文敘述日本文化，由於日本文化比美國文化更接近華人文化，所以在翻譯這個文章時如能直探其原，當然比轉譯自第三文字要高明，也更能達到譯入文導向（Target Language Oriented）的目的，所以比較講究一點的譯者，就會透過各種形式和管道[20]把它們的日文原譯找出來，不能用像國內翻譯美國電影對白那種敷衍的態度，凡碰到非英語部份，一概標以「外語」[21]了事。

原文	中譯
Two Kinds of Knowledge There are two kinds of knowledge[22]. One is explicit knowledge, which can be expressed in words and numbers and shared in the form of data, scientific formulae, product specifica-tions, manuals, universal principles, and so forth. This kind of knowledge can be readily transmitted across individuals formally and systematically. This has been the dominant	知識的兩種形式 　　知識的形式有兩種，一種是可由語言、數字表示，並可以藉數據、公式、產品說明書、原理等形式共享的顯性知識。這種知識能方便地在個人之間正式且系統化地傳播，它是西方人普遍熟悉的知

---

20 在網路發達的今天，這一點的難度並不太高。

21 比較好的會告訴觀眾是德語或法語，還是西班牙或義大利語，下焉者則連廣東話都分辨不出，直接標以外語敷衍之。

22 此句與其譯為「有兩種知識的形式」，還不如譯為「知識的形式有兩種」貼近中文。

form of knowledge in the West. The Japanese, however, see this form as just the tip of the iceberg. They view knowledge as being primarily tacit, something not easily visible and expressible.	識種類。而日本人只將這種知識看為知識冰山的一角，他們主要把知識看成隱性，不明顯也不易表達，
Tacit knowledge is highly personal and hard to formalise, making it difficult to communicate or share with others. Subjective insights, intuitions and hunches fall into this category of knowledge. Furthermore, tacit knowledge is deeply rooted in an individual's action and experience, as well as in the ideals, values or emotions he or she[23] embraces.	隱性知識高度個人化而難以歸納。主觀感覺、直覺等都屬於這一類。它植根於個人的行動、經驗、理想、價值觀及感情中。
To be precise, there are two dimensions to tacit knowledge. The first is the "technical" dimension, which encompasses the kind of informal and hard-to-pin-down skills or crafts often captured in the term "know-how". Master craftsmen or three-star chefs, for example,	更精確地說，隱性知識有兩個向度，一個在技術方面，它包括非正式、難以定位的技能，例如工藝大師或大廚師經過多年的經驗所造就的專長，很

---

23 由於英文的單數人稱代名詞有性別之分，故每有需要表達男女泛稱時，都要麻煩地用起 *...he or she...* 或 *...he and she...*，華文界亦有人在寫作時東施效顰，用起「⋯⋯他與她⋯⋯」的句法來，其實早期英文中也沒有這種矯枉過正的用法，即令今天，也仍有以 he 來代表男女全稱者，猶如 1966 年至 1969 年間的電視影集 *Star Trek*（星際爭霸戰）開場白中的 *...to bravely go where no man has gone before*，此舉在文法上並無錯誤，只是那些堅持要分別 *chairman* 及 *chairwoman* 可能會有意見罷了。

develop a wealth of expertise at their finger-tips, after years of experience. But they often have difficulty articulating the technical or scientific principles behind what they know. Highly subjective and personal insights, intu-itions, hunches and inspirations derived from bodily experience fall into this dimension.

難用科學或技術的原理表達出來。極為主觀的個人見解、直觀、心血來潮、親身體驗來的靈感等都屬此類。

Tacit knowledge also contains an im-portant "cognitive" dimension. It consists of beliefs, perceptions, ideals, values, emotions and mental models so ingrained in us that we take them for granted. Though they cannot be articulated very easily, this dimension of tacit knowledge shapes the way we perceive the world around us.

隱性知識的另一個向度在認知方面，它包括信仰、見解、理想、價值、感情和心態等，已深深植入我們的內在，雖然不能用語言清楚表示，但卻決定了我們觀察世界的方式。

The difference in the philosophical tradi-tion of the West and Japan sheds light on why Western managers tend to emphasize the im-portance of explicit knowledge whereas Japa-nese managers put more emphasis on tacit knowledge. Western philosophy has a tradi-tion of separating "the subject who knows" from "the object that is known", epitomized in the work of the French rationalist Descartes.

西方與日本哲學傳統上的不同說明了西方重顯、日本重隱的原因。西方哲學裡有個將「能知的主體」（能）與「所知的客體」（所）分開的傳統，這種思想表現在法國理性主義學派笛卡爾的著作中，它將能與

He proposed a concept that is called after him, the Cartesian split, which is the separation between the knower and the known, mind and body, subject and object.[24]	所[25]，心與物等分開來。
Descartes **argued**[26] that the ultimate truth can be deduced only from the real existence of a "thinking self", which was made famous by his phrase, "I think, therefore I am." He assumed that the "thinking self" is independent of body or matter, because while a body or matter does have an extension we can see and touch but doesn't think, a mind has no extension but thinks. Thus, according to the Cartesian dualism, true knowledge can be obtained only by the mind, not the body.	笛卡爾認為最終真理可由一個「能思想的自我」得到，即我思故我在[27]。他認為「能思想的自我」應獨立於身體及物質，因為身體或物質有可觸及的實體而不能思維，而思想則沒有實體而能思維，因此，根據解析二元論，真正的知識應來自思想而非身體。

---

24 本句甚長（28字），若照原文直譯，應作「他提出一種以他為名的觀念，稱為解析二元論，該觀念即主張能與所，心與物、主與從的分立。」筆者以簡筆譯之，以期靠近中文。

25 「能」與「所」乃是譯自梵文的佛經用詞，「能」是「心、主體、觀察者」，而「所」則是「物、客體、受觀察者」，能與所這對名詞的出現要比西方的 *the knower and the known, mind and body, subject and object, the observer and the observed* 早上千餘年。

26 Argue 一般作辯解、爭執、爭論的意思，但此處卻應作說明、主張解。見第3.3節「一字多義的處理」。

27 笛卡爾認為必須對一切的觀念和意見懷疑，然而有一點是無容置疑的，那就是「我」必須先存在，才能夠懷疑到週遭的一切，而懷疑即是在思想，所以我思故我在，他以此出發，引申出許多哲學命題。

In contrast, the Japanese intellectual tradition placed a strong emphasis on the importance of the "whole personality", which provided a basis for valuing personal and physical experience over indirect, intellectual abstraction. This tradition of emphasizing bodily experience has contributed to the development of a methodology in Zen Buddhism dubbed "the oneness of body and mind" by Eisai[28], one of the founders of Zen Buddhism in medieval Japan.	相形之下[29]，日本思想傳統強調人的「全性」的重要性，它尊重個人的經驗，而不是抽象的思維。這種傳統有助於發展榮西所創之禪宗「身心合一」修煉法。榮西為中世紀時日本禪宗祖師之一。
Zen **profoundly**[30] affected samurai education, which sought to develop wisdom through physical training. In traditional samurai education, **knowledge was acquired when it was integrated into one's "personal character"**.[31] Samurai education placed a	禪宗深深影響了日本武士道教育，這種教育是經由體力鍛煉來培養人的智慧，在傳統的武士道教育中，知識是以融入人的個性的方式而獲得的，因

---

28 即榮西，為十二世紀時日本禪宗始祖；禪宗自達摩初祖起算，榮西為第五十三代。見 http://homepage.ac.com/iihatobu/busseki/eisai.html

29 *In contrast* 在此譯成「相形之下」顯然要比譯成「對比之下」要優雅；同類的片語 *on the contrary* 譯成「反之」也比譯成「相反地」更貼近中文。

30 傳統中譯英文副詞時，多會帶上「地」，即所謂的副詞字尾，但是副詞不一定要加上這個字尾，本篇下工夫之處，在於原文中有九個一般人會譯成「……地」的副詞，但在譯文卻只出現了兩個「……地」。參見第3.8.1節「副詞字尾的處裡」。

31 此句包含了兩個被動語態，為了符合中文表達習慣，均以主動語態譯出，被動語態的處理原則詳見第3.1節「被動語態的處理」。

great emphasis on building up character and attached little importance to prudence, intelligence and metaphysics. Being a "man of action" was considered more important than mastering philosophy and literature, although these subjects also constituted a major part of samurai education.

此它極為重視個性的培養，而忽視悟性，智力和其他形而上學的東西。雖然哲學與文學課程也是武士道教育的一部份，但是有行動力要比精通哲學與文學更重要。

The Japanese have long emphasized the importance of bodily experience. A child learns to eat, walk and talk through trial and error. He or she learns with the body, not only with the mind. Similarly, a student of traditional Japanese art - for example, calligraphy, tea ceremony, flower arrangement or Japanese dancing - learns by imitating the moves of the master. mind become one while stroking the brush (calligraphy) or pouring water into the kettle (tea ceremony). A sumo wrestler becomes a grand champion when he achieves shingi-ittai, or when the mind (shin) and technique (gi) become one (ittai).[32]

日本人長期重視人的切身體驗。小孩藉著不斷嘗試來學習吃飯、說話和走路，他們不光是用思維而且用身體來學習。同樣，學習日本傳統藝術（書道、茶道、花道及傳統日本舞蹈等等）的學生也是藉模仿老師的動作來掌握這些技藝。大師之成為大師乃是因為他們在揮毫和倒茶之間也能身心一致。相撲選手就是由「心技一體」而成為勝者。

---

32 本段是最能看出譯者用心的部份，因為光靠原文的描述，絕不足以捉住其中想要描繪的日本文化的味道，譯者透過網路以及幾位熟諳日本文化的人士之助，不但忠實轉譯了原文所傳達的每一個訊息，而且讓譯文更將出色生輝，可臻信、達且雅之境。

2.3 本章習作

譯文核校習作

請就以下五篇譯文發表看法與評論，如其中有不理想處，請修正或重譯。

原文	待核校之譯文
Most of these books, as well as several chapters, mainly in, but not limited to, journalism and broadcasting handbooks and reporting texts, stress the "how to" aspects of journalistic interviewing rather than the conceptual aspects of the interview, its context, and implications.	大多數的這類書和一些章節強調如何進行採訪，而不是研究採訪的概念性問題，比如採訪的概念性問題，比如採訪的背景以及含義。這些章節主要見於，但也不限於，報章雜誌、廣播手冊以及新聞報導的書籍中。
No one looking ahead 20 years possibly could have foreseen the ways in which a single invention, the chip, would transform our world thanks to its applications in personal computers, digital communications and factory robots.	如果 20 年前的人們預想現在的情況，恐怕誰也無法預見到僅積體電路塊一項發明，一旦將其運用於個人電腦、數位通信和工廠機器人身上，會給世界帶來怎樣的變化。
Conflict, defined as opposition among social entities directed against one another, is distinguished from competition,	戰爭衝突與競爭不同，前者可以定義為社會實體之間彼此對立的抗爭，後者可定義為

defined as opposition among social enti-ties independently striving for something which is in inadequate supply.	各個實體在單獨獲取供應不足的物資時所產生的對抗。
Many authors have argued for the in-evitability of war from the premise that in the struggle for existence among animal species, only the fittest survive.	許多作家根據動物世界為生存而進行的鬥爭中具有適者生存的規律這一點，論證戰爭是不可避免的。
Having evolved when the pace of life was slower, the human brain has an inher-ent defect that prevents it from absorbing several streams of information simultane-ously and acting on them quickly.	由於在其進化期間，人類的生活節奏較為緩慢，人腦形成了固有的缺陷，不能同時接收來自多個管道的資訊並迅速進行處理。
We have only to look behind us to get some sense of what may lie ahead.	只要回顧過去，就能知道未來會是什麼樣子。

翻譯考量習作

在第 2.2.1 節「讀者為中心重於原作者為中心」中，有一則《閱微草堂筆記》內故事的英譯例子，以下這則英譯[33]乃是譯自同一篇原文，請針對它就以下三點發表看法與評論：

1. 靠近原文或靠近譯入文，
2. 以原作者為中心或以譯文讀者為中心，
3. 重原文形式或重原文內容。

---

33 摘自「王茜翻譯的閱微草堂筆記」，見2011/9/30之 http://www.wangqian.com.cn/ancient/3.htm

如有需要，亦可對照第 2.2.1 節中之譯文或照你自己的方式修改下文。

In the city Ningbo there was a guy whose surname was Wu. He enjoyed visiting whorehouses. Later he met a fox spirit and often dated her. But at the same time he still patronized the whorehouses. One day, the fox spirit told him: "I can transform my appearance. Whoever you are drawn to, I can transform myself into her appearance after I see her for even once. Therefore, if you think of any girl, I can transform myself into her appearance immediately. Isn't it better than dissipating your money on prostitutes?" They took a crack, and she really transformed herself into another girl immediately and precisely. Therefore, Wu stopped patronizing the whorehouses.

Once he told the fox spirit: "It is so delectable to sleep with different girls. However, it is always a pity that the girls are no more than illusions." The fox spirit answered: "It is not the case. Lustful and sultry amusements are as transient as lightning and stone fires. Not only the girl I transformed is an illusion, but the girl herself is also an illusion. Not only that girl is an illusion, but I myself am also an illusion. The well-known beauties in the history of thousands of years were also illusions. The white poplars, the green grasses, the yellow soils and the dark green mountains, weren't they once also glitzy places of amusement? One makes love with beauties, buries them with earth, and parts with them...all these happen in just a fraction of a second. The passion between two people may be counted in minutes, in days, in months or in years, but the moment of departure will arrive sooner or later. At the moment of departure, whether they have been sticking together for dozens of years, or they have just met each other, they will have to let go, and everything between them will be over. Aren't the days spent with sensuous girls as fugitive as spring dreams? Even though the affection between the two has always been profound and they cling to each other throughout their lives, time will rob the woman of her pleasing appearance and cover her with white hairs, making her no longer look like before. Therefore, the dark eyebrows and the rosy cheeks of the old days are still illusions. So, now why on earth do you only accuse the girl I transformed as illusory?" Wu was enlightened. A few years later, the fox spirit left him, and he never went to whorehouses any more.

第三章
常見的翻譯問題及其處理

本章提綱

3.1 長句的處理

　　較長的句子往往含有比較複雜的文法，致使結構複雜，分析起來很不容易，意思也不容易把握，讓人讀到了後面就忘掉了前面，很不可取，不信的話，讀完下面這一句長達 58 字的句子[1]，看能了解多少：

1　葉乃嘉，《商用英文的溝通藝術》，新文京圖書出版公司，2002/12。

As you know, your year's guarantee is one which covers defective workmanship or materials which would reveal itself under normal use conditions within twelve months, likewise, it exempts the company from mechanical failures due to accident, alteration, misuse or abuse, and time also accounts for a certain amount of deterioration which obviously cannot be covered by our guarantee.

再看看修改後的例子，把原文斷成四句之後，篇幅少了三分之一，是不是易懂而且容易翻譯得多了？

Your one-year guarantee covers defective workmanship. It also covers materials under normal use conditions within 12 months. The guarantee exempts the company from mechanical failures due to accident, alteration, misuse or abuse. Certain amount of deterioration through time obviously cannot be covered.

您這一年期的保證範圍涵蓋貨品出廠時的缺陷，並涵蓋正常使用下 12 個月以內的耗材，保證範圍不涵蓋因事故、改裝、不當使用或濫用所造成的機件故障，當然亦不涵蓋使用期間的特定折耗。

有些翻譯的教材會選用長而複雜的英文句子，煞費功夫地翻譯出來，一方面是讓學習者曉得，翻譯工作有時真的不簡單，真的要下功夫，不要是掉以輕心；一方面有「揚刀立威」的意思，告訴學習者：「你瞧，沒那麼簡單吧？！我的翻譯功力可不是三腳貓的工夫！」

其實，以翻譯長句的方式來學習，讓學習者經歷困頓，固然可使他

們日後在碰到比較簡單的文章時，變得游刃有餘，但也可能使一些人誤以為英文能寫成這麼複雜，非得功力高深不可。殊不知纏夾的長句絕不是寫作能力的表現，反而可能是思路不清的佐証。

像下面這個長達 39 字的句子就是個彆腳英文的例子：

In 1975 psychologist Robert Ader at the University of Rochester School of Medicine conditioned mice to avoid saccharin by simultaneously feeding them the sweetener and injecting them with a drug that while suppressing their immune systems caused stomach upsets.

這個句子充分顯出寫作者沒有清楚敘事的能力，可是，類似的寫作方式在一些科學論文期刊的作品裡卻所在多有。請記住，文字的目的在於達意，而不是要考驗讀者分析文句的能力。要讓讀者更易理解作者想要傳達的意思，短句確實比長句較能勝任，但是身為翻譯者也無從要求原作者把句子寫得簡化一點，只好自力救濟。

選上這個例子的譯者幾經轉折，翻譯如下：

1975 年，羅賈斯特大學醫學院的心理學家 Robert Ader 在使老鼠對排斥糖精形成條件反射的試驗中，餵食老鼠糖精的同時給它們注射了一種藥劑，這種藥在破壞老鼠的免疫系統的同時還會引起腹痛。

能夠翻譯成這樣已經超出原文的成就了，肯定花了不少心力。但是，「對排斥糖精形成條件反射」又是什麼呢？依你之見，應該怎麼翻？

　　我倒是有個比較簡單的方法，就是從根做起，先救一救原文，把那一大句切割成比較短的三個小句如下：

> In 1975 psychologist Robert Ader at the University of Rochester School of Medicine conduct an experiment. In that experiment he conditioned mice to avoid saccharin by simultaneously feeding them the sweetener and injecting them with a drug. The drug, while suppressing the mice's immune systems, caused stomach upsets.

　　1975 年，羅賈斯特大學醫學院的心理學家 Robert Ader 做了一個實驗，在實驗中他用同步餵食糖精和注射藥劑的方式，造成老鼠排斥糖精，該藥劑在抑制老鼠免疫系統的同時還會引起老鼠的腹痛。

　　沒錯，在翻譯應用文字時，不需要像翻譯文藝創作那樣，大費周章地斟酌文字的藝術性或者角色說話的特點，這種情形下，翻譯是可以這樣來的，直逼文意而不隨原文的句型結構起舞。

3.2 連接詞的處理

　　在英文中，除了冠詞 *the*，沒有任何字比 *and* 這個連接詞（Conjunction）更常出現，以 Mark Twain 的〈*The Advanture of Tom Sawyer*〉為例，*and* 在全文中共出現了 3,040 次，稍微落在 *the* 的 3,730 次後面，而遠遠趕在冠詞 a 的 1,832 次之前。

　　and 有下列幾組意義，有了這麼多的意義可以選用，翻譯 *and* 的時候應該可以比較得心應手才是。

1. 又
2. 與（及、和、跟）
3. 同（連同、同時）
4. 且（而且、並且）
5. 而（然而、而且）

其中「而」的適用度最廣，因為它有轉折（即：然而）的作用，也有對等（即：而且）的效果，但要是懶惰地一路「而」到底，也會製造不少累贅字詞。

如果一定要把這個句子譯成下面那樣，就嫌太生硬了：

You should open your eyes and see the world.（你應該睜開眼睛並且看看這個世界。）

因為該句的意思不外是：

You should open your eyes to see the world.（你該打開眼睛來看看世界。）

另外，*and* 還可以引申成與 *then*（於是、然後、接著）同義，又有一個比較鮮為注意的就是，*and* 也可以是不具任何意義的虛字（functional words，不求甚解者敷衍式地把它譯為「功能字眼」），本身並無意義，可以省略不譯，要不然也應避免公式化的譯法。又，既然 *and* 是連接詞，而逗號也有連接的作用，有時將兩者視為同類，也是理所當然。

以下且用不同的例子來一一說明：

Mary gave him a tin basin of water **and** a piece of soap, **and** he went outside the door **and** set the basin on a little bench there; then he dipped the soap in the water and laid it down; turned up his sleeves; poured out the water on the ground, gently, **and** then entered the kitchen **and** began to wipe his face diligently on the towel behind the door.

譯文一	譯文二
瑪麗遞給他一臉盆水和一塊肥皂。於是，他走到門外，把臉盆放在那兒的一個小凳子上。然後他把肥皂蘸了點水，又把它放下；他捲起袖子，輕輕地把水潑在地上，轉身走進廚房，用門後面的一條毛巾使勁地擦著臉。	瑪麗給他一盆水和一塊肥皂，他到門外，把臉盆放在那兒的一張小凳子上，然後把肥皂蘸了水，放下，捲起袖子，輕輕把水潑在地上，接著走進廚房，用門後的一條毛巾使勁擦起臉來。

　　短短的七十字原文中，*and* 就多達六個，不可說不多，在中文裡這樣重覆使用同一個字，未免顯得聱牙透頂。所以，譯文一裡把各個 *and* 分別翻成「和」、「於是」、「又」及「，」；在稍經改良後的譯文二裡，除了把第一個 *and* 譯出之外，把其他的 *and* 都以「，」帶過。

　　又如以下的所有例句裡的 *and*，有哪個是需要大費周章地找個中譯來套用的？

1. And... Ladies and Gentlemen...
2. And now for a commercial break...
3. And now for something completely different...
4. And now for some good news...
5. And now, Adieu. Britain's longest-running political drama is finally coming to an end.

另外 *or* 這個連接詞雖有「或者、也許」之意，但有些時候也不見得就必須譯出來，尤其是跟在 *or* 後面的句子稍長的時候。

What brings joy into your life? Do you know? Are you aware of that which makes you happy? Or are you so busy fulfilling your daily obligations that you put off to some future time those things that make you feel good?

譯文一	譯文二
你知道什麼給你生活帶來快樂？你是否清楚什麼使你幸福？還是你如此忙碌於日常的義務而把那些使你感到快活的事推延到將來？	你可知道什麼給你的生命帶來喜悅？你可清楚什麼能讓你快樂？你是否忙於盡日常的義務而把那些使你感到快活的事往後延？

譯文一中把 *or*...譯成「還是……」可算是比譯成「或者……」、「也許……」要有創意了，但是像在譯文二那樣乾脆取消 *or* 不譯，反使譯文更加中文化而可讀。

3.3 助語詞的處理

英文中的某些字（像 *again, listen, look, now, say, then, well* 等），雖然各有我們原本熟悉的意思，但是我們很常把它們當作發語或助語詞使用，在這種用法下，這些字大多沒有實際的中文譯意。以下就將它們分項敘述。

Again

Again 的最基本意思是「再……」，例如：

The Old Lancaster Road was the original stage coach road from Philadelphia to Lancaster. It branched off from Market Street, and then turning to the right at 52nd Street, and then **again** turned somewhat to the left.

老 Lancaster 路本來是從 Philadelphia 到 Lancaster 的驛馬車道，它從 Market 街分出，到了五十二街右轉，然後再稍轉向左。

但是 *again* 沒有義務非得是「再……」不可，它有時只是發語詞，只是一種說話的習慣，不具實際的意義：

Again, highly simplified here, under certain conditions these coagulate into matter. Those electromagnetic units of high enough intensity automatically activate the subordinate coordinate points of which I have spoken.

　　這還是非常簡化的說法：在某種情況下，這些電磁能量單位凝固成了物質，那些具高強度的電磁能量單位自動引發了我前面所說的次調和點。

　　口語中常會用到的 *but then again...*，有緩衝前文的意味，可以翻做「可是，話說回來……」，而 *then again...* 和 *and then again...* 就有兩重意思，其中之一是有加強前文所描述的事物的意味，可以譯成「再說嘛……」。另外一個就和 *but then again...* 相同，用於緩衝前文，這兩種語意幾乎相差一百八十度，可是[2]其中微妙分別，還是得依上下文來判斷，以下有幾個例子供讀者推敲：

Then again, the present commercial depression has affected ours, a new industrial country, more than yours, an old one.

　　話說回來，當前的商業衰退對我們這個新興工業國家的影響比對你們這個老工業國家要大。

　　這裡的「話說回來」，完全可以代以「再說嘛」，端看上文如何引導。下例的語意也可以因其上文而變。

And then again, some people may never get it.

　　再說嘛，有些人就是永遠搞不懂。

2　這裡這個「可是」就恰恰可以翻成 *but then again...*。

　　原文中的模糊語意，有時是原作者所有意營造出來的，譯者無從效勞，也就只好跟著裝迷糊，用「再說……」這種宜於兩面倒的譯法來敷衍：

> Well, **then again**, all they have to do is get some more money from the city, making their jobs safe for a few more years...

　　再說，只要他們從政府那兒多搞些錢，讓工作多保幾年就……

　　But then again... 就比較不那麼模糊，原因是有 ***but...*** 在主導整句話的語意：

> ...It went surprisingly well. But then again, not knowing how a traditional band setup produces music first-hand, I can't directly compare.

　　……進行得非常好，但是話說回來，我沒有親身了解傳統樂團如何製作音樂，無法直接比較。

> TV ads are less effective. But then again, it depends on who's making them.

　　電視廣告的效果比較小，可是話說回來，那也得看是誰做的廣告。

I adore kitties and I am glad to see this one gets a very happy ending, a new home, and loving owners.... Our society is cruel to some animals, but then again, we sometimes find babies in dumpsters.... Go figure.

我喜歡貓，很高興能看到這隻貓有個好結局，有個新家和新主人……，我們的社會對某動物很殘忍，但是話說回來，我們不也有時會在垃圾堆裡發現棄嬰嗎……大家自己想想吧。

佛經中常見的「復次……」就是標準的 *again* 或是 *repeat* 的意思。若是一見到文中有這類用法的 *again*，就一律譯成「再次的」，那未免是太過懶惰。

Say, Look, and Listen

Say 可用作發語詞，不具實際的意義，多了它，句子的涵義不會增加，少了它，句子的涵義也不會減損，它的存在只代表了一種說話的習慣，因此就可有可無，自然也就可譯可不譯。例如，下面兩句中的 *say...* 都譯成了「我說……」，其實，沒有加上「我說……」，也無傷原意。

· Say, I really like to accept your offer. But I'm afraid that something may come up and force me to leave this place.
（我說，我真的很想接受你的提議，但又怕有狀況出現，迫使我離開本地）

> · Say, how about creating your own profile here and let others to say hi to you as well?（我說，你何不在這裡給自己做個介紹，好讓別人也來向你搭訕？）

Look 的作用也和 **say** 一樣，像下面第一句沒有譯出 **look...** 來的方式，是完全合理的。電視或電影看得多的人就會發現，有些譯字幕的人硬要把 **look** 譯成「瞧⋯⋯」，其實可說是多此一舉，若真要譯，也可以像第二句那樣，譯成「依我看⋯⋯」。

> 1. Look, why don't you go to a grocery store and pick up some pork tomorrow?（你明天何不到店裡去買點豬肉？）
> 2. Look, if you don't already have a date, let's go out and have a dinner together this Friday night.（依我看，如果你還沒有約會，那這個禮拜五晚上我們出去吃個飯吧。）

現在輪到 listen。

以下三個例句的前兩句中，**listen** 都不譯出，因為，若要照勉強翻譯 **say** 和 **look** 的方式那樣，把 **listen** 硬翻成中文，會造成一種不太禮貌的語氣，像下面第一句那樣。

當面叫人家「聽著⋯⋯」是很不得體的，與原文的意思全不搭調，因此，在第二句不譯為宜，若非譯不可，就不如像第三句那樣，譯成「我說⋯⋯」。

1. Listen, you have the wrong number!（聽著！你打錯電話了！）
2. Listen, let's meet at the front desk later and then plan on what to do on our trip back to Taipei.（我們待會兒到櫃檯見，然後打算一下回台北的路上要做些什麼。）

3. Listen, why don't we go to Washington DC together this weekend and see if there is any new development.（我說啊，這個周末我們何不一起到華府去瞧瞧有什麼進展。）

至於把第三句中的 *listen* 翻譯出來，是有原因的，這個句子確實有不耐煩的意味在內。

另外，出現在本小節幾個例句中的 *and*，都用作連接詞，而且都是虛字，因而不予譯出，此點可參照第 3.7.1 節「*And* 的處理」。

Now

把 *now* 當成現在，好像是天經地義：

Now our time in the dining room was over and we were lead down a corridor and into a room....

如今，我們在餐廳的時間結束了，就被帶經一條走道，進到另一個房間……

但有時 *now* 也只是一種說話的習慣，或是開始說話時引起大家注意的發語詞，不具實際的意義：

Now: This is highly simplified, but the subjective experience of any consciousness is automatically expressed as electromagnetic energy units. These exist "beneath" the range of physical matter. They are, if you prefer, incipient particles that have not yet emerged into matter.

　　這是非常簡化的說法，但是，任何意識主觀的感受確實會自動變成電磁能量的單位，這些單位存在於物質事物的「底層」，你們可以稱之「尚未轉變」物質的初素。

　　Now, this is not to be a technical book, so this is not the time nor place to discuss thouroughly the action , behavior or effects of these coordinate points.

　　本書無意成為技術讀本，是故此間實不宜透徹討論「調和點」之行為和效能。

　　以下這些例子中的 *now* 都屬於虛字，不必譯出：

- Now people, people...why all the hate? Can't we all just get along? （各位！各位……為什麼要恨？難道大家就不能好好相處嗎？）
- Now, the soul is never diminish, nor basically are any portions of the self. （靈魂不滅，自我任何的部分基本上也不滅。）
- Now: A whole book could easily be written upon this subject. （光是這個主題就夠輕易寫上一整本書。）
- Now anything that appears in physical terms also exists in other terms that you do not perceive. （任何出現在物理狀態東西，也出現在其他你所無法感知的狀態。）

Well and Then

用 *well* 起頭來回答問題是一種常見的說話習慣，因此 *well* 的使用場合甚多，在以下三個例子中，後兩句裡的 *well* 雖然都譯做「好……」，其中第三句裡的 *then* 還譯成了「那麼……」，但其實它們只做助語詞用，沒有譯出的必要。

1. Well, we certainly support greater emphasis on finding explosive devices, but not at the expense of another area of aviation security. (我們當然支持花更多努力去找出爆裂物，但也不該犧牲其他方面的飛行安全。)

2. Well, I think the only things that are certain is that some people are intelligent, some people are average, and some people are just plain stupid. (好，我想唯一可以認定的是：有些人聰明，有些人普通，而有些人擺明了就是笨。)

3. Well then, we certainly hope that Iran will take a few days to think over a very serious proposal. (好，那麼，我們當然希望伊朗會花幾天的功夫來考慮一個嚴肅的建議。)

Then 固然可以翻成「那……」或「那麼……」，但許多時候它只用於銜接語氣，是不具實際意義的助語詞。如下例：

There is a storm on the way and no its not a hurricane, well then again maybe it is a hurricane.

有個風暴在成形中……不對……不是颶風……哦……也許是颶風。

本節最前面的 *again* 條目中，還有其他 *then* 的例句可供參閱。

3.4 被動語態的處理

在中文裏原本很少使用被動語態（Passive Tense），但由於受到西潮的影響，中文裏出現被動語態的情形也就增多了。英文中使用被動式的地方固然比中文多得多，但也不必以為那就是英文的特色。

如果連教授翻譯的教師也只知道「英譯中不得逕直譯成被動語態」，而誤認為「中譯英不妨多採用被動語態」，當然也就不免有人受到錯誤的啟迪，認為使用被動式才算洋化，但是這真是天大的冤枉。有這類誤會的翻譯者，不但在「英翻中」時把英文裡的被動式句型照單全收到中文來，還變本加厲，在「中翻英」時把中文裡的非被動式句型轉用英文的被動式句型來表示。

下面引用的是一篇中文論文的英文摘要，其中的七個句子，每一句都是以被動式「拼湊」而成，作者可能還自認為這樣才算擺脫中式英文的窠臼，也才更像英文，殊不知整段文字在識者的眼中，十分慘不忍賭：

In this paper, a customer relationship management (CRM) platform based on data mining method is constructed to understand customers in detail. An on-line register mechanism is developed. Three web services, data mining, data preprocess, and decision support, are built over Internet to provide data mining service with XML format exchange. The systematic UML analysis and design are used to develop and decompose the entire CRM system. An intelligent data mining algorithm is developed for classification. A simple fuzzy discrimination index (SFDI) and fuzzy entropy are constructed for attribute selection. Finally, the real customer data from a cosmetic company is employed to justify the proposed CRM platform and shows good results.

即使不用看上文的中文原文，也知道原來的中文決不會寫成這個樣子。碰到這樣的文字，真正熟悉兩種語文差異的譯者當然知道要怎麼改進：

The researcher constructs a data-mining based customer relationship management (CRM) platform with an on-line register mechanism to support detailed customer behavior understanding. This internet platform provides data mining service with XML format exchange. The complete system, as designed via a systematic UML analysis, consists of three web functions (i.e. data mining, data preprocess, and decision support). It uses an intelligent data mining algorithm for data classification A simple fuzzy discrimination index (SFDI) is built in the system along with fuzzy entropy for the purpose of attribute selection. The proposed CRM platform is validated with the real-life customer data from a cosmetic company.

大幅修改的結果，文中的被動句由七個減到了兩個，文字顯得更順暢，不像先前那樣一路被動，難以卒讀。

　　被動語態常出現在老式的英文裏，曾經是一種流行的寫作方式，但經過有識之士幾十年來的宣導，已經使被動語態的市場縮小了許多。下面這段引文就強調了主動語態要比被動語態可取：

> Our editors find that one of the greatest weaknesses of admissions essays is their frequent use of the passive tense.
>
> ...Overuse of the passive voice throughout an essay can make your prose seem flat and uninteresting. Sentences in active voice are also more concise than those in passive voice.
>
> —GradSchools.com Information Center[3]

　　事實上，主動語態能夠更清楚、更直接地表達文意，也較被動語態簡短有力，比較下面兩個同義的句子，就可以很明顯地分辨出孰優孰劣：

> Passive: A decision was made by his family...
> Active: His family decided...

　　當然，被動語句是無法、也毋須全面避免的，但是，在任何寫作和翻譯中，如果不是要刻意經營出一種被動的態勢，就應該儘可能少用老舊僵化的被動式。同時，翻譯的時候，在可能的情況下，大可一改英文的被動語態，將之以更切合中文的習慣轉譯出來。而在中文裡無法避免被動語句時，也不用死命抓住「被」字，舉凡「經（過）」、「遭（到）」、「受（到）」、「讓」、「給」等等，都是被動的表示，而

3　http://www.gradschools.com/info/cyberedit/lf_verbtense.html, Retrieved on 2006/9/15.

且都比「被」更具有本土的味道，需要時不妨交替使用，增加文字的多
樣性，例如：

原文	建議修訂
該環境評估報告被鑑定後，歸入評估不完整之列。	該環境評估報告經（過）鑑定後，歸入評估不完整之列。
警察被槍擊的案子並不是第一次發生。	警察遭（到）槍擊的案子並不是第一次發生。
調查顯示，該弱勢團體的權利仍然不被重視。	調查顯示，該弱勢團體的權利仍然不受重視。
進口牛肉有問題的事先別被民眾知道。	進口牛肉有問題的事先別讓民眾知道。
經濟罪犯的海外銀行帳戶早就被凍結了。	經濟罪犯的海外銀行帳戶早就給凍結了。

3.5 一字多義的處理

　　字典是翻譯者的基本工具，即使是已經認識的字，有時也需要查一查字典，看看有沒有更恰當的字義可以使用，不該偏執地一律使用自己先前學得的、習慣的使用的字義。

　　以下用 *complain, fair, great, intimate, sly, storm* 等字來示範英翻中時一字多義的難局。

Complain

看看下文：

> ... The Times newspaper agrees, **complaining** that quality has suffered as student numbers soared, with close tutorial supervision giving way to "mass production methods more typical of European universities."

……《泰晤士報》對此有同感，它抱怨說，由於學生人數激增，教學品質受影響，個別指導不得不讓位於「歐陸大學慣有的大量生產方式」。

整體上，這段譯文譯得相當妥貼，只是有一個毛病相當礙眼，那就是：《泰晤士報》有什麼立場來「抱怨」歐陸大學的教學方式呢？

應該是人家的作為有礙於你，基於切身的不滿，你才有立場抱怨。翻譯者不該一見到了 *complain*，就直覺地想到「抱怨」，而要推敲「抱怨」在此是否合理，只要查查字典就可以發現，*complain* 還意味著「抗議、評論、挑毛病、反對」等等，換作是你，你會挑哪一個意思呢。

Fair

Fair 雖然可以譯成「公平」，但是也有「好」、「不錯」的的意思，因此，與其譯為「這不公平」」或「那不公平」，*It's not fair* 及 *That's not fair* 也可以翻譯成「真差勁」，至於其中的 *it* 及 *that* 都是虛字，可以不譯。

Great

有人動輒把 *great* 翻成「偉大」[4]，但是，以下面幾句為例：

> · She has a *great* mother.
> · There are many *great* atheletes.
> · He is a *great* actor.

先不提母親應該到什麼程度才稱得上偉大，且問，這世界上哪有這麼多「偉大」的運動員或演員？

Great 除了有「偉大、崇高、龐大」之意，還有「嚴重、主要、知名、很好、優秀、絕佳、完全、強力、過分」等等意思，

甚至還有當成反語用時的「糟糕」意味，例如：

> · Oh, that's great. Look at what he just did. （這下可好，瞧他幹的好事。）

「偉大」不是隨隨便便就可以賦予的層級，所以請別再把 "This is a great movie." 翻成「這是一部偉大的電影」，或把 "Clinton is a great politician." 翻成「Clinton 是一個偉大的政治人物」了。

此處最接近的意思應是「很好、優秀」，而非一般「大、偉大或龐大」之意。

4　源自中國大陸的電影字幕以及網路文字的譯文尤其如此。

Intimate

　　像 intimate 這個形容詞，大部分人所知道的意思是 close（親密、親近），但其實它還有 comfortable, cozy（舒適）、detailed, exhaustive（詳盡）、familiar（熟悉）、friendly（友善）、in-depth, profound（深入）、thorough（完整）、warm（溫暖）、confidential, personal, private, secret（私密）、甚至還有作為動詞使用時的 indicate, imply（暗示）和 suggest（建議）等諸多意思。

　　在與原文對照翻譯的時候，譯者應該在各個涵義中選擇一個最適當的，不要像某些不專業而又懶惰的翻譯者一樣，不願意查字典，就一廂情願地把「親密」或「親蜜」硬套在所有出現 intimate, intimately, intimacy 的句子裡。

　　現在，請看看下面這些例句裡衍生自 *intimate* 的字中，到底有沒有可以算得上是「親密」或「親蜜」的？[5]

1. A decorative fireplace and classic chandeliers provide a warm **intimate** feeling to the space. (**cozy**)
2. It's difficult to have an **intimate** feeling in such a large theatre, yet it depends on the number of people in the volume, so this theatre has an intimate feeling in spite of its size. (**private**)
3. To help enforce the feeling of **intimacy**, the red upholstered seats are closer together than at other theatres. (**warm**)
4. All of this he narrated with the nasal accent of a native New

---

5　讀者可以參考一下各句末括號中的字義。

Yorker, with all of the confidence and all of the command of a performer who knows his art **intimately**, and who knows how to make it feel intimate to an audience. (**thorough**)

5. He finds some remote, desolate, beautiful parts of Africa -- places that we viewers will probably never go, but now feel **intimate** to us because of what we saw in this film. (**familier**)

如果讀者不能解讀以下這兩句，就有勞查查字典去。

· Thomas's great facility and strength as a poet lay in his ability to internalize his fury and make it feel **intimate** to his readers.

· Many original paintings and portraits, prints and ceramics give the house a very **intimate** feeling and an old world atmosphere.

Sly

Sly 一般多譯成「狡猾、狡黠」等，比較口語的意思可以是「滑頭」，有負面的意味，殊不知 sly 也有「機伶、聰明」的、較正面的意義，還有「小心、神秘、防衛性」等中性的意思。

1. I smile slyly from the compliment as she hands me my gun. I put it back in my holster and adjust my jacket. （她把槍遞還給我時，我對她的恭維防衛性地笑笑，把槍放回槍套

裡，然後整了整夾克。）

2. A smile slyly exchanged over a table top had the power to get the heart into a frenzy. （在檯前互換的一個神秘微笑有讓人心陷入熱情的魔力。）

下面這個例子是教女性如何挑動男子興趣的技術指導文字，請斟酌一下其中的 *sly* 有無狡猾或狡點的意味？

Lick your upper lip...bite bottom lip...with a **sly** look in your eyes and place one hand in front of your face as if you were in deep thought but are using it to hide your blushing. Let your hair fall over your face, and look at the guy through your eyelashes.

Storm

在 1992 年波斯灣戰爭（Gulf War）中，美軍的主要攻擊行動有個響亮的代碼--Dessert Storm，Storm 一字有「爆發、暴怒、風暴、攻擊，突襲」等多個意思，而翻譯的人竟出人意表，沒有聯想到這場大規模軍事行動跟「攻擊、進擊或突擊」的關係，反倒把它和沒有多大關係的「風暴」套在一起，這種半吊子的翻譯可說是跌破專家眼鏡，可是一盲引眾盲，各個華文華語媒體不加思考，紛紛跟進使用，真個是：

媒體力量龐大，專家無力回天。

從此，*Dessert Storm* 就以沙漠風暴之名，正式列入歷史。

沙漠攻擊行動結束後，就是收拾戰場了，這時的行動代碼就叫做 Dessert Shield，*Shield* 一字也有「保護、阻擋、防禦、盾牌」等多個意思，這一次翻譯的人倒是沒有選上「盾牌」，他把 *Dessert Shield* 譯成沙漠防禦，要比上一個翻譯者稱職得多。

只是我以為，要是論對仗的工整，還是「沙漠盾牌」比較對得起「沙漠風暴」。

言歸正傳……

以上只是用幾個隨手捻來的例子，來說明一字多義在翻譯上所製造的問題，其實英文翻成中文時，一字多義乃是常態，負責任的翻譯者碰到自己無法解讀的原文，不會吝惜一查字典，一來是為了免得誤導讀者，二來也要想到天下之大，能人輩出，率爾操斛，難保不會貽笑方家。

從事翻譯工作的人最少要有一本好的字典。電子字典是很好的工具，像內建在 Microsoft-Word 裡的英英同義字典就非常好用，可以幫助譯者省時省力、又快又準地找出字義，以往所謂「電子字典不如傳統紙本字典」的觀念，早已落伍。有了電子計算機以後，堅持使用算盤實在沒什麼道理。

3.6 人稱代名詞的處理

在英文裡需使用主詞的地方，比在中文裡多很多，為了避免重複，往往需要用代名詞來代替前文所提到的人事物，因此，應該仔細閱讀全文，找出其中具有指代意義的詞，根據上下文確定它們指代的人、事、物。

有些情形下，不妨適時把代名詞還原成它們各自代表的東西，然後明確地翻譯出來。但有時候，中文句子可以省略主詞，為求譯文更為中化，遇到人稱代名詞（Personal Pronoun）過多之處，為了讓中文的文意

較為通順，原文中的代名詞及關係代名詞也可以、甚至不用一一譯出。例如 *Have you had your lunch, yet?* 雖然有生手會譯成「你吃過你的午餐了嗎」，但其實只要譯成「你吃過午餐了嗎」就足夠了。

　　請看下例：

...Sid's fingers slipped and the bowl dropped and broke. Tom was in ecstasies. In such ecstasies that **he** even controlled his tongue and was silent. **He** said to **himself** that **he** would not speak a word, even when his aunt came in, but would sit perfectly still till she asked who did the mischief; and then **he** would tell, and there would be nothing so good in the world as to see that pet model "catch it." **He** was so brimful of exultation that **he** could hardly hold **himself** when the old lady came back and stood above the wreck discharging lightnings of wrath from over her spectacles.

譯文一	譯文二
……希德手一滑，糖罐子掉到地上摔碎了。湯姆簡直高興得要命，但他閉著嘴，一言不發。他心裏想他還是什麼不說為好，就這麼靜靜地坐著，等他姨媽進來，問這是誰闖的禍，那時他再說出來。看那個模範「寵兒」吃苦頭，那真是最大快人心的事。當老太太走進來，站在那兒望著地上的破	……希德手一滑，糖罐子就摔碎了，湯姆樂昏了，當下他還忍著高興，一氣不吭，要自己先一句話都別說，就這麼靜靜坐著，等姨媽進來問這是誰闖的禍，才說出來。世上再也沒有比看那個模範寵兒「就逮」那樣大快人心的事了。老太太回來，站在地上的碎片前，眼

| 碎的罐子，從眼鏡上面放射出憤怒的火花，他[6]真是高興到了極點，幾乎按捺不住了。 | 鏡架後射出憤怒的電光，湯姆簡直是高興得快按捺不住了。 |

　　短短的 108 字原文中，代表湯姆的代名詞（*he, his* 或 *himself*）就多達十個，幾乎佔了全文的 10%，如果全數翻譯出來，簡直不知道要把中文糟蹋到什麼程度。譯文一中已經把「他」減少了一半，但五個還是不算少，譯文二則精簡多了，全段只出現了一個「他」，而且這樣的簡化方式並沒有礙及文意。

　　下面這個例子有 41 個字，其中代名詞（*he* 或 *his*）出現了三次，連接詞 ***and*** 也出現了三次：

> The boy ran around and stopped within a foot or two of the flower, and then shaded his eyes with his hand and began to look down street as if he had discovered something of interest going on in that direction.

　　那孩子跑過去，停在離花一兩尺的地方，接著手搭涼棚朝街上看去，好像發現那邊有什麼有趣的事情。

　　譯文雖然連一個代名詞或連接詞都不譯，但是行文不減流暢：

6　譯文中還使用這個「他」來代表湯姆業已不怎麼妥當，因為這個「他」離開上一個提到湯姆的地方已經很遠了，其代替的力量已經很弱，不如重新提起湯姆來鞏固一下文意。

> If **you** have created a job, a relationship, or anything that is not bringing **you** joy, look inward and ask why **you** feel **you** must be in a relationship with anything or anyone that does not bring **you** joy. Often it is because **you** do not believe **you** deserve to have what **you** want.

譯文一	譯文二
如果你創造了一份工作，一種關係或其他一些並不給你帶來快樂的東西，反躬自問一下為什麼你會覺得必須與那些並不給你帶來快樂的人打交道。經常是因為你相信你還不應得你想要的東西。（84 字）	你若是投入了一份工作、一段戀情、或任何不讓你愉快的事，反問自己為何覺得有必要應酬那些不讓你愉快的人事。原因多半是你不信自己配得到自己所想要的。（71 字）

原文只有 54 字，代名詞 *you* 就多達八個，幾近全文的 15%，若是像譯文一那樣幾乎全數譯出，實在不能算是好譯文，譯文二把「你」減半，其他的「你」以「自己」代之，這樣的方式使文意更為流暢。

3.7 關係代名詞與疑問代名詞的處理

中文裡沒有類似關係代名詞（Relative Pronoun）的詞類，但是在英文裡用到關係代名詞的場合極多，這在英文結構中是無法避免的。不巧的是，英文的關係代名詞和其疑問代名詞（Interrogative Pronoun）恰好是同一組字（見表 3-1）

表 3-1　關係代名詞表

人	事、物	時	地	原因	方法
who whom whose which	what which	when	where	why	how

　　疑問代名詞與關係代名詞一樣，都可引導名詞子句，也在它們所引導的子句中扮演主詞的角色，因此造成了許多人翻譯時的混淆。現在用些簡單的例子逐步澄清兩者的差異。

　　例一：

　　疑問代名詞：I already told the detective <u>about when</u> I saw that person.
　　關係代名詞：I already told the detective (at the time)[7] when I saw that person.

　　第一句中的疑問代名詞是做為限定詞用，在這種限定詞角色中，它們有時也被稱為疑問形容詞（interrogative adjectives）。這是它比較容易與關係代名詞混淆的例子，一定有人不會察覺，只是 ***about*** 一字之差，第一句就譯成「我已經告訴過警探我什麼時候看到那人」，而第二句則應譯成「我看到那人的時候已經告訴過警探」。再看例二：

　　疑問代名詞：I know <u>where</u> he is going.

　　關係代名詞：I know the place where he is going.

---

[7] ***At the time*** 可省略。

　　第一句很簡單，直譯成「我知道他要去哪裡」即可，而第二句中的 *where* 是修飾 *the place* 的，整個句子有「我知道他要去的地方叫做什麼」之意。但是話說回來，由於英文的簡化趨勢，第二類句型中的 *the place* 常會被省略，因此，中文翻譯者又回到原點，再度混淆。

　　例三：

　　疑問代名詞：I don't know when he will come.
　　關係代名詞：I don't know the time when he will come.

　　第一句直譯成「我不知道他什麼時候會來」即可，而第二句中的 *when* 是修飾 *the time* 的，有「我不知道他來的時間」之意，其中暗示了「知道他大概什麼時候會來，但是對他來的正確時間則不太清楚」的意思。

　　同理，英文的簡化趨勢常會把第二類句型中的 *the time* 省略，翻譯者還是難免混淆。

　　我們只好用另外的規則來判別這兩種詞類。在例一中，省略了 *I know the place where he is going* 裡的 *where*，意思保持不變，但要是省略了 *I know where he is going* 裡的 *where*，意思就變成了「我知道他要去」，與原句大不相同。

　　I don't know he will come 意思是「我不知道他會來」與例二中 *I don't know when he will come* 的意思大相逕庭，而 *I don't know the time he will come* 雖然讀來有些異樣，但保持了 *I don't know the time when he will come* 的意思。因此：

　　能夠省略不譯而不影響文意的叫關係代名詞。

　　省略不譯會改變文意的的叫疑問代名詞。

　　但這也只是權宜之計，並不全面。我們權且放下這難以釐清的細

節，多讀、多寫、多用功，任何語言只要變成了我們直覺的一部分，就可以不假思索地應用自如。君不見我們說母語的時候，豈不是很少考慮到文法啊、語法啊這些枝節。

而英翻中時，原文句子中若有代名詞和其他具有指代意義的詞，應根據上下文確定它們指代的內容是什麼；又，在許多情形下，為了讓中文的文意較為通順，原文中的代名詞及關係代名詞可以、甚至不用一一譯出。請看下例：

Out of our emotional experiences with objects and events comes a social feeling of agreement that certain things and actions are "good" and others are "bad", and we apply these categories to every aspect of our social life-from what foods we eat and what clothes we wear to how we keep promises and which people our group will accept.

譯文一	譯文二
與事物的情感經歷使*我們*產生了一種社會認同感，即認為某些事情或行為是好的，其他的是壞的。*我們*還把「好」和「壞」的分類推而廣之，運用於社會生活的方方面面，從*我們*吃的，穿的，到*如何守信*以及*與什麼人為伍*等。（97字）	判別好惡的社會認同感隨*我們*在情緒上對事物的體驗而來，*我們*還把這種好惡的分類引申到社會生活的各方面，從吃的、穿的、到然諾和交遊的狀況等。（69字）

　　原文中的七個人稱代名詞（*our, we*）到了譯文一就減成了三個，其他的代名詞（*what, how, which*）從四個減成兩個，譯文二裡的人稱代名詞雖沒有比譯文一要少，但其他的代名詞就一個也不剩了，譯文二精簡了近三分之一，讀者不妨比較這兩個譯文的可讀性高下如何。

How

　　本節所要提到的關係代名詞翻譯中，*How* 的問題是最小的，但還是難免有人混淆了它的角色，非得把它翻成「如何」不可，例如，就會有人把下面的句子譯成「你難道不同意這就是人們為何意外而死嗎？」

　　Don't you agree these are the ways how people are killed by accident?

　　其實 *how* 在做為關係代名詞的時候，是根本不用譯出來的，所以上句可以譯成：「你不同意有人就是這樣枉死的嗎？」

　　以下的幾個譯例中，就沒有一個把 *how* 翻成「如何」的：

1. So I guess those are the ways how we're connected.（因此我猜我們就是那樣接上線的。）
2. As young researchers advance in their career through friendly competition, the system would be gradually transformed into the one in which friendly competition is the norm. I believe that is the way how the reform should take place.（年輕的研究者能透過友善的競爭在生涯上邁進，系統就會漸漸轉型，使得友善的競爭成為常態，我相信這就是轉

型應有的方式。）

3. This is a very important moment for countries that are oil exporters to use their windfall gains either to reduce their public debt, or to increase effective and high-quality investments or to save. It is the way how countries will strike this balance between saving and investing and reduce the public debt that will determine the country's medium term growth rate.（這是產油國以獲利來減少公債、增加有效且高品質的投資、或增加儲蓄的極重要一刻，國家要達到儲蓄和投資間的平衡、減少會影響國家中程成長率的公債，就該這樣。）

When

When 這個表示時間的關係代名詞在英文裡使用 *when* 的場合非常多，許多翻譯者在遇到 *when*...的時候，常常制式地把它譯做「當……」，殊不考慮中文裡不但不需要這麼泛濫的「當……」，甚至幾乎沒有「當……」的必要，例如：

When are we leaving?（我們什麼時候走？）
We'll leave when everybody arrives.（大家到齊了就走）[8]。

這兩句話都用到了 *when*，可是，它們的中文譯句裡都沒有出現「當」。可以想見，會有些人硬是要把第二句譯成：

8　參見第 3.5 節「人稱代名詞的翻譯」。

當大家到齊了我們就走。

這樣的翻譯雖然沒什麼錯，但是你若要從眾多翻譯者間出類拔萃，就應該講究一點，讓英文的歸英文，中文的歸中文。看看下面的例子翻譯成中文時，省去「當」，於文意無損，但是在中文的文意上，就流暢得多了。

It is wrong to curse a flower and wrong to curse a man. It is wrong not to hold any man in honor, and it is wrong to ridicule any man. Your must honor yourselves and see within yourselves the spirit of eternal validity. You must honor all other individuals, because within each is the spark of this validity. When you curse another, you curse yourselves, and the curse returns to you. When you are violent, the violence returns.

譯文一	譯文二
詛咒一朵花和詛咒一個人都是錯誤。不尊重任何一個人和嘲笑任何一個人都是錯誤。你必須尊重你自己，看到你自身永久有效的精神。你必須尊重其他所有的個人，因為在他們每個身上有著這種有效性的閃光。當你詛咒他人時，你也詛咒自己，這詛咒轉回向你。當你使用暴力，暴力也會轉回你。	罵花是錯的，罵人也不對。不尊重人是錯的，嘲弄人也不對。要尊重自己，認清有個永遠安穩的靈魂在你裡頭。要尊重別人，因為每個人都有這種安穩的內在光輝。咒別人就是咒自己，咒力會回到你身上，使用暴力，暴力就會反噬。

如果硬要用「當」，依照英文中 *when* 出現的頻繁程度，你的中譯文就可能「當」得厲害了。

Who

下面這個譯例不是虛構的，而是出現在一本翻譯的新時代（New Age）類書裡的文字：

This is who I am. This is who I really am.
這就是我是誰，這就是我真正是誰。

其實只要稍有用心就可以知道，上例中的 *who* 是關係代名詞而非疑問代名詞，*This is who I am* 更貼切的翻譯，乃是「這就是我」、「這就是我的本質」或「這就是我的本性」等等，這個句子若出現在一般的談話中，也可以譯成「我就是這樣」，至於 *This is who I really am* 就更簡單了，直接譯成「這就是真正的我」就結了。

文字有自己的社會生命，會進化也會退化，而翻譯是一種文字工作，一般從事文字工作的人士，也許不見得有能力促進文字的進化，但是，奉勸諸位文字工作者至少也別做文字退化的推手。

Why

以應付考試為目標的英文教學常會教導固定的句型，學生們只要把一些「常考句型」背熟，自然就能應付那方面的考試需要，這種填鴨式的教學方式有它的價值，但是也僵化了學生們的大腦，比如說，*That's the reason why...* 就硬被套上了「那就是為什麼……的原因」的帽子，搞得難以翻身。

　　讓我好奇的是，我們幾乎看不到有人把 *That's the place where I was born.* 翻譯成「那就是在哪裡我出生的地方」，把 *That's the time when he receive his gift.* 翻譯成「那就是什麼時候當他收到禮物的時間」，或把 *That's the person who show up in the class.* 翻譯成「那就是誰出現在課堂上的人」，甚至也極少有人把 *That's the way how I conduct the experiement.* 翻譯成「那就是我如何做實驗的方法」，為什麼卻有千千萬萬的人偏偏要把 *That's the reason why it is bothering me so much.* 翻譯成「那就是為什麼這件事如此困擾我的原因」？弄得就連並非翻譯自英文的本土文章，都「那就是為什麼……的原因」起來了。

　　翻譯不是一種標準程序，好的翻譯者不應被這些陋習和積非所限，就像照著食譜學做菜的人，要記得食譜並非必須嚴格遵行的聖典，它只不過是前人做菜經驗的紀錄，我們自然不用銖兩計較於其中所說的要用多少醋多少油，何況，說不定我們還會因為稍加增減變化而另闢蹊徑。

　　當然，我們自己的方法也不能太離譜，就像做菜的時候，用醬油來代替鹽巴是可以湊合的，千萬不要一意孤行地把糖當鹽使用。

　　先看一個彆扭的翻譯例子：

Summer is hot. That is the reason why I don't like it.
夏天很熱，那就是為什麼我不喜歡它的原因。

　　要使譯作更順暢可讀，變通一下當然值得鼓勵。而進一步來說，別人照著葫蘆能夠畫出瓢來，我難道就不能比他畫得更傳神嗎？況且，「那就是為什麼……的原因」也不過是前人想出來的彆腳公式而已，如今既然連它的祖宗 *That's the reason why....* 都常被有識之士簡化成 *That's why....* ，我們為何就不能推翻「那就是為什麼……的原因」呢？

　　但是，把 *That's why...* 譯成「那就是為什麼……」除了是換湯不換藥

之外，還使中文譯文有如斷了氣，沒有結尾的句子顯得更乏善可陳，例如：

Summer is hot. That is why I don't like it.
夏天很熱，那就是爲什麼我不喜歡它。

那麼，到底要怎麼翻才比較自然呢？試用「因此」看看，沒錯，***That's the reason why...***和 ***That's why...***都有「因此」的意思，像下面這個譯文，是不是就好多了？

夏天很熱，因此我不喜歡。

由於本書所鼓勵的，是不拘泥於固定的形式，所以也不強調「因此」是 ***That's the reason why...***和 ***That's why...***的最佳出路，以下的句法也都值得交互使用：

這就是……的原因
正因如此，才……
就因爲這樣……

請看下例：

Those of you who are willing to look upward and find your vision will find your lives even more accelerated. If you think you are busy right now - be prepared! Things will happen even faster, and that is why wisdom and discernment are becoming increasingly important. That is why you will want to look at each day and compare it to your higher purpose.

譯文一	譯文二
你們那些願意向上尋求自己夢想的人會發現自己生活加速得更快。如果你認爲現在已經很忙了。準備好！事情會發生得更快，<u>那就是爲什麼</u>智慧和分辨力正<u>變得愈加重要，那就是爲什麼</u>你得把每一天都與自己更高的目標相聯繫。	你們之間那些想提升自己願景的人，會發現自己生命的步調加快。若你自認現在已經夠忙了，還有得瞧呢！事情會來得更快，<u>就因爲這樣</u>，智慧和判斷力<u>變得更重要，也正因如此</u>，你會要檢視自己每天過得是否符合你更高的目標。

再看一個例子：

You will see the reason why people want you to step down after you watch the TV news tonight.

從下面的譯文中，你會做什麼選擇？

1. 你看了今晚的電視新聞後，就知道大家要你下台的原因了。
2. 等你看了今晚的電視新聞，就知道大家爲什麼要你下台了。
3. 看了今晚的電視新聞後就知道爲什麼大家要你下台的原因了。

3.8 一些偏執譯法和誤用

　　本節主要是在指出常見的、最為一般青澀翻譯者所誤譯的和偏執的譯法。

3.8.1 冠詞的處理

　　英文字句前常要冠上冠詞（*a, an* 或 *the*），中文句子就沒有冠詞，由於中文並無相類的冠詞，因此英文冠詞成了一般英文學習者的難題。

　　冠詞 *a, an, the* 和連接詞一樣，屬於虛詞（Functional Word）。凡是英文普通名詞，可數而且是單數時，其前必加冠詞。不定冠詞 *a*、*an* 加在單數名詞之前，則表明其後的名詞乃是泛指該事物的全體，此時冠詞不必譯出。例如：

　　A spear or a robot is as much a cultural as a physical object.（矛和機器人既是物理體，同樣也是文化現象。）

　　若加定冠詞 *the*，則表示其後名詞乃是「特指」。「泛指」即非特定的泛稱，「特指」即特別指定的對象。

　　例如在 *The horse is a useful animal* 中，冠詞 *the* 特指馬類，冠詞 a 則是泛指 *useful animal*，故應該譯成「馬是有用的動物」，而不可譯成「這馬是一個有用的動物」。*The TV is a gift from my brother* 中，冠詞 *the* 特指該 *TV*，冠詞 *a* 則是泛指任何 *gift*，故應該譯成「那電視是我弟弟送的生日禮物」。

　　這兩個例子當然不足以概括大部分的情況。下面這段 250 字的原文有 28 個 *the* 和 11 個 *a*，且看看其後的譯文如何對待這麼多的冠詞。

原文	中譯
About midnight Joe awoke, and called **the** boys. There was **a** brooding oppressiveness in **the** air that seemed to bode something. **The** boys huddled themselves together and sought **the** friendly companionship of **the** fire, though **the** dull dead heat of **the** breathless atmosphere was stifling. They sat still, intent and waiting. **The** solemn hush continued. Beyond **the** light of **the** fire everything was swallowed up in **the** blackness of darkness. Presently there came **a** quivering glow that vaguely revealed **the** foliage for **a** moment and then vanished. By and by another came, **a** little stronger. Then another. Then **a** faint moan came sighing through **the** branches of **the** forest and **the** boys felt **a** fleeting breath upon their cheeks, and shuddered with **the** fancy that **the** Spirit of **the** Night had gone by. There was **a** pause. Now **a** weird flash turned night into day and showed every little grass-blade, separate and distinct, that grew about their feet. And it showed three white, startled faces, too. **A**	夜半光景，喬醒了，叫另外兩個孩子。空氣悶熱逼人，似乎要變天。儘管天氣又悶又熱令人窒息，幾個孩子還是相互依偎在一起，盡力靠近那堆火。他們全神貫注默默坐著，等待著。周圍還是一片肅靜。除了那堆火，一切都被漆黑的夜色吞噬了。不一會兒，遠處劃過一道亮光，隱約照在樹葉上，只一閃便消失了。不久，又劃過一道更強烈的閃光。接著又一道。這時候，穿過森林的枝葉，傳來一陣低吼聲，幾個孩子仿佛覺得有一股氣息拂過臉頰，以為是幽靈過去了，嚇得瑟瑟發抖。一陣短暫的間隙過後，又是一道悚目驚心的閃光，把黑夜照得亮如白晝，他們腳下的小草也歷歷可辨；同時，三張慘白、驚懼的臉也

deep peal of thunder went rolling and tumbling down **the** heavens and lost itself in sullen rumblings in **the** distance. **A** sweep of chilly air passed by, rustling all **the** leaves and snowing **the** flaky ashes broadcast about **the** fire. Another fierce glare lit up **the** forest and an instant crash followed that seemed to rend **the** tree-tops right over **the** boys' heads. They clung together in terror, in **the** thick gloom that followed. A few big raindrops fell pattering upon **the** leaves.

畢露無遺。一陣沉雷轟轟隆隆當空滾過，漸去漸遠，消失在遙遠的天邊。一陣涼風襲來，樹葉沙沙作響，火堆裏的灰，雪花似地四處飛撒。又一道強光照亮了樹林，響雷緊隨其後，仿佛就要把孩子們頭頂上的樹梢一劈兩半。之後，又是一團漆黑，幾個孩子嚇得抱成一團，幾顆大雨點劈哩啪啦砸在樹葉上。

　　我們無力從無窮無盡的文字分析中理出冠詞翻譯的公式，因為本書提供的是翻譯的藝術，不是文字解剖的技術。從事翻譯工作要想勝任愉快，就一定得超越剖析文字結構的青澀階段，進而要能直覺式地了解原文，這種功力只能從多讀、多寫、多練習中發展。

3.8.2 副詞字尾的處理

　　常讀中國古典白話小說的人應該會注意到，不論是形容詞、副詞、所有格等，中文裏原本使用的字尾都是「的」，到了五四白話運動時期，洋文中譯日漸蓬勃，因為需要對應西洋文字中形容詞、副詞及所有格的不同詞性，有人開始倡議以「的」、「地」和「底」分別作為形容詞，副詞和所有格的字尾，其中「的」是固有的，也就沒什麼問題，而「你底眼睛……」、「我底希望……」、「他底饅頭……」等等，也風

行過一段時日，只是如今業已式微，只有在一些新詩裡見得到。獨有「OO 地」自當時起大行其道，直到今天。

以英文為例，其副詞絕大多數是由形容詞末綴上 -ly 而成，譯成中文時相當方便，只要化形容詞字尾「的」為副詞字尾「地」就行了。久而久之，「OO 地」成了制式化副詞標誌，不求甚解者好像認定了非得要「OO 地」才算副詞，這當然純是誤解。

例如，以下第一句中的 *gradually* 譯成「逐漸」就很得體，沒道理定得在其後加個「地」。而第二句更不用為了要遷就「地」而把「發展緩慢」改成「緩慢地發展」。

1. Developing countries have **gradually** become the main force in antidumping disputes against China.（開發中國家逐漸成為反傾銷爭議中對抗中國的主力。）
2. There was little demand for commercial aviation and it **developed slowly** until after World War II.（二次大戰後商用飛行的需求有限，因而發展緩慢。）

還有，中文傳統副詞中，有一種疊字的型態，像「淡淡、徐徐、悠悠，漸漸、緩緩、慢慢、靜靜、悄悄」等等，根本沒有必要接「地」。

1. Upon returning to the room he sits down **silently** in the corner with legs crossed and slowly puffing on his pipe.（他一回房就靜靜翹著腿坐在角落裡，慢慢抽著煙斗。）
2. Before I could answer, he walks up **sneakily** behind another person who is not wearing a shirt....（在我來得及回答之前，他悄悄走到另一個沒穿上衣的人後面……）

3. Lightly spread this two-color type eye shadow on your eye-lids. （把這種雙色眼影<u>淡淡</u>敷在眼瞼上。）

另外，「然」則是中文形容詞和副詞兩用的字尾，像「突然、果然、忽然，誠然、竟然、驀然、必然、偶然」等，作為副詞時，也沒有接「地」的必要。

1. The car **suddenly** began accelerating and was heading towards a soggy, grassy area. （汽車<u>突然</u>加速衝向一片濕草地。）
2. Knowledge and technology will **surely** become the basic source of competition for the future enterprise activities. （知識與技術<u>必然</u>會成為未來企業活動競爭的基本資源。）
3. This is **actually** a very good detective crime thriller that will attract more female movie goers. （這<u>誠然</u>是部會吸引更多女性觀眾的、很不錯的警匪懸疑片。）

總之，在不會影響文句流暢的地方，「地」能省則省。

3.8.3 其他翻譯瑕疵的處理

About

把 *About* 翻成「關於……」幾乎已經成了公式，沒錯，*About* 的最常見意思是「關於……」，但是我們又怎麼能閉著眼睛把 *It's not about money, it's about principle.* 譯成「那不是關於錢，那是關於原則」？再不

濟也可以譯成「那不關乎錢，而是關乎原則」，若能譯成「那不是錢的問題，那是原則的問題」就更好了。

About 在有些地方也算是虛字，例如：

1. This is about Mark's stunning discovery about Sony's actions.
   這是 Mark 對新力行動的驚人發現（= This is Mark's stunning discovery about Sony's actions.）

2. This is all about a means for unscrupulous people to make money by trading on our privacy. And I am not talking about the criminals.
   這全是不道德的人用出賣我們的隱私來賺錢的法子，而我說的還不是罪犯哦（= All this is a means for unscrupulous people to make money by trading on our privacy. And I am not talking about the criminals.）

　　所以，翻譯這門功課，實在不能停頓於「咬定句型，以不變應萬變」的入門階段，那些國、高中時期英文課所教的翻譯公式，有許多都該隨我們英文程度的成長而翻新了，光靠那些把式實在不足以勝任正式的翻譯工作。

Damn

Damn 常被譯成「該死」，其實 *damn* 只是某些人慣用的口頭語，有咒罵的語氣，與該不該死倒沒有絕對的關係，只是有些人沒有自己的主張，因為前面的人既然這樣子譯，也就依著葫蘆畫瓢罷了。其實此字發

音與「他媽的」（damnit）相近，可以考慮音譯。不然，與其一律譯成「該死」，不如換點更有創意的譯法，如「要命」、「要死」、「去死吧」、甚至「夭壽」、「短命」、「天殺的」或「遭天譴的」等等，都不見得不比「該死」高明，全看說話者語氣的輕重。請看下例：

"That score is settled -- damn you."

「這下可了帳了……去死吧，你！」

Must

Must 雖然有「必須、一定」的意思，也有推測的意思，作推測語時並不非得譯成「一定……」，要是譯成「肯定是……」，這推測的意味就多了幾分，要是譯成「多半」，推測的意味就更濃了，也更白話了一點。

1. Your friend told me that she must be crazy to act the way she did.（你的朋友告訴我說她肯定是瘋了才會那樣。）
2. If she's really as pretty as you say, why doesn't she have a boyfriend? There must be something wrong with her.（她要是像你講的那麼美，為什麼沒有男朋友，多半是哪裡不對勁。）

Shall and Will

英文動詞有時態之分，其中代表未來式的助動詞 *shall...* 和 *will...* 多被譯成「將……」，這種譯法就像把 *when...* 譯為「當……」一樣，是中文受西洋文字污染後的退化產品，中文是用副詞來描述時間的，不在動詞上用工夫。

有人一見到 *will...*，就像套公式一樣，一定要「將……」一下，例如：

Tomorrow I will go to New York to attend an important meeting reguarding our our status in the World Trade Organization membership。（明天我*將要*到紐約參加一個討論我們 WTO 會員現狀的重要會議。）

其實，在一般說話的場合也不會把「明天我要去……」硬說成「明天我將要去……」吧？在此提醒大家，翻譯未來式時，不見得要用「將……」，翻譯過去式時，也不見得要用「已經……」，中文裡的「……了」就已經是過去式，例如：「他們到家了」，而「會……」則代表未來式，例如：「我們會去看你的」。

Versus (vs.)

早期皇冠雜誌連載過一套漫畫，叫做《諜對諜》，原題就叫做「Spy vs. Spy」，「versus」有「對抗」、「相對於……」的意思，凡是兩國相爭、兩個球隊對決、兩名候選人競選等兩方抗衡的情況，都可以用 versus，例如：

· US vs. Iraq
· Dallas Cowboys vs. Washington Redskins[9]
· Bush vs. Gore, etc...

可是，本地電視台的新聞節目中，竟然充斥了像以下這類的說法：

警察 vs. 目擊者
記者 vs. 受訪者

事實上，警察跟目擊者沒有對立的關係，記者與受訪者也多半站在合作的立場，除非他們各自針鋒相對，要不然正確的用法應該是：

警察 and 目擊者
記者＆受訪者
警察 vs. 槍擊要犯
搶犯 vs. 人質

由於始作俑者的一時失察，加上各台不求甚解，一陣跟風，大家竟然習以為常，喧賓奪主，而至顛倒是非，就像誤用「凸顯」的人多了，竟然反過來糾正使用「突顯」[10]的人。

9　美國的兩個職業橄欖球隊。
10　「突顯」可以解作「某件事很突出，以致顯出了重要性」，而「凸」字一向僅用於說明「某樣東西鼓起來」，除了用來形容形狀上「凹凸不平」、「凸出一塊」之外，幾已不做他用。「凸」字有時可以用「突」字代替，如「突出一塊」，反之，「突」字則不宜代以「凸」字。

3.9 本章習作

長句處理之習作

　　讀讀下面這一句長達 58 字的超長句子，針對原文的中譯提出評論與看法，再把這一大句改寫成比較短的幾個小句後，試行翻譯，比較自己的譯作與原譯之差異，並提出解釋。

原文	暫譯
Through the study of instruments, as well as painting, written documents, and so on, we can explore the movement of music from the Near East to China over a thousand years ago, or we can outline the spread of Near Eastern influence to Europe that resulted in the development of most of the instruments in the symphony orchestra.	通過對圖片、文字記載以及樂器等的研究，我們可以瞭解一千多年以前近東音樂傳入中國的情況，也可以勒出近東音樂的影響波及歐洲並導致交響樂的大部分樂器發展和演變的大致輪廓。

處理 **and** 之習作

　　翻譯下面這兩段充滿 ***and*** 的原文，在譯文中盡量消除 ***and***，或使 ***and*** 以本節中所介紹的不同面貌出現，最後請對自己的譯作提出說明與評論。

　　On Saturday, shortly after noon, the boys were at the dead tree again. They had a smoke and a chat in the shade, and then dug a little in their last hole, not with great hope, but merely because Tom said there were so many cases where people had given up a treasure after getting down within six inches of it, and then somebody else had come along and turned it up with a single thrust of a shovel. The thing failed this time, however, so the boys shouldered their tools and went away feeling that they had not trifled with fortune, but had fulfilled all the requirements that belong to the business of treasure-hunting.

When they reached the haunted house there was something so weird and grisly about the dead silence that reigned there under the baking sun, and something so depressing about the loneliness and desolation of the place, that they were afraid, for a moment, to venture in. Then they crept to the door and took a trembling peep. They saw a weed-grown, floorless room, un-plastered, an ancient fireplace, vacant windows, a ruinous staircase; and here, there, and everywhere hung ragged and abandoned cobwebs. They presently entered, softly, with quickened pulses, talking in whispers, ears alert to catch the slightest sound, and muscles tense and ready for instant retreat.

被動語態處理之習作

　　下面四段原文中共出現 13 個被動語態，請在中譯這些段落時，盡量用非被動語態的方式來表達，試試看你能取代掉幾個，若有無法取代者，請說明原因。

1. If you **were not told** that it was an FBI agent describing what Americans had done to prisoners in their control, you would most certainly believe this must **have been done** by Nazis, Soviets in their Gulags, or some mad regime--Pol Pot or others--that had no concern for human beings. Sadly, that is not the case. This **was the action taken** by some Americans in the treatment of their prisoners.

2. Occasionally it is not clear whether a term is **being used** to certify that work relating to the goods **was performed** by someone meeting certain standards. But it is clear that a certification mark may only be used upon the services to certify that the work **was performed** by the performer who meets certain standards.

3. This survey **is conducted** by the School of Public Health on studying the behavior in drinking alcohol and some health habits among university students. The study **has been conducted** since 2005 with focus on first-year undergraduate student. The study in 2006-07 **will be focused** on more health issues and follow up of the first survey.

4. If you drink and drive and **get caught**, you could face fines, loss of driving privileges, or other penalties. If you drink and drive and don't **get caught**, the results could be much, much worse. Drivers, passengers, people in other cars, and pedestrians are all at risk when you, or any body else, drive while impaired. By making the right choices - recognizing

that alcohol consumption impairs your driving ability, and planning ahead and getting a designated driver - crashes **can be prevented** and **lives saved**. If controlling your intake of alcohol is a problem, see your doctor, a counselor, or join a step program.

人稱代名詞處理之習作

下面的原文只有 89 字，卻有 14 個 *you, your* 和 *yourself*，譯文中的「你、你們」也有十個之多，請針對原文的中譯提出評論，嘗試以減少代名詞的方式翻譯，比較自己的譯作與原譯之差異，並提出解釋。

原文	暫譯
Are **you** setting it up so that people are pulling on **you**, so that **your** time is full, but is not filled with the things **you** want? **You** have the power to change that drama. It comes from **your** compassion for who **you** are, and from **your** sense of inner freedom. Many of you have set up lives for yourselves that are not joyful because you believe that you are obligated to others, that you need to be needed, or that you are enslaved by one situation or another.	*你*有沒有作過這樣的安排讓別人佔據*你*的時間而並不是為了*你*想要的事？*你*有力量去改變這出戲劇，那力量來自*你*對真實自我的體認和對內在自由的感知。 *你們*很多人為自己營造了並不快樂的生活只因為*你*相信*你*對別人有義務，*你*需要被需要，或*你*受制於這種或那種的情景。

關係代名詞處理之習作

試譯出下面的七個句子，看看自己對關係代名詞的譯法有沒有逃出一般公式化的窠臼。

4. Casablanca is one of the greatest love stories of all time, toping Gone with the Wind and West Side Story. It has a very well written script. That **might be the reason why** six of the top 100 most memorable quotes of movies came form Casablanca.

5. I found that taking the light train is like taking a city bus. Such train goes super slow, just like the metro transit buses do. I guessed **this could be the reason why** the light rail is part of the metro transit association because a light train is not a real train.

6. Another map of great interest is *Tasmania during the Ice Age,* which will takes us back to **the time when** you could walk from the mainland to Tasmania, **when** the Aboriginal people lived in a harsh and icy world.

7. There's too much of hype about SARS, and that the whole thing will blow over in no time. People are breaking their holiday plans anyway and so SARS need not necessarily be a reason for this anymore than **it can be the reason why** domestic travel is going up.

8. Highly qualified personnel , excellent technical potential, fast transfer of electronic data, top quality finished product, short task completion time and punctuality **these are the ways how** we gained the trust of our best known clients.Can you imagine living all your life without knowing **who you really are**? You saw yourself as **who you think you are and who you really are** at the same time.**What I said** isn't really **what I wanted to say. What I really mean** is I knew this girl was perfect for me but I just didn't have the courage to take the next step.

冠詞處理之習作

翻譯下面這兩段有不少冠詞的原文，並請對自己在譯作中處理冠詞的方式提出說明與評論。

Someday is **a** science fiction short story by Isaac Asimov. **The** story is set in **a** future where computers play **a** central role in organizing society. Humans are employed as computer operators, but they leave most of **the** thinking to machines. Indeed, whilst binary programming is taught at school, reading and writing have become obsolete.

The story concerns a pair of boys who dismantle and upgrade an old Bard, a child's computer whose sole function is to generate random fairy tales. **The** boys download a book about computers into **the** Bard's memory in an attempt to expand its vocabulary, but **the** Bard simply incorporates computers into its standard fairy tale repertoire. **The** story ends with **the** boys excitedly leaving **the** room after deciding to go to **the** library to learn writing. As they leave, one of **the** boys accidentally kicks the Bard's on switch. **The** Bard begins reciting a new story, ending with **the** words: "the little computer knew then that computers would always grow wiser and more powerful until someday-- someday-- someday-- ... "

副詞字尾處理之習作

翻譯下面這七個英文句子，並請說明自己在譯作中處理副詞的方式。

9. I have dated so many guys who have always turned around and hurt me. Now I decide to have someone who can really treat me **nicely**.

10. Our mission is to provide materials that **greatly** improve student performance in the classroom and to encourage a habit of reading, responsibility and good citizenship.

11. About fifty or sixty million years ago , salt water **gradually** invaded fresh water lake and river on which whale originated.

12. To those who have contacted me in the past and who visit here **occasionally**, I would appreciate an email from you as I lost email addresses during the hard drive crash.

13. Overlooking the importance of the resources that interact with the client in the sales process is a critical mistake **frequently** made in organizations. Most companies use very few resources dedicated to selling, and even less focused **exclusively** on selling additional services to current clients.

14. A mistake commonly made among home buyers is locating the house they want to buy first. It is often the case that potential buyers **accidentally** choose a home out of their price range. Time and **possibly** money is wasted by beginning the approval process to only find that the buyer is unable to afford the payments.

15. It can affect a woman not only **physically**, but **emotionally, psychologically, spiritually**. It also **really** touches on all aspects of her life and also her family and relationships.

第二篇

中英雙向翻譯實務

第四章
致詞類文的翻譯

　　許多國際會議中，多會請講者提供講稿，轉交口譯者事先準備，以減少因錯譯而產生不必要的誤會，尤其在聯合國開會或絕大部分的政治協商會議中，更是必要。而一般如下例的開幕致詞，難度不高，有經驗的翻譯者應該可以順手捻來，即席譯出。

原文	英譯
各位長官、各位貴賓、各位參賽選手、各位師長、各位同學： 　　歡迎各位貴賓、各位參賽選手蒞臨＿＿＿大學，參加＿＿＿年國際燃料電池車競賽。 　　＿＿＿年，我們承辦第二屆燃料電池車競賽時，只有 7 隊臺灣車隊參加，本屆延續前兩屆競賽精神，擴大為『國際型』的燃料電池車競賽活動，以提供國際交流機會。 　　同時，除了原有的『競速賽』之外，增加『節能賽』以激發台灣的燃料電池車實用研發。本屆參賽者有馬來西亞＿＿＿大學，而臺灣共	Officials from our Sponsors and supervising organizations, honored guests, boys and girls, friends and families, ladies and gentlemen: 　　Welcome to ＿＿＿ University. This is the ＿＿＿ International Fuel Cell Car Race Award. 　　In ＿＿＿, there were only 7 Taiwanese teams when we hosted the 2nd Fuel Cell Car Race Award, This time we expand the scale and make it international in order to provide an international culture exchange opportunity.

有＿＿車隊參賽，盛況可期。

我們有這個機會共同承辦＿＿年國際燃料電池車競賽，特別感謝教育部、經濟部能源局與工業技術研究院以及各位貴賓的指導，更感謝各位選手的熱情參與。

敬祝 活動愉快，圓滿成功！

Except for the model car racing, this time we add an energy conservation contest with a hope to stimulate the fuel cell car research and development in Taiwan. Our participants, this time, include the University of ＿＿ from ＿＿ and 11 teams around the island of Taiwan. We are anticipating an exciting event.

We are honored to have this privilege to host this international fuel cell car racing event. Special thank is given to the Ministry of Education, Energy Bureau and Industrial Technology Research Institute.

Thank you for your participation.

And let's wish for a joyful and successful game.

　　對於上面這種簡短的致詞，有現場口譯經驗者，可能隨聽隨譯，沒有大礙，但是若要詳實得體，還是建議先取得講者的原稿，先做功課，才比較容易藝驚全場。非口譯界的朋友不要以為這是學藝不精才出的下策，其實，至於像林肯的蓋茲堡演說那樣的講稿，即使口譯者再藝高膽大，也難以即席傳譯，就算有時間慢慢翻譯，也是要煞費苦心的。

美國內戰末期的蓋茨堡戰役，於 1863 年一月一日至三日在賓州小鎮蓋茨堡的街上及其周圍地區持續了三天，此次戰役犧牲了超過七千位戰士，是美國內戰的轉捩點。賓夕法尼亞州購下 17 英畝（69,000 平方公尺）的土地作為墓園之用，以為這些葬送於烈日沙場的英靈善後。後來美國國會決定把這一片的戰場建為國家公墓。治喪委員會幾乎是事後才想起邀請林肯參與揭幕式。

林肯總統應邀從華府到蓋茨堡參加十一月十九日的典禮，於演說順序中排名第二，類似於現今邀請貴賓於開幕式剪綵的傳統，該次典禮有一萬五千至兩萬人參與儀式。

儘管林肯這場演說名垂青史，但當日視之為「蓋茲堡演說」者，並非林肯總統的簡短致詞，而是時任國務卿的艾佛瑞特（Edward Everett）長達兩小時的演講。

林肯在所發表的獻詞雖然很短，只有十句話 272 個字，但卻是闡釋民主信念的最動人的演詞之一，獻詞中簡述了這場內戰，重提國家在這場艱苦戰爭中的作用，以及對此觀念的影響，即「不分聯邦軍或邦聯軍，蓋茲堡陣亡將士的犧牲無一白費」。

美國國會圖書館（The Library of Congress）內藏有該講詞的原稿，除了英文原文之外，還有包括中文的二十八種文字的譯稿，下面這篇就是其館藏的中譯本：

八十七年以前，我們的祖先在這大陸上建立了一個新的國家，它孕育於自由，並且獻身給一種理念，即所有人都是生來平等的。

當前，我們正在從事一次偉大的內戰，我們在考驗，究竟這個國家，或任何一個有這種主張和這種信仰的國家，是否能長久存在。我們在那次戰爭的一個偉大的戰場上集合。我們來

到這裡，奉獻那個戰場上的一部分土地，作為在此地為那個國家的生存而犧牲了自己生命的人永久眠息之所。我們這樣做，是十分合情合理的。

可是，就更深一層意義而言，我們是無從奉獻這片土地的──無從使它成為聖地──也不可能把它變為人們景仰之所。那些在這裡戰鬥的勇士，活著的和死去的，已使這塊土地神聖化了，遠非我們的菲薄能力所能左右。世人會不大注意，更不會長久記得我們在此地所說的話，然而他們將永遠忘不了這些人在這裡所做的事。相反，我們活著的人應該獻身於那些曾在此作戰的人們所英勇推動而尚未完成的工作。我們應該在此獻身於我們面前所留存的偉大工作──由於他們的光榮犧牲，我們要更堅定地致力於他們曾作最後全部貢獻的那個事業──我們在此立志誓願，不能讓他們白白死去──要使這個國家在上帝庇佑之下，得到新生的自由──要使那民有、民治、民享的政府不致從地球上消失。

像這樣受到推崇的文字有興趣翻譯者當然不少，以下是另一個譯本[1]

八十七年前，我們的祖先在這個大陸上創立了一個新國家，她孕育於自之中，並奉獻於人類生而平等的主張。現在，我們正進行一場偉大的內戰，它正考驗著這家或任何孕育於自由並為相同主張而奉獻的國家，是否能長久存在，我們聚集在這場戰爭中的一個偉大戰場上，我們前來此地要將這個戰場的一部分士地奉獻給為了國家的生存而犧牲生命的人們，作為最

---

[1] 余玉照譯。

後安息之所。我們這樣做是完全恰當正確的。 然而，從更廣的意義上來說，我們不能奉獻－我們不神化－我們不能聖化－這塊士地，因爲那些曾在此奮戰過的勇士們，活著的和去世的，已經將它化爲神聖了，非我們微薄的力量所能予以增減。世界將不大會注意，對不會長久記得我們在此所說的話，但它永遠不會忘記勇士們在此所做的事。我們生者毋寧應該奉獻於在此戰鬥過的人們業已卓絕地推展但未竟全功的志業。我們應該在此獻身給仍然留在我們前的偉大任務－我們要從光榮的死者身上，取得更大的熱忱來奉獻於他們已爲之鞠躬盡瘁獻出一切的使命－我們在此下定最大決心要使這些死者不致白白犧牲－務使我們的國家，在上帝的庇佑之下，獲得自由的新生－ 並願民有、民治、民享的政府將永存於世。

　　筆者也不惴淺陋，提供一己之譯，供大家比較。

Address Delivered at the Dedication of the Cemetery at Gettysburg－蓋茨堡演說辭

原文	中譯
Four scores and seven years ago our fathers brought forth on this continent, a new nation, conceived in Liberty, and dedicated to the proposition that all men are created equal.	八十七年前，我們的先人在這大陸上建立一個新的國家，這個國家孕育於自由，致力於「人生而平等」的理念。

Now we are engaged in a great[2] civil war, testing whether that nation, or any nation so conceived and so dedicated, can long endure. We are met on a great battlefield of that war. We have come to dedicate a portion of that field, as a final resting place for those who here gave their lives that that nation might live. It is altogether fitting and proper that we should do this.

But, in a larger sense, we cannot dedicate, we cannot consecrate, we cannot hallow this ground. The brave men, living and dead, who struggled here, have consecrated it, far above our poor power to add or detract. The world will little note, nor long remember what we say here, but it can never forget what they did here. It is for us the living, rather, to be dedicated here to the unfinished work which they who fought here have thus far so nobly advanced. It is rather for us to be here dedicated to the great task remaining before us--that from these honored dead we take increased devotion to that cause for

現在我們在進行一場大型的內戰，考驗著這樣一個國家，或任何如此孕生、致力於如此理念的國家是否能長久生存，我們齊集在這個戰爭的偉大戰場上，把戰場的一部分獻給那些為國犧牲者作為長眠之地，這樣做，是十分地合宜而且正當的。

可是，廣義地說，我們不足以奉獻這片土地、不足以使這片土地神聖、不足以使它尊嚴；在此奮戰過的、在生的和已逝的勇士們，早已使斯土神聖得遠過於我們的微薄能力所能增減。世人不會在意，也不會久記我們在這裡所說的話，然而將永遠不會忘記這些人在這裡的事蹟。我們這些在生者該做的，是為奮戰於此的人早已英勇推動、而尚未完成的工作盡力，我們是為眼前所留

---

2 作者把此處的 *great* 譯成「大型」，以別於前兩篇譯文的「偉大」，主要因為作者認為任何戰爭都不該以偉大來頌揚。

which they gave the last full measure of devotion that we here highly resolve that these dead shall not have died in vain--that this nation, under God, shall have a new birth of freedom--and that government of the people, by the people, for the people, shall not perish from the earth.	下來的偉大使命－先烈們全力輸誠的肇因 —— 盡更大的力量，在此我們堅定信念，使他們不致白白的犧牲，使這個國家在上帝庇佑下，得到自由的新生，使民有、民治、民享的政府不致在地球上殞滅。

第五章
心靈類文的翻譯

本章提綱

原文：You Can Live Joyfully

譯文：你能快樂生活

　　新時代運動者指出，公元二千年後，將進入一個科學新發現與古老智慧漸形合流的時代，在此時期，人類對自我與自然的認識將更完整與深入，為了這個時代的來臨，大家理應在更遼闊的思想環境下接受薰陶，庶幾不再以科學為檢驗真實性的唯一工具，並且不再歧視科學對之無能為力的心靈現象。

　　本章所選譯的範例是摘錄自《Living with Joy》的第三章 You Can Live Joyfully，此書歸入新時代類，記錄了一位自稱為 Orin 的靈界眾生透過通靈人士 Sanaya Roman 所傳達的訊息，Orin 自稱為 a being of light（光體），不具人身，他傳遞的訊息具有很高的生活智慧。原文接近於談話的形式，以文章的標準來說，比較鬆散，讀來容易，譯起來卻較費周章。

You Can Live Joyfully —— 你能快樂生活

原文	中譯
I will speak of joy, compassion and higher purpose, for many of you are searching for peace and a sense of inner completion.	由於你們很多人都在尋求平靜和內在的成就，我就來談談喜悅、愛心和更高的

Most of you are aware that peace comes from your inner world, and that the outer world is a symbolic representation of that which is within. You are all at different levels of perceiving the process by which you create what you experience.

What is the path of joy? There are many lifepaths you can choose, just as there are many ways you can serve on a planetary level. There is a path of will, a path of struggle, and also a path of joy and compassion.

Joy is an inner note that you sound as you move through the day.

The path of joy deals with present and not future time. Are you holding an image of what life will be like some day when you are happy, but not feeling that sense of well-being right now, today?

Many of you fill your time with activities that are not soul directed, but activities of the personality. You may have been taught that being busy creates self-worth. There are two kinds of busyness, however.

目標。

　　各位多數都知道平靜來自內心，外在的世界乃是內心一種圖象式的顯現。對於「自造自受」的過程，各位的覺察程度各有不同。

　　喜悅之路是什麼？正如在這個世界你們有許多方式工作一樣，也有許多生活之路可以選擇，有遂心的路、勞苦的路，也有喜悅和愛心的路。

　　喜悅是你在生活當中由內心發出的訊息。

　　喜悅之道只照應當下而非將來。各位會否光想像「將來哪一天你快樂的時候，生活會有何改變」，卻沒有在今天、當下就體會到那種適意的感覺？

　　許多人把時間花在不以心靈為導向、而以形體為重的行動上。可能有人教過你，忙碌能創造個人價值。但繁忙

Personality-directed activity is often based on "shoulds" and is not done to benefit your higher purpose, while soul-directed activity is always done with your higher purpose in mind.

　　The personality is often distracted by the senses, which capture its attention from moment to moment. The phone call, the child, the constant voices, the emotions of others -- all are energies that grab your attention throughout the day, and can distract you from your inner-directed messages.

可有兩種，形體導向的行動往往是「做你該做的」，無助于你達到更高的目標；而心靈導向的活動則總是與你心中更高的目標相應。

　　感官不斷吸引形體的注意，形體因而時常分神。電話、孩子、呶呶不休的話聲、別人的情緒等，全是成天抓住你注意力的能量，它們會分散你對內在訊息的注意。

True joy comes from operating with inner-directedness and recognizing who you are.

　　You may have many reasons why you cannot change your life right now. If you do not begin to create reasons why you can, change will always be a future thought, and you will not be on the path of joy. In this world you have chosen to come into, you have been given physical senses and an emotional body. Your great challenge is not to be distracted by that which

　　真正的喜悅來自內心，來自認清自己的本質

　　你可能有很多理由不能當下就改變生活，你要是不開始製造些理由，改變就永遠是個未來的念頭，你也就不會走上喜悅之路。在這個你選擇投身的世上，你被賦予了物質的感官和具有情感的身體。你主要的挑戰，在於「避免被迎面而來、接踵而至、或是向你召喚呼引的事物所迷惑，反要

comes in front of you, or that which is pulling on you or calling to you, but instead to find your center and magnetize to yourself all those things that are in alignment with your inner being.	找到自己的核心，把與你內心一致的事物吸引過來。」
The path of joy involves valuing yourself and monitoring where you put your time. If every single person spent time only where he accomplished the greatest good for himself and the person he was with, the world would change in a day. It is important to spend time in ways that promote your highest good. If something is not for your highest good, I can guarantee that it is not for the highest good of the planet or others either. You may ask, what am I here to do that will bring me joy? Each one of you has things that you love to do. There is not one person alive who does not have something he loves to do.	喜悅之道在於珍視自己，和檢視自己把時間運用在何處。 如果每一個人都把時間用於對自己和身邊的人最有益的地方，這世界會在一天內改變。花費時間牟取自己的最高利益方式非常重要。任何事若不符合你的最高利益，我可以保證它也不會對地球或他人最有益。 你可能會問，我在這兒做什麼才能得到喜悅呢？每個人都有自己愛做的事。世上沒有人不有自己愛做的事。
You will have joy only when you focus on having it and settle for nothing less.	只有一心想得到喜悅而不退求其次時，你才能得到

What is your highest vision and how do you find it in your life? Most of you have many distractions that need not be. If you were to sit for even five minutes each day, reviewing what you set up for the day, and ask how each appointment, person or phone call fits into your higher purpose, in a few short months you would be on the path of your destiny and would discover ways to double your income. Of course, you will need to act upon this wisdom.

If you do not know what your path is, you can create a symbol for it. Imagine that you are holding it in your hands as a ball of light. Bring it up to your heart, then into your crown chakra at the top of your head, and release it to your soul. Very shortly, it will begin to take form. You will find that at just the thought of higher purpose you will begin to magically and magnetically rearrange your day. Suddenly friends who took your time will no longer look so interesting, as you bring in new friends and change the nature of your friendships with old acquaintances.

它。

你的最高理念是什麼，又要怎樣在生命中找到它？多數人都為許多不必要的事分心。你若每天靜坐五分鐘，檢查一下當天的安排，自問如何將每個工作、每個人或每通電話都與你更高的目標一致，短短幾個月，你就會踏上幸運之路，並且發現收入倍增的辦法。當然，你得力行這個智慧之舉。

要是你不知道你的道路是什麼，不妨替它創造一個象徵，想像自己像托著一個光球般地托著它。慢慢捧到心口然後升入頭頂的脈輪，然後把它釋入靈魂。很快它就會成形，你會發覺，只要一想到更高的目標，你就會開始神奇而無從解釋地重新安排日子，就在引來新朋友，改變與舊交的交往習性的同時，突然間，那些會消耗你時間的朋友不會再吸引你。

Compassion is caring for yourself; valuing yourself and your time. You do not owe anyone your time. When you take charge of yourself and affirm that you are a unique and valuable person, the world will affirm it to you also.

If you find yourself in power struggles with people -- strangers, loved ones or close friends -- go into your higher self. Stop for a moment, take a deep breath, and don't get caught in their desire for a confrontation. Remember, it's their desire, not yours.

Many of your challenges on the path of joy will be to step outside of power struggles and come from a deep level of compassion. If a friend snaps at you or is unfriendly, step back, and with a sense of compassion, try to experience life from his perspective. You may see his tiredness, or his defensiveness, which has nothing to do with you, for you only represent another character in his play. The more you can step outside and not be pulled into power struggles, the more peaceful and abundant

「愛心」意味著關心自己、珍惜自己和把握時間,你並沒有欠人時間,只要你主控了自己,並肯定自己的獨特和價值,這個世界也會這樣肯定你。

你要是發現自己與別人發生衝突,不管是陌生人、愛人或好友,就進到更高的自我中,停一會兒,深呼吸,不要被他們想要交鋒的欲望所俘虜。記住,要這樣的是他們,不是你。

能懷抱深深的慈悲從爭鬥中脫離,會是你喜悅之路上的考驗項目,如果朋友冒犯你或是不友善,退一步,懷著同情心從對方的角度體驗人生,你就會發現他的疲乏或戒心不是因你而起,因為你僅是他劇本裡的一角,你越能從鬥爭中解脫,不被牽扯進去,你的生命就越平靜富足,你也就越能處在一個用愛心去復建他人的位置上。

your life will be, and the more you will be in a position to heal others by being in your heart with compassion.

Go inward for a moment and ask yourself what you can do tomorrow, specifically, to bring more joy into your life. Ask what you can do to let go of a power struggle or an issue that is going on in your life and draining your energy. What can you do tomorrow to free up a little more time to find inner peace?

You have so much to be grateful for, your excellent mind and your unlimited potential. You have the ability to create anything you want; the only limits are those you create for yourself. Wake up in the morning and affirm your freedom. Hold up your higher vision and live the most joyful life you can imagine.

省察一下內心，問問自己明天要怎樣才能給人生帶來更多喜悅，問自己要怎樣才能拋開權力競爭或生活中榨損你精力的事情。明天要怎樣才能多騰出些時間去尋找內心的平靜？

有那麼多東西值得感恩，像絕佳的頭腦和無限的潛能。你有創造萬事萬物的能力，所有的侷限全是你自己造成的。明早醒來就宣告你的自由吧，掌握更高的憧憬去過你所能想象的最喜悅的人生吧。

第六章
學術類文的翻譯

本章提綱

> 原文：品質成本管理方法
> 譯文：Cost of Quality Management

　　寫作論文原本就是求取博士學位者生涯中不可避免的一部分，此外，幾乎每一個研究所都要求其碩士學生寫作畢業論文。論文是表現高等教育及專業研究成果的最具體方式，對於大部分研究生說來，畢業論文是一項重大工程，攸關是否能順利取得學位。

　　自 1990 年代中期以來，國內大學教育趨向普及化，研究所教育也不再那麼難以企及，加上兩岸理工科技及管理學門、乃至文學及社會科學領域的研究水準不斷提高，基礎研究與國際間的交流與合作日趨頻繁，研究者對提高自身溝通能力和技巧的要求日益迫切，以致有愈來愈多學者、學生、專門技術研發人員以及文學及社會科學領域的研究人員，開始面臨以英文撰寫論文的課題。

　　儘管華人世界的高等教育普遍發展，但是用英文來寫作任何文獻，對非以英語為母語的人士來說，都是很大的考驗，因此，論文英譯就成為一個註定要崛起的行業。

　　以本書作者來說，每年都要接到許多同事、朋友、學生的請託，進行各學門中英論文的翻譯及校閱，數量直追以翻譯為糊口事業者。

　　翻譯或校閱任何學門的論文，都需要對該學門有基礎以上的了解，不能率爾操觚，有些人誤認為找個通英文的英語國家人士，價錢還可接

受，即可放心交付任務，這是絕大的謬誤，除非你自己的英文已經在水準以上，只是需要找個人來修正一般的文法錯誤，這樣做可能只是白費金錢。

對於自己熟悉的學門如理工、管理、電腦等類，筆者自可獨立作業，對於不熟悉的學門，筆者通常的作法是請原作者一起坐在電腦之前，邊譯邊與作者溝通其所想要表達的原意，這種做法極為繁重費時，但也是唯一負責的作法。

論文的翻譯絕對不要拘泥於逐字逐句的對譯，而是要以原文內容為重，因此，讀懂原文並消化之後再從新寫作的方式，除了不至於翻出中式英文或是西式中文以外，還可以加快翻譯的速度。

以下謹介紹一篇管理類論文的翻譯，供有意此業者參考。

因篇幅所限，本書只取譯該論文之部分，順著論文中出現的瑕疵，按部就班，在註腳中詳細註解了論文寫作時應遵守的部份原則，並說明了翻譯時捨棄部分原文不譯的原因，除善盡了翻譯的責任，也在譯文中改良了論文原有的品質[1]，這一篇範例不只在文法上做小小的修正，還顧到了論文的邏輯和修辭，對論文寫作本身和論文的英譯，都極有幫助。

1　當然，再好的譯者也沒有辦法從根解救論文的缺失，充其量不過是做個化妝與小針美容的工作，先天太過不足的論文是無法起死回生的。所謂 *garbage in, garbage out*，即此之謂也。

Cost of Quality Management 品質成本管理方法

原文	英譯
1. 前言 　　在今日競爭益趨激烈的網路時代中，不僅交易模式丕變，企業管理模式與思維亦應隨之改觀，方能確保企業求創新求改進原動力的長存，而在諸多新興管理手法中，[2]「品質成本管理法」因強調企業在提昇品質的同時亦可降低成本，一改傳統高品質即高成本的迷思，而獲諸多歐、美企業的青睞與驗證，結果發現，企業導入品質成本後確可達成品質提升、同時降低成本的顯著成效。 　　相較國外[3]產學界多年來在實際執行品質成本制度所累積的豐富經驗，國內[4]學術界在此領域的發展亦不遑多讓，[5]成果亦	1. Introduction 　　Cost of Quality (COQ)[6] management system stresses that a business is able to reduce its cost without suffering a quality loss. This emphasis breaks the traditional myth of "high quality means high cost" and wins the hearts of many European and American enterprises. 　　Internationally, there have been many researches regarding COQ implementations. The academia in Taiwan has also contributed local research effort in this area and has provided local enterprises with the results that can serve as references for COQ implementations. Compiled in Table 1 are the international research findings about the COQ implementation status. This research

---

2　原文到此之前全是應酬性的敘述，與論文宏旨無關，不論是中文或英文，加上此段都使論文鬆散，為求札實，盡可略去。

3　所謂「國外」，到底如何翻成英文？是 *foreign* 還是 *international*？所稱的國外又到底是哪一國之外？故應直指國名。

4　應直指國名，不然翻成英文時所稱的國內（*domestic*）到底是哪一國？

5　類似「不遑多讓」等個人評論，不宜出於學術倫文之中，宜略去。

6　在使用論文專業範圍內的關鍵詞時，可在其第一次出現處用括弧將該關鍵詞之縮寫括在裡面，以利後文引用。

多已提供國內企業於導入品質成本制時作為參考。表一即列示國內外產學界歷年來針對品質成本實施程度調查之結果。	team uses question naire to conduct a wider and deeper survey regarding current COQ implementation status among top 500 manufacturers in Taiwan.
2. 品質成本報導制之理論探討 吾人[7]若以消費者與生產者兩個不同的層面來看品質成本的定義，大致可區分出 Juran 的消費者觀點，以及 Morse 等人所提出生產者觀點的兩種看法，除此之外，Ortreng 另提出運用附加價值的觀念，可將品質成本視為企業分配資源工具的主張，因之，除預防成本屬於有附加價值的成本外，其餘評鑑、內部失敗、及外部失敗成本，都是無附加價值的成本[Ortreng, 1991]。	2. About COQ Reporting System In addition to Juran's consumer aspect COQ and Morse et. al's provider aspect COQ, there is Ortreng's added value COQ. This added value COQ can be deemed as a business's tool for resource distribution. When comes to added values, except for the prevention cost that can add value to the business, all the other costs such as those induced by assessment, internal failure, and external failure have no added value [Ortreng, 1991].
3. 研究設計與研究方法 本節將就本研究施測工具、研究架構、問卷變數設計與抽樣方法等相關內容依序說明如下：	3. Research Design and Research Method This section describes the tools used in this research in addition to research structure, questionnaire variable

---

7 「吾人」這個第一人稱代名詞，不文不白，可能是 1910 年代白話文運動期間翻譯西文時，用來承接外文裡的第一人稱（如英文中的 *We, I* 等）的，但是在許多情況下，中文句子裡的主詞即使省略也不致影響文意，因此這個怪異的代名詞早就可以從任何文章中淘汰。

3.1 施測工具

　　為配合本研究期望獲得具普遍性、一般性之影響企業實施品質成本制之主要因素，與企業實施品質成本制後所能獲得之效益的實證結果，決定採用問卷作為本研究之驗證工具。

3.2 研究架構

　　為達成本研究建構企業「品質成本系統參考指標」之目的，故設計本研究架構如圖一所示。

3.3 問卷變數設計

3.3.1 企業經營體質調查

　　設計此變項之目的，主要用以探討『何種企業』較易／適合導入品質成本制。而此變項之內涵，則源自於彙整(1)國內、外文獻資料之所得，及分析(2)台灣相關實證研究結果而得（見表五），茲分述本研究操作化構面如下文所示：

design and sampling method.

3.1 The Survey Tool

　　The researchers decided that questionnaire survey is the best tool for acquiring 1)[8] universal and general factors that affect the COQ implementation, and 2) the proof of benefits for business to implement COQ.

3.2 Research Structure

　　For the purpose of constructing a COQ System Reference Indicator, this research is structured as shown in Figure 1.

3.3 Questionnaire Variable Design

3.3.1 Business Management Quality

　　Business Management Quality is a variable that identifies the type of businesses fittest for COQ implementation. The contents of this variable is 1) compiled from international literatures and 2) extracted from the surveys in Taiwan (Shown in table 5). The operation phase of this research is numerated in the following subsections.

8　括號通常都是用一對，但在用「i, ii, iii...」、「a, b, c...」或「1, 2, 3...」等項目符號與編號分條列舉大綱或分段時，可以只放括號的右半邊「）」在各該項目符號與編號之後。

3.3.1.1 資訊化程度之差異

此變項設計理念主要來自於國外學者[9] [Sullivan, 1983], [Tsiakals, 1983]，提及利用電腦資訊系統，除可簡化現行會計系統流程，尚可用於協助品質成本系統之構築與導入，因此將其視為影響企業是否容易導入品質成本制的重要因子。

此操作變項之設計，主要參考國內學者[10]劉 OO 所提資訊系統五大發展階段予以設計：(1)啓始運作階段；(2)系統規劃階段；(3)系統整合階段；(4)網路連結階段；(5)經營革新階段[劉 OO 1996][11]。

3.3.1.1 Informationization Extent

The concept of Informationization Extent comes primarily from Sullivan [1983] and Tsiakals [1983], which indicates that using computerized information system not only simplify the current accounting system workflow, but also help in COQ construction and implementation. Therefore, the informationization extent is deemed an important factor that affect the COQ implementation.

The operation variable is designed as per five development stages of an information system:

1. Initial Operation Stage
2. System Design Stage
3. System Integration Stage
4. Network Connection Stage
5. Operation and Renovation Stage

---

9 學術無國界，不用作此強調，且所謂「國外」，到底如何翻成英文？是 *foreign* 還是 *international*？所稱的國外又到底是哪一國之外？論文中不需指明被引用者是何身分，只要提出所引文獻的作者姓名及文獻出版年即可。

10 文中所稱的「學者」會不會只是學生？省去稱謂可以免除判定錯誤的麻煩。

11 資訊系統五大發展階段為早已存在之理論與實務，並非始自 1996 年該論文。

3.3.1.2 品管意識成熟度／TQM 執行水準

此變項之設計，則因獲國內陳 OO 與邱 OO 二位學者的實證研究證實，品質成本與 TQM 的實施的確存在顯著的正相關，故將之置入自變項當中[陳 OO 1993]，[邱 OO 1999]。

因本研究尚欲區分出何種品管執行程度，方達需導入『品質成本』之需求，故又將之區分為以下兩個構面：

(1)品質內在重視度：包含品質主管位階、品質意識成熟度與 TQM 執行程度。

(2)品質外顯成熟度：指標包括是否通過 ISO 或其他系統、產品認證，以及是否獲頒品質相關獎項等。

3.3.1.2 QC Awareness Maturity / TQM Execution Standard

QC Awareness Maturity / TQM Execution Standard is being used as an independent variable for it has been verified by [Chen, 1993] and [Chiou, 1999] via an empirical study, which indicates that the implementation of COQ and the execution of TQM are positively relevant. This research also aims to identify, within a company, the extent of QC execution that will call for the COQ implementation. So the variable is further divided into two phases:

1. Internal Value of Quality (including the rank of quality manager's position, the maturity of quality awareness, and the extent of TQM execution.)

2. Explicit Maturity of Quality (including whether or not pass the ISO or any other certification, whether or not awarded with quality related award)

3.3.2 企業品質成本實施現況 　　此變項之衡量方式，主要利用 ASQC[12] 協會所頒佈之品質成本分類辦法，在列示出所有的成本項目後，並利用流程型品質成本模式預先予以歸類，再請填答者依該公司實際執行狀況，利用李氏五點量表予以填答之。	3.3.2 Business COQ Implementation Status 　　The measuring of Business COQ Implementation Status is based on the COQ classify standard issued by American Society for Quality Control (ASQC). The research team lists all the cost items and classify the items with cost of process COQ model. And then, ask the survey participants to answer the questions based on his or her company's practical execution status using a five-point Likert Scale.
4. 研究結果	4. Study Results
相較國外產學界多年來在實際執行品質成本制度所累積的豐富經驗，國內產學界在此領域的成就亦不遑多讓，成果並多已提供國內企業於導入品質成本制時	The results of this study as presented in the followings include: 1. COQ implementation status in Taiwan 2. The patterns of COQ information gathering and compilation

---

[12] 有些人動輒使用英文字縮寫，認為只要寫出來就該有人認得，事實上即使是專業人士對自己專業中使用的專用縮寫也不見得能夠完全清楚，因此，在論文中使用任何縮寫時，應該在題目、摘要或關鍵詞中至少出現一次全稱。作者雖可以自己擴充縮寫詞，但也必須在該縮寫詞第一次出現時用括弧將全稱括在裡面。若縮寫字實在很多，最好建立一個縮寫字參照表（nomenclature），以供讀者閱讀時參考。

之參考，並於其後依序說明[13]本調查所得現今企業在品質成本制度上的實施情形，內容包括：

1. 品質成本制度之推行現況，
2. 品質成本資料之蒐集與彙整模式，
3. 品質成本管理體系之執行現狀。

3. Current execution status of COQ management system

　　本次調查主要針對台灣五百大企業在品質成本制度上的實施情形，其中將依序介紹：

1. 受訪廠商品質成本的實施現況，
2. 品質成本制度實施目的，
3. 企業未能推行品質成本的原因，
4. 品質成本制度的推行模式，
5. 品質成本體系的主導單位，
6. 品質成本年度目標值的決定依據，以及

　　This research is concentrated in the study of COQ implementation status among top 500 Taiwan Enterprises. For the Surveyed businesses, this paper will discuss:

1. their COQ implementation status,
2. their purpose for implementing COQ,
3. their reasons for not implementing COQ,
4. their COQ implementing patterns,
5. the department that conduct their COQ implementation,

---

13 本段已在前文出現過，若欲重複，應以不同之寫法出之，不宜用寫作新聞稿充篇幅的方式原文照錄。譯文中已將此段漏去不譯。

7. 企業推廣品質成本時對教育訓練所做的投資等項目。[14]	6. the basis for their annual COQ goal , and 7. the amount they invest in COQ-oriented education and trainings.
(一)多數[15]企業目前仍傾向採取自行開發的方式導入品質成本制 　　有鑑於表八中彙整樣本廠商未能實施品質成本制的原因，以「缺乏一套有具體可行的導入模式」為目前所面臨到最嚴重的問題點，而在本調查中亦針對那些宣稱已實施品質成本制度的廠商，進行該制度導入模式之現況蒐集，問卷結果如表九所示，其中亦以「自行發展出的系統」為填答比例最高的項目（約佔77.78%），至於一般人認為較可行的導入模式「購買資訊公司所提供之套裝軟體」竟僅佔全體	Finding 1: Businesses tend to develop their COQ system in-house. 　　For those businesses that claim to have implemented COQ, this research surveys their COQ status and compiles the results in Table 9. Table 9 shows that "using a system developed in-house" takes a share of 77.78% to top the list. As for the pattern generally agreed to be more feasible, "purchasing an off-the-shelf software package," barely make the list. This finding indicates that industry and academia should be up to speed in development of a proper COQ information system.

---

14 內容可以分成數點來陳述時，使用「列舉」的表達方式會比較清楚。如果所陳述的每一點都自成段落，則各點可以用段落方式分列，並在每一段落前使用數字或符號標示。因為論文本身有固定的難度，寫作者不妨以「文字表情」（例如較佳的版面排列、使用黑體、斜體、加底線等方式）來增加其易讀性。又，對英文較無把握者在寫作英文論文或英譯論文時，使用列舉的表達方式可以省去不少文字轉折之間的修辭困擾，值得多多考慮使用。

15 到底多少才算多數？人言人殊。論文中宜以明確數據佐證，凡不能以數據說明者，不宜提出。

已實施 COQ 廠商的 5.56%，再次突顯「品質成本資訊系統」的開發，實乃當前產學界責無旁貸且已刻不容緩的任務[16]。

㈡企業在品質成本教育訓練的投資仍嫌不足

品管大師[17]Dr. Juran 曾道：「品質始於教育，終於教育」，可見[18]品質的觀念實與教育、訓練與實踐等息息相關，由表十二中可看出目前企業在品質成本制的投資仍然不足，僅有不到六成的廠商會定期實施品質成本教育訓練，且由於受矩陣式組織管理制度之影響，制度之推行多以專案方式進行，品質成本制教育訓練之參與對象，亦僅限於各部門參與專案之人員（佔 30.56%）；而教育訓練之實施方式，則並未

Finding 2. The business's investment to COQ-related training still falls at the lower end.

Table 12 shows that less than 60% of the surveyed businesses conduct regular COQ trainings. This means over 40% of the businesses surveyed disregard that the quality is deeply related to education and training and simply do not invest enough money in such aspect. The participants of COQ trainings are mostly limited to COQ-related project personnel (30.56%), which indicates that the industry is influenced by the concept of matrix organization management system and consider the COQ implementa-

---

16 「責無旁貸……刻不容緩」云云，非論文用辭，用於新聞寫作則無可厚非，用於論文則過於「濫情」，本句可改寫成「當前產學界實宜加速『品質成本資訊系統』之開發工作」，並已依此英譯。

17 論文中不需指明被引用者是何身分，只要提出所引文獻的作者姓名及文獻出版年即可。

18 事實的真相不會由一個人的說法就足以證明，類似「由某人的說法得知……」或「由某人的說法

有顯著之特定方法，不論是「派員至專業單位或公司受訓（佔 25%）」、「由公司內部之品管專才自行訓練（佔 19.44%）」以及「禮聘外界專家來公司演講授課（亦佔 13.89%）」三者之間並未存有顯著差異[19]，但相信隨著網際網路之興起，將大幅影響企業對於此制度的教育訓練方式與比重。

tion a project rather than a program. The statistics also shows that among the surveyed businesses that provide their staff with COQ-related trainings, 42.86% of the them choose to have their staff trained outside by professional training organizations. The remaining two training options are both in-house, which add up to 57.14%.[20]

There is a reason to believe that the web-based training will prevail as time goes by.

可見……」這類的語法，應該盡量用「某人的說法旨在表示……」、「某人的說法表達了……」或「某人的說法意在指明……」等方式取代。又，此段敘述既未引出處，又與論文的鴻旨無關，英譯文中已予刪除。

[19] 25% 與 13.89% 間之差異超過 50%，焉可謂「未存有顯著差異」？譯文中已將之除去不譯。

[20] 譯文之百分比以「定期實施品質成本教育訓練之廠商」為基底，而原文中之百分比則為以「所有受訪廠商」為基底，故兩者有所不同。

第七章
文藝類文的翻譯

本章提綱

7.1　傳奇小說一段

7.2　鬼故事一則

7.3　博君一笑

　　翻譯文藝創作類的文章，其難度永遠是最高的，不是一般初入門的翻譯者所能勝任愉快，一些經典的英文文學作品，常常不乏術業專精的翻譯名家願下工夫去譯，好的譯作也就時有所見。下面這段文字取自馬可吐溫的《湯姆歷險記》，其後所引的兩種譯文，各擅勝場，均可稱為上選。

　　Now the battle was at its highest. Under the ceaseless conflagration of lightning that flamed in the skies, everything below stood out in clean-cut and shadowless distinctness: the bending trees, the billowy river, white with foam, the driving spray of spume-flakes, the dim outlines of the high bluffs on the other side, glimpsed through the drifting cloud-rack and the slanting veil of rain. Every little while some giant tree yielded the fight and fell crashing through the younger growth; and the unflagging thunderpeals came now in ear-splitting explosive bursts, keen and sharp, and unspeakably appalling. The storm culminated in one matchless effort that seemed likely to tear the island to pieces, burn it up, drown it to the tree-tops, blow it away, and deafen every creature in it, all at one and the same moment.[1]

譯文一	譯文二
這時候，天空中風、雨、閃、雷交加，狂暴至極。閃電把天空也照亮了，把天宇下的萬物映襯得分外鮮明；被風吹彎的樹木、白浪翻騰的大河、大片隨風飛舞的泡沫以及河對岸高聳的懸崖峭壁的模糊輪廓，都在那飛渡的亂雲和斜飄的雨幕中乍隱乍現。每隔一會，就有一棵大樹不敵狂風，嘩啦一聲撲倒在小樹叢中；驚雷如潮，震耳欲聾，驚魂奪魄，難以言狀。最後的這一陣暴風雨更是威力無比，似乎要在片刻之間，把這個小島撕成碎片，燒成灰燼，淹沒樹頂，再把它吹個無影無蹤，要把島上的生靈都震昏	這時空中的激戰已經達到了高潮，天空閃電，火光不息，下面一切都照得狀分明，清晰得連影子都沒有。樹木低頭彎腰，大河波濤洶湧，白沫泛起。水花大片飛濺，對岸懸崖高聳的輪廓，全都透過飛馳的流雲和斜斜的急雨，時隱時現。每過一會就有一棵大樹敗下陣來，喀嚓一聲，倒在年輕的矮樹叢裡。響雷再接再厲。爆炸聲驚天動地，無法形容的威力讓人心膽俱裂。暴風雨使出了無比巨大的力量，這時到達了巔峰，彷彿要在這同一時刻裡，把小島劈得粉碎，燒成灰燼，還把它淹到樹頂，再捲入大河，而且還

1　Mark Twain, "The Adventure of Tom Sawyer,"

震聾。對這幾個離家出走的孩子們來說，這一夜實在夠他們受的了。[2]	要把島上所有的生物都震聾。這一夜，對這幾個離家出走露宿荒島的年輕人來說，真是夠受的哩。[3]

　　許多人不喜歡讀翻譯的東西，想是因為沒有逢到好的譯作，試想，如果讀者因為讀到你的譯作而對翻譯的東西重燃信心，你的成就感豈同小可。

7.1 傳奇小說一段

　　作者在第一章中介紹了自己的一部英文小說《*The Legend of Two Heros*》的寫作背景，該節從小說中的一篇（*The Adventure of Lee*）內摘錄了一段文字。如今，筆者再以原作者的身分，從小說的另一篇（*The Adventure of Chou*）中摘錄一段文字，並把它翻成中文。

原文	中譯
The wind howled horribly around the house. But both Hung and Fan were sleeping soundly. It was almost midnight. Chau was awaken by the snores of his roommates. He knew that he had to sleep more in order to recover for the next stretch of the journey. However, he was not able to fell asleep again	屋外的風呼哮怒吼，老洪與小范都睡得很熟，接近半夜，趙生被兩人的鼾聲吵醒了，他知道自己得多睡一會兒，恢復體力明天才好上路，但就是很難再睡著。

2 鄧秋蓉譯，《湯姆歷險記》，天津教育出版社，2005/3。
3 徐樸譯，《湯姆歷險記》，新潮文庫（446），志文出版社，2001/8。

easily.

Suddenly he heard a noise from the next room. It sounded like something was dragging. With nothing better to do, he sat up and peeked through a crack on the wall. There was candlelight in the next room.

"Is Lady San still up and working?" Chau thought. ""I thought she said she was tired. Guess it is not easy to run this tavern alone. There are so many things to take care of.""

Lady San pulled out a wooden box from under a bed. That box looked just like a small coffin. She opened the box and took something out of it, then spread things on the ground in front of the bed.

Chau became curious. He saw a cup, a scroll, a small wooden donkey, a wooden figurine of a man, and some miniature farm tools.

Lady San unrolled the scroll under the flickering candlelight and read it with a rhythmic tone in a language unknown to Chau. She then took a sip from that cup, puffed into the

忽然間，他聽到隔壁房有聲音，好像拖東西的響動，趙生反正也沒事做，就坐起來從牆上的隙縫偷看，隔壁房有燭光。

趙生心想：「難道三娘子還在做事？她不是叫累了嗎？一個人經營這家店畢竟不容易，要做的事情那麼多。」

只見三娘子從床底下拉出一個木盒，那木盒看起來像是個小棺材，她打開盒子拿出一些東西散放在床前地上。

趙生好奇起來，他看到了一個杯子、一個小木驢、一個捲軸、一個小木偶和一些小農具。

三娘子在閃爍的燭光下解開捲軸，用一種有節奏的音調唸一種趙生不懂的語言，然後，她用杯子

wooden donkey and the wooden man, and said, "Wake up, little friends," said Lady San gently. "Let's start to work."

A bizarre thing happened. Both the donkey and the little man started to move around. Theman hitched the donkey to the plow. He then walked behind the donkey and started to harrow. It was not very long before a patch of earth was fully tilled. The little farmer then hitched the donkey to a thick, flat board. He stood on the board and drove back and forth across the plowed area. This made the area a smooth seedbed.

Lady San handed the little farmer a bowl of seeds. The farmer did not seem to need any instruction. He planted the seeds in the seedbed. Then Lady San went back to the scroll and read on. This time, a piece of dark cloud rose from within that wooden box. The cloud followed the movement of Lady San's waving hands and sailed to above the seedbed. After a crack of lighting followed by a low roar of thunder, rain started to fall. The seeds sprouted. The new plants grew very fast. Soon, Chau

啜了一小口，噴向木驢和木偶，說：「醒來吧！小朋友們，要開工了喔！」

怪事發生了，木驢和木偶都動了起來，木偶將犁套在木驢上，然後開始翻土，沒多久，一塊田就翻好了，之後，小農夫將厚重的木板套在驢身上，他站在木板上，趕著驢在犁好的這塊土地上來回走動，把地整城平坦的苗床。

三娘子給小農夫一碗種籽，小農夫好像不需要任何指示，把種籽撒在田裡，然後三娘子繼續將捲軸唸下去，這時候，有一小片烏雲從木盒中升起，烏雲隨著她招手之勢飄到田上，幾道閃電過後，隨之而來的是雷鳴聲，雨開始降下來，種籽發芽了，長得很快，沒多久，趙生

was able to recognize the plants from their appearance.

　　"It's rice," thought Chau.

In just a few moments, the stalks of the plants were turning yellow, and their heads had many fine grains. The farmer cut those plants with a sickle. When he finished harvesting, he threw the plants into the air. This made the grains fall apart from the lighter straw. The farmer then gathered the grains and put them into a basket.

　　Chau was frightened by what he saw. He tried to wake the other two in the room without alerting Lady San. But he was not able to bring Hung and Fan back to consciousness. He was scared. Than he realized, "it must have been the wine."

　　Chau went back to peer through that crack. The farmer was cleaning up his tools as Lady San took that basket of grains and set it on the table.

　　"You may retire after you put those things away, my friend," said Lady San with a sweet voice and sounded just like a loving

就認出了莊稼的長相：「原來是稻子。」

　　過沒多久，稻稈轉黃，稻穗垂了下來，農夫用鐮刀收割，收割完後，他把稻子向空中拋擲，這樣一來，稻米就和稻草稈分開了，然後，他把稻米收集起來，放在一個籃子裡。

　　趙生看了，心裡害怕，他試圖在不驚動三娘子的情形下把其他兩人叫醒，但洪范兩人怎麼都叫不醒，他愈來愈恐懼，這才想起：「肯定是酒有問題。」

　　趙生回去偷看，小農夫正在收拾工具，三娘子把那籃米放在桌上，像慈母對小孩一樣甜甜地對小農夫說：「你收完東西之後就可以休息了，我的小朋友。」

mother talking to her child. She then grounded the grains with a small stone mill. When the flour was ready, she made a few dozen rice cakes with it.

At the same time, the farmer was putting things away and setting everything back to normal. Finally, he drove the donkey into the wooden box, then climbed into that box himself.

"Now you can have a good rest. Until nexttime," said Lady San as she closed the box. "Thank you, my little helper. I have to go to bed, too. Good night."

Chau drew back to his bed after Lady San put off the candle. He was very uneasy. All he could do was sit there in silence and wait for morning to come. After a long time, he still had not gotten over his fright. The wind shrieked loudly around the house. Every now and then, he would try to wake up his friends but in vain. It was a long night, indeed. At last, Chau was too tired to stay up any longer.

He had a few nightmares and woke up

然後，她用小石磨把米磨成粉，用那粉做成幾十個米糕，在那當兒，小農夫也在把一切歸位，最後，它把小木驢趕進木盒裡，自己也爬了進去。

三娘子說道：「下回見，你可以好好休息了，謝謝你們，我的小幫手，我也要去睡了，晚安！」

趙生縮回自己的床上，心裡很不安，只能靜坐在床上等天亮，過了很久，他還是沒法擺脫內心的恐懼，風在屋外怒號，每隔一段時間，他就試去叫醒他的朋友，但都沒有用，真是長夜漫漫，終於趙生疲倦得再也撐不下去了，他做了幾個惡夢，驚醒了好幾次，最後他累到

several times. Finally he became so tired and confused that he was not able to distinguish a nightmare from reality.

沒法子分清到底是夢是真。

In the morning when it was about time for breakfast, tavern guests gathered in the dining area. These guests were in groups and all busy minding their own business. Chau was not the type of person who could talk to strangers comfortably. He sat in a corner with Fan and Hung and chatted with them absent-mindedly. Chau did not mention what he saw last night because he was not sure if what he saw was real. As a matter of fact, he would rather believe it was just a nightmare.

Shortly Lady San entered the dining room with a full tray of rice cakes. Chau then realized it was not a nightmare last night. But he was too scared to bring it up. After all, who knew what kind of witchcraft Lady San might have. She might even have a gang that worked with her. Chau decided to pretend that everything was normal and he did not know what others didn't. He believed that revealing what he saw was very risky and could make things

次日早餐時分，店裡的住客聚在飯廳裡，這些客人各自三五成群。趙生不是個能跟陌生人暢談的人，他心不在焉地跟小范和老洪坐在角落閒聊。趙生沒有提起昨晚所見，因為他不敢確定自己所見的是真是假。其實，他寧願相信昨晚只是做了個惡夢。

不多久，三娘子端著一整盤米糕走進來，趙生這才省悟昨晚的事不是夢，但是他不敢說出來。畢竟，誰又曉得三娘子會有什麼樣的魔法，甚至也許還有一群手下跟著她呢。

趙生決定假裝一切如常，自己知道得並不比別

worse.

"I am under a religious oath and am not suppose to eat before noon," said Chau to Lady San. "And, I have an appointment with my friends in the city. I must leave now. If you don't mind I'll take a rice cake with me."

人多，他相信透露實情不但有風險，而且可能把事情弄得更糟，他跟三娘子說：「我在神前許過願，午前不食。我還和城裡的朋友約好，現在就得走，可以的話，讓我帶一塊米糕走。」

"That's all right," said Lady San. She didn't seem to mind. "Let me help you out."

Chau put a rice cake into his pack, bade farewell to his two friends and other guests, and then checked out.

"Have a nice trip," said Lady San as she closed the door behind Chau.

Chau walked to his horse and sprang into the saddle. Then he took the reins, gave the animal a nudge, and sped away. He rushed over a slope, hid his belongings with the horse behind a tree, then sneaked back to the tavern. He peeped though a window into the dining area. Lady San was not there. All the guests were devouring their breakfast. The mysterious rice cakes in that tray were almost gone.

三娘子看來並不在乎：「沒關係，讓我送你出去吧。」趙生把一塊米糕放在背包裡，向他那兩位朋友和其他的客人道過別，方才結帳出門。

三娘子在關門前對趙生說：「祝你旅途愉快。」。

趙生跳上馬，拿起韁繩，夾了一下馬腹，騎馬快速離開。他越過一個斜坡，把東西和馬藏在一棵樹後，然後潛回小店，隔窗窺視飯廳裡的動靜。三娘子已經不在那裡，所有

的客人都狼吞虎嚥在吃早餐，那盤神秘的米糕就快被吃完了。

"This is really good," one said after finishing a rice cake.

"I've never had a better rice cake than this," another commented.

"It is very tasty, indeed," others followed.

For a while after these people enjoying the food, nothing peculiar had happened. Chau started to suspect that he might have been a little carried away with what he saw last night.

"I may have been worried for nothing," thought Chau. But he decided to observe a little longer.

Not long after these guests had finished their breakfast, Lady San came in to offer them tea.

"I see all of the rice cakes are gone. Have you all tasted my rice cakes?" asked Lady San.

"Yes, and they are really good," said the

一個客人吃完米糕：「真好吃。」

另一個客人說：「我從來沒吃過比這更好吃的了。」

其他人也附和：「的確很好。」

這些客人吃完東西以後，一時間並沒有發生什麼特別的事，趙生開始懷疑自己對昨晚的所見是不　緊張過度了，他想：「我也許是在瞎擔心。」

但他還是決定再多觀察一下。客人們用完早餐沒多久，三娘子走進來奉茶，她問：「米糕全光了，每一位都嚐過了我的米糕嗎？」

客人們答：「是啊，真好吃。」

guests.

"They are delicious, indeed," said Fan. "Maybe we can have some more to take with us for lunch."

"I wonder why Chau had to leave in such a hurry," said Hung. "We should take more and share with him if we meet him on the road."

小范說：「確實好吃，也許我們可以帶一些當午餐。」

老洪說：「我真納悶那姓趙的為什麼要急著走，我們該多帶點，在路上遇到他好分給他一些。」

"Of course! I can arrange that," said Lady San as she took an incense stick out from under the rice cake tray and lit it up. "This incense is very soothing. Take a few deep sniffs. Its aroma can wake you up thoroughly and fill you with plenty of strength."

That incense emitted some thick smoke. Shortly the entire dining area was covered with a thin fog.

All of a sudden, the guests began to moan. One-by-one, all the guests but two young men fell onto the ground and started rolling back and forth. As Lady San and those two young men stood there watching, those poor guests started to transform. Hair of different colors started to grow on their arms, faces,

「當然！我可以準備。」三娘子邊說，邊從盛米糕的托盤底下拿出一支香點著：「這香很能安神，深深吸幾口，它的香氣可以提神醒腦，讓你精力充沛。」

那支香散發出濃濃的煙，不多久，整個飯廳瀰漫了一層薄霧。

突然，客人們開始呻吟，除了兩個年輕人以外，大家一個接一個倒在地上，來回打滾。，三娘子和那兩名年輕的漢子站在一旁觀看，可憐的客人

and bodies. Their ears started to stretch out and got bigger and bigger. Their limbs lengthened and their hands and feet were turning into hooves. Tails popped out from their buttocks. Their faces extended out to become long snouts. Their clothes were torn apart by their expanding bodies. One-by-one, they all turned into donkeys!

Then Lady San summoned the two young men to drive all of the donkeys to the courtyard as she swept away those torn pieces of clothes. At the end, the gang put away the belongings left behind by those poor men.

們開始變形，他們的手上、臉上、身上各處開始長出各色的毛髮，耳朵展開來，愈變愈大。四肢變長，手和腳都變成蹄，屁股長出尾巴，臉伸長，變成了長長的吻部，一個接一個，他們都變成了驢子。

而後，三娘子邊清掃裂成片片的衣服，邊交代那兩名年輕人把驢子全趕到庭院裡去，最後，他們收拾了那些客人們留下的物品。

Chau was almost frightened out of wit. He knew that he was in great danger. He carefully sneaked away from the tavern. As soon as he believed it was far enough, he started to run as fast as he could over the hill to where his horse was. He jumped on the horse and rushed away as if he were chased by a fierce beast.

趙生幾乎被嚇傻了，自知處境非常危險，他小心潛離小店，一覺得自己已經走得夠遠了，就開始沒命地跑過斜坡，到他藏馬的地方，跳上馬火速離開，簡直就好像有猛獸在追他。

The wind was blowing. Clouds flew across the sun. Chau slowed down to give his horse a break. His mind was so occupied by what had just happened that he lost his way. He found himself wandering on a vast grassland. Then, nervously he tried to find a way out. But dark gray clouds hid the late morning sun. Chau lost his orientation entirely.

風在吹著，浮雲飄過太陽，趙生慢下來歇一下馬，他滿腦子都在想剛剛發生的事，結果迷路了，發現自己在一片廣闊的草原上遊蕩，然後他才慌慌張張要找出路，但烏雲遮住了近午的日頭，趙生完全迷失了方向。

這部英文小說的原文本是根據古老的中國故事再創作而成，寫成英文之後，又回過頭來翻譯成中文，這種在兩種文字中反復跨越的工作，甚是有趣，都由筆者身為作者兼譯者，獨力完成，想來有此經驗的人士，應該不多，有意於此者，不妨一試其中甘苦。

7.2 鬼故事一則

我們再探一探英譯中文文言文的情趣，接續第二章中的狐仙故事，翻譯《閱微草堂筆記》裡的一則幽默鬼故事，首先錄出原文：

交河及孺愛，青縣張文甫，皆老儒也，並授徒於獻。嘗同步月南村北村之間，去館稍遠，荒原闃寂，榛莽翳然。張心怖欲返，曰：「墟墓間多鬼，曷可久留。」俄一老人扶杖至，揖二人坐，曰：「世間何得有鬼，不聞阮瞻之論乎？二君儒者，奈何信釋氏之妖妄。」因闡發程朱二氣屈伸之理，疏通證明，詞條流暢，二人聽之皆首肯，共歎宋儒見理之真，遞相酬對。

竟忘問姓名。適大車數輛遠遠至，牛鐸錚然，老人振衣急起
曰：「泉下之人，岑寂久矣。不持無鬼之論，不能留二君作竟
夕談。今將別，謹以實告，毋訝相戲侮也。」俯仰之頃，欻然
已滅，是間絕少文士，惟董空如先生墓相近，或即其魂歟。[4]

　　這段文字像第 2.2.1 節裡所引用的狐女故事一樣，有文化上難以跨越
的問題，像阮瞻、程朱、宋儒、二氣屈伸等等，實在沒法翻譯得得體，
只好把原文也用對待狐女故事同樣的方法來處理。避去那些難以傳達的
成語典故，先把原文轉成白話，再行翻譯。

A Ghost Story

白話譯文	英譯
交河的及孺愛和青縣的張文甫兩位都是老讀書人，一起在獻縣教書。有一個月夜，兩人在南村和北村之間散步，離開了教書的學館稍遠的地方，荒郊野外又暗又安靜，路上怪樹雜草掩映。姓張的心生恐懼，想要回頭，就說：「墳場裡常有鬼類出沒，怎麼可以停留？」 　　沒多久，有一位老人扶著拐杖走來，向兩人做揖請他們坐下。老人說：「世間怎麼可能有鬼，沒聽	Ji of Jiao-ho county and Chang of Ching County were two old scholars. They each held a teaching position in the County of Hsian. One night, the two took a moonlight walk in between two villages and found themselves in a remote field away from the private school they boarded. The place was dark, quiet, and overgrown with wiered looking trees as well as vegetations. Chang was

---

過阮瞻的理論嗎？兩位都是讀書人，怎麼會相信佛教徒的妖言妄語。」

說著就詳細述說了程頤和朱熹的陰陽二氣消長的道理，引經據典地加以證明，說理流暢，頭頭是道，兩人聽了連連點頭表示同意，一起讚嘆起宋儒對真理所見之高明，接著雙方互相應對問答，竟然忘了互問姓名。

恰好有幾輛大車從遠方駛來，牛鈴的聲音清脆響亮，老人抖了抖衣服，急忙站起來說：「我是陰間

scared and wanted to go back. He said, "graveyard are full of ghosts, we should not stay."

Not long after, an old man with a walkingstick walked up to them. The old man bowed and asked the two to be seated, then said, "how can there be ghosts in the world? Haven't you ever heard of the famous Chan's theory of ghostlessness? You two are both learned scholars and should not take seriously the Buddhist's nonsense about ghosts."

The old ma,n then, elaborated some ancient scholars' yin-yang energy theory with extreme proficiency. The speech make the two nodded and exclaimed over the insightful views of the Song Dynasty scholars. They chatted delightfully and ended up forgetting to ask each other's name.

Several wagons approached from a distance at that moment. The cawbells clank briskly. The old

的人，孤單寂寞了好久，要是不用無鬼的理論就沒辦法留兩位下來談心打發時間。如今要告別了，說出實話，請別見怪說我是在戲弄和羞辱兩位。」

俯身抬頭之間，老人就銷聲匿跡了。

　　那個地方很少讀書人，只有一位董空如先生的墳墓在附近，那老人也許就是他的陰魂吧。

man fluttered his cloth and stood up quickly, said: "I have been deceased and been surrounded by loneliness for too long. Without making use of the agnosticism, I would not be able to keep you two here for such a long and enjoyable conversation. Now, I am telling you the truth as we are bidding farewell. Please don't take it as an offense." The old man took a slight bow and disappeared swiftly.

There were rarely any learned men in that neighborhood except that a tomb of a Mr. Dong was nearby. The old man could very well be Dong's ghost.

7.3 博君一笑

其一

　　某男子粗通英文，初訪美國，班機抵達前，空服員發 I-94[5] 給入境乘客。

---

[5] I-94 即美國出入境紀錄卡，有中文版，凡獲准入境美國的非移民身分外國人士都要填寫，以供美國海關及移民單位存查。

此人填至 *Sex* 一欄[6]，尋思之後，乃下筆曰：*Once a week.*

填妥後請座旁洋人代為檢視，洋人見之笑曰：*This item should be filled in with male or female.*

此人似有所悟，乃填下：*Female.*

洋人奇曰：*Shouldn't it be male?*

此人乃解釋：*I only do it with females.*

男子到達紐約下褟某飯店，晚飯後到樓下精品店參觀，看到一件樣式新潮的衣服。

他不確定是女裝還是男裝。即問一男服務員 *For girl or boy?*

服務員回答：*Unisex.*

男子露出錯愕的神情，原來他聽成了 *You need sex.*

服務員見狀，一個字母一個字母解釋：*That's "U ... N ... I ...SEX."*

這次他聽成 *You and I Sex*，忙答：*I am sorry, I can only have sex with women.*

服務員覺得好笑，曖昧應道：*I am sorry, too.*

他見人家一再道歉，自己應有禮貌，遂表達再三致歉的意思：*I am sorry three.*

服務員有些不解：*What is this sorry for?*

此人為示文明，有些無奈：*I am sorry five.*

次日男子打算去看自由女神像[7]，他帶著參觀處的聯繫電話 666-2613，他上了計程車。

司機問道：*Where do you want to go, Sir?*

他想，自由應該是 *Free*，女神大概是 *Woman*，於是回答 *Free*

6　其實 I-94 上的 Sex 欄是這樣的：| 5. Sex (Male or Female) | | | | | | |，空格只有六個，填不下 *Once a week.*，填個 *Weekly* 倒是剛好。若怕鬧笑話，可向空服員索取中文版 I-94 填寫。

7　The Statue of Liberty.

woman!

司機道：*Hey man, here in America, nothing is free!*

此男操著重重的口音說：*But I have this telephone number. You see, It's* *"sex... sex... sex... two... sex... one... free."*

男子有在美久居的意思，便從人所勸去考駕照。第一次路考時，他有些緊張。

看到地上向左轉的標線，不敢自作主張，乃問考官：*Turn left?*

考官答：*Right!*

各位猜猜他會往哪個方向轉？

其二

這個流傳在大陸的笑話。說到某單位首長第一次為部屬上英語課。

為了要了解學員程度以便因才施教，便在黑板上寫了一句：*How are you?*

他說：「誰來說說這句英文意思？」

結果依例沒人出頭，他就點了自己的副手回答。

副手看這幾個單字，*How* 是「怎麼」，*Are* 即「是」，*You* 是「你」。

連在一起雖沒把握，但也勉強回答：會不會是……『怎麼……是……你』啊？

首長有點哭笑不得，卻又不好指正，便說：「再來一句試試……*How old are you?*」

副手見上司不置可否，以為答對，又見 *Old* 即「老」。

這次比較有信心：這句應該是『怎麼老是你』吧？

其三

　　第 2.2.2 節「原文內容重於原文形式」中提到，五四時期把 *democracy* 音譯成「德謨克拉西」，把 *science* 音譯成「賽恩斯」，*inspiration* 音譯成「煙士披裏純」，比較那些上古時代的怪異音譯，下面這些英文讀音的現代妙譯，是否有趣不少？

Come on, let's go.	快馬拉死狗
Digital	低級透了
Electronic	伊拉克戳你
Sentimental	山東饅頭
Sometimes	三太子
What's your name?	花枝魷魚麵

　　以下這些音譯，更是展現了童趣：

・Was 我死
・Knees 你死
・Does 都死
・One dollar 完蛋了

第八章
雜誌專文的翻譯

本章提綱

8.1　科技類文

8.2　管理類文

8.1 科技類文

科技類文的翻譯大可不必逐字逐句地直譯，而要以原文內容為重來意譯，以下的範例就是採取先消化原文後再從新寫作的方式譯出，在資訊快速成長的環境中，這種譯法比較能夠爭取時效，重點是：譯者必須對文章所介紹的主題有較深入的了解，對原文與譯入文皆具有直覺式的閱讀和寫作能力，不必苦苦剖析文法結構，才能譯得順利。

即時環境安全監控系統—Realtime Environmental Monitoring System

原文	英譯
1. 系統介紹　　由於相關性資料庫和即時性緊急狀況資料的整合是大規模電腦化環境安全監控系統的主件，因此有用及地	1. Introduction　　The integration of relevant databases and real-time information during emergencies is a key element for large-scale computerized emergency planning and response

理資訊系統之處。

地理資訊系統是傳統資料管理系統和圖解式操作系統的組合，比之傳統資料管理系統，它有更具智力的資料結構和管理系統。

地理資訊系統提供按圖索驥的資料處理方式，使用者不需要直接操作資料庫中之資料記錄，如此一來更可為護資料庫的使用安全。地理位置、相對位置和描述性資料是智慧型地理資訊系統的三種基本元件。

在電腦化環境安全監控系統裡面，地理資訊系統能被用來在地圖上顯示定點上感應器的讀數，並藉此發出警告信號（如：在地圖上的事件地點閃動的不同顏色之圈符）以供緊急應變決策支援之用。

systems. Therefore, a system without a relational management capability is incomplete. At this point, a geographic information system (GIS) is introduced. The GIS moves one step ahead of a conventional relational database management system (RDBMS) through its graphical presentation.

The GIS differs from other mapping systems by the degree of intelligence built into its database structure and management system. The system provides graphical database handlers that can preserve database integrity by not requiring users to manipulate data tables directly. Geographic location, relative position, and descriptive data are three basic elements required to make a mapping system fully intelligent. Within a Computerized Emergency Response System, the GIS can be used to display the sensor readings on maps and floor plans and thereby issues warning signals (such as blinking icons of different colors in the event location on the displayed map) to facilitate emergency response decision making.

電腦化環境安全監控系統發展過程中最引人入勝的是虛擬工具的引入，虛擬工具是一種具有實際工具外觀和作用的軟噓，其控制板上有與實際儀器相同的控制桿、控制鈕、闖關和儀表板等，可做為系統輸入和輸出的界面，習於操作實際儀器者能輕易操作這種以軟體設計成的虛擬工具。

One of the most exciting advances in computerized environmental monitoring is the introduction of virtual instrument (VI). A Virtual Instrument is a software module that can create the look and functions of a physical instrument. People accustomed to the instrumentation of a typical work area can interact with a panel of instruments created with software to simulate physical instruments. A front panel in the virtual instrument toolbox constructed with knobs, slides, switches, graphs, and strip charts, can serve as an interactive interface for system inputs and outputs. Those who are familiar to the practical instrument can easily operate the vertural instrument designed with computer software.

2 系統概觀

所有的環境安全監控系統均應包括下述之系統前端、通訊系統和使用者界面（見圖1）。

2. System Overview

An Environmental Monitoring/ Emergence Response System (as shown in figure 1) should consist of a system front end, a communication system, and a user interface, as described in the following overview.

2.1 系統前端

　　監控系統的前端是一組組的感應器，用來感知化學物質、放射線、移動物體、設施保全、氣體濃度、氣象狀況等等。

　　監控系統能就既定的感應器抽樣頻率執行統計分析，系統能依設定的時間間隔自動請取資料，例如：化物汽體感應器可每隔 30 秒檢查一次，空氣品質每分鐘檢查一次，氣象資料每五分鐘檢查一次，等等。系統也可預設讀數範圍，例如：請數在 1 至 10 之間為第一級；讀數在 11 至 20 之間為第二級；等等。系統隨後可將收得的資料與預設的指標作比較，如果續數超出預設指標，系統可就其潛在風險警示使用者。

2.1 The Front End

　　The front end of a monitoring system is an array of physical sensors that send electrical signals to the data acquisition hardware. Sensors are needed to detect information such as radiation, motion, building security, gas concentration, meteorological conditions, etc.

　　The monitoring and response system can perform static analysis at a given sensor sampling frequency. A user can program the system so that data are retrieved automatically at specified time intervals (for example, chemical vapor detection sensors may be checked every 30 seconds, air quality once a minute, and meteorological information every five minutes). The system can also be programmed to define reading ranges. For example, readings between 1 and 10 can be set as class 1；those between 11 and 20 as class 2；and so on. The system then compares the collected data to a predefined threshold (or the standard for quality control). If the data reaches the threshold, the system will alert users of a potential environmental hazard.Each sensor within the monitoring network is linked to a computer that stores sensor information on storage media. The saved information may be a log of all sensors or only of those that have sensed a critical threshold.

2.2 系統通訊

　　來自感應器的資訊能以透過無線電、行動電話、區域網路、大區域網路乃至網際網路的任一組合方式傳輸到電腦，在某一定點的感應器讀數能在整合後分配到其他定點上。

2.2 System Communication

　　Information from the sensors can be transmitted from a remote sensor to the computer in a combination of the following ways, so that one site can integrate sensor readings on its system and distribute them to other users

• via radio, mobile phone, or other media,

• via a communication package,

• through Local/Wide Area Networks (LAN /WAN) and/or

• throught Internet

2.3 使用者界面

　　監控系統經由圖式使用界面收集資料，並將資料顯示在主監視器上。

2.3 The User Interface

　　The monitoring and response system collects and displays the data onto main monitors via a Graphical User Interface

　　圖式使用界面能讓操作員經由特定資料感應器的分析、測試等很快地分析所得的資料，圖式使用界面也能依操作員的特殊需要來設定顯示的方式。監控系統的操作能夠完全以滑鼠進行。

　　典型的圖式使用界面包含受監視區域之電子地圈，地圖上顯示的主要資訊包含空氣品質、水品質、及噪音水平等等。操作員可用滑鼠在電子地圖上的定點打開視窗，籍以顯示該處的詳細環境資訊，亦可先進入感應器分配位置的放大圈，再在特定感應器位置上另開視窗，以顯示那個感應器的詳細資訊。電子地圖上的閃動物件也能夠被用作緊急狀況位置的指標，這些閃動物件也能經由滑鼠定位而顯示與該物件相關之詳細資訊。

(GUI).The GUI display allows operators to analyze data by quickly finding, testing, and analyzing specific data sensors. In addition, a GUI display can be tailored to the specific needs of the operator. The operation of the monitoring system could be solely mouse dependant.

　　Typical GUI displays would contain maps of the community display key information about air quality, water quality, noise levels, etc. for the monitored areas. By pointing and clicking a mouse at certain locations on a map, a user can open windows that give detailed environmental information or a magnified map of that location showing the sensor distribution. The user can then click at a sensor location for more detailed information about that sensor. Flashing objects on the display maps could also be used as indicators of emergency locations and conditions within the industrial community. These flashing objects can also be clicked on to reveal more detailed information.

感應器資料能在地理資訊系統上以圖符、區域、線、圓周、或文字標示等圖層的形式表達，這些感應器數據的圖像能經由圖式使用界面依系統設計時所定的規則隨時改變。系統能定期更新圖層，使用人可依圖符閃動、顏色和文字標示的變化來觀察感應器的成應狀況。

The sensor data can be associated with a GIS to create graphic overlays such as icons, areas, lines, circles, or word labels. All these graphic displays can be altered dynamically by the GUI's interpretation of sensor readings based on rules formulated during system design. The system can update the graphic overlays periodically. One can then observe sensor detections in the form of blinking icons, color changes, and the appearance of words on the screen.

圖式使用介面能擴大成為多媒體使用介面，多媒體使用介面在圖式使用介面上附加了聲音和影像的能力。

The GUI can be expanded into a Multimedia User Interface (MUI). The MUI enhances the GUI's video with the addition of audio.

3 系統元件

大規模環境安全監控系統需要具備下列主要的硬體和軟體元件。

3.1 應用硬體

應用硬體模組是全體系統的骨幹，選用應用硬體組時應評估其資料擷取、控制、通訊、分析、監控、顯示和資料儲存的能力。

3 SYSTEM ELEMENTS

The major hardware and software elements required for the construction of a large-scale environmental system are categorized in the following:

3.1 Application Hardware

An application hardware package, the skeleton of the entire system, should be evaluated on its capabilities for data acquisition (DAQ), control, communication,

3.1.1 資料擷取和控制硬體

　　資料擷取硬體由感應器（轉換器）和信號調節器組成。感應器可感得具體的自然現象並發出電子信號，信號須經轉變成資料擷取板能接受的形式。最普通的信號調節方式是將信號放大以增加資料的解析度，另一種普遍的信號調節方式是線量化，許多感應器對測量的現象不作線性反應，為了使取得的資料具有意義，必須用特殊的硬體或軟體組件將該資料線量化。資料擷取硬體規格還包括頻道數、取樣頻率、頻道範圍、精確度、和雜訊容受度，這些因素都會影響數位化信號的品質。

analysis, storage, and monitoring and displaying.

3.1.1 Data Acquisition and Control Hardware

DAQ Hardware consists of sensors (transducer) and signal conditioning elements. The sensors sense physical phenomena and emit electrical signals. The signals must be converted into a form that the data acquisition board can accept. The most common type of conversion is amplification of low-level signals to increase their resolution. Another common signal conditioning process is linearization. Many sensors respond non linearly to the phenomena being measured. In order to get a meaningful measurement, the result must be linearized in hardware (or in software) with specialized modules. Other than resolution and linearity, data acquisition board specifications also include the number of channels, sampling rate, range, accuracy, and noise. All of these affect the quality of the digitized signal.

3.1.2 通訊硬體

任何有用的環境系統都需要一組中央電腦網路或多組電腦網路（區域網路或大區域網路）的組合來支援資料通訊。

位於工業區內各處的感應器能經由同軸電纜或其他介質傳送資料至一節點上的接收器內，粗纜線則會將節點接收器上的資料傳送到電腦網路內加以分析。

由於粗纜線較易在安裝時或壞天氣下損壞，無線電頻率／微波傳輸是通訊的較佳選擇，典型的無線電傳輸系統包括無線電收發機和碟型天線，資料可被送至信號

3.1.2 Communication Hardware

While the communication hardware's importance has been greatly challenged by today's mobile phone and Internet technologies, the hardware elements introduced in this section still hold vital positions in many serious environmental systems. A central computer network or the combination of multiple computer networks (Local Area Network or Wide Area Network) is needed as the main structure to support data communication. Remote sensors located throughout the industrial community could transmit their data through twisted pair or coaxial cables to a receiver at a node collector. Trunklines would carry data from node collectors to the computer network for analysis.

Since trunklines are more prone to being damaged during installation or bad weather, radio frequency (RF)/ microwave transmission is a better alternative for communication among the networks in the community. This data transmitting methodology

調節接收器然內，然後被傳
送到電腦網路內加以分析。
中央電腦網路提供 Internet 連
線將工業區外的電腦網路連
結起來，並藉此將資料傳送
到其他的機構去作環境品質
或緊急狀況之分析和查證，
移動式和固定式的視訊會議
中心也能用此通訊環來改良
緊急狀況反應之協調工作。

can eliminate the need for trunklines. A typical setup of a RF transmission system is a parabolic dish antenna equipped with transceivers. The data are then sent to a signal-conditioning receiver and finally ported to the computer network for analysis. The central computer network would provide a communications link to networks outside the industrial community to supply data to authorities or other institutions for analyzing and verifying environmental quality or emergency situations. Video Tele-Conference Centers (both mobile and stationary) can also use the established communication link to improve emergency response coordination.

3.1.3 分析用硬體

　　任何需要快速執行的應
用軟體均可自分析用硬體之
計算能力獲益。需要高頻率
信號和即時反應的應用軟體
在使用數位信號處理器的個
人電腦上已屬可行。
　　今日的浮點數位信號處

3.1.3 Analysis Hardware

　　Any application that needs to run faster can benefit from the computational power of analysis hardware. Applications requiring high frequency signals and realtime response are now possible on the PC using digital signal processing hardware. Today's digital signal processors are 32 bit accurate

理器有 32 位元的精確度，它們有較定點（整數）處理器更具彈性，用浮點處理器發展的應用程式不需要其他的附加軟體來維持浮點的精確度，因此浮點應用程式較易發展，且在與浮點處理器共用時可執行得更快。

with floating point format. They have a much higher dynamic range than fixed point (integer) processors. The applications developed with floating point processors do not require software overhead to maintain floating point accuracy. Therefore, floating point applications are simpler to develop and can run faster with floating point digital signal processors.

3.1.4 高存量儲存體

環境安全監控系統會自感應器中取來所有的資料，將之存入高存量儲存體中以供長程的統計分析，此分析可按週、按月或按年進行，分析結果能用圖式使用介面以圖像方式將感應器附近之環境品質作一表達。由於需要儲存大量的資料，儲存體可選用數位影音光碟（DVD）和高存量的硬碟。DVD 價格低廉，並可長期保存，允為目前最佳的儲存介質。

3.1.4 Mass Storage Media

The environmental monitoring and control system will take data from the sensors and save the data in mass data storage media for long term statistical analysis. This analysis could be weekly, monthly, and yearly. The results could be graphically expressed (using a GUI) to show environmental quality levels for a given sensor or group of sensors. Since the resulting data volume can be tremendous, the mass data storage media should consist of high storage capacity hard drives and digital video disks (DVDs). The DVDs are generally used for backing up data from the hard drives,

	thus creating space for the data from the sensors.
3.1.5 顯示用和監測用硬體 　　顯示系統需要在電子地圖上顯示許多感應器的讀數和來自不同類型感應器的分析結果，系統的操作員也需要經由虛擬工具控制板來發出指令或控制信號。	3.1.5 Displaying and Monitoring Hardware 　　The display system needs to display, on maps (using distinctive icons), many sensor readings and analyzed results from different types of sensors. The operator of the system would also need to issue commands or control signals via the VI panels.
由於單螢幕不足以顯示這許多資訊，所以需要用到多螢幕的電視牆。錄影機網路應該也應被加在網路上以利此高科技的電腦工具之應用。	Since a single screen display would be inadequate, a wall of multiple screens is required. A video camera network should also be constructed online to add a human touch to this hightech computerized application.
3.2 應用軟體 　　應用軟體是使用者和資料擷取系統間的環節，它將個人電腦和資料擷取硬體轉成完整的資料擷取、分析和顯示用的系統，應用軟體組需就其資料擷取、通訊、分析和資料表達的能力來評估。	3.2 Application Software 　　Application software is the link between users and the data acquisition system. Software transforms the PC and data acquisition hardware into a complete data acquisition, analysis, and display system. Formerly, an engineer or scientist often constructing a block diagram for an application might have to convert it into program

設計好應用程式流程之工程師有時仍須程式設計師協助將流程寫成程式碼，流程圖式程式即是用來彌補此種不足的應用程式，用流程圖式程式能將可執行之流程圖塊連接起來。

code. Often, he/she would need to consult a computer programmer. After investing the time to accomplish the preliminary task, the person might still be faced with the difficulty of maintaining or modifying the code to meet long term needs. To remedy this dilemma, Block Diagram Programming (BDP) has been introduced. With a BDP utility, one can actually draw the program in diagram form by connecting executable blocks.

流程圖本身就是程式，它決定了虛擬工具的各項功能，和流程圖一樣容易修正和維護。由於流程圖式程式對習於流程圖者很方便，它已經被用在一些商用資料擷取系統和使用者界面組件上。

The block diagram (or flow chart) itself is the program. It determines the functionality of the virtual instrument, and as a pictorial representation, it is self documenting and therefore easy to modify and maintain. Since the BDP method appeals to those who are comfortable with flow charts, it has been implemented in some commercial data acquisition and user interface modules.

3.2.1 資料擷取系統

資料擷取系統讀入具體的自然現象並利用驅動軟體將其數位化，驅動軟體將應

3.2.1 Data Acquisition System.

Data Acquisition system acquires readings of real-world phenomena and converts it into digital form via driver software. The

用程式寫作的困難減到最低。應用程式的使用者只需知道驅動軟體是否可與應用軟體或程式語言配合。程式師則需知道驅動軟體是否提供必要功能的指令。

driver is written and organized to minimize the difficulties in application software programming. The user of a prewritten application needs to know if the driver works with the application software or the programming language. On the other hand, the writer of a program needs to know if the driver provides commands that perform the needed functions.

3.2.2 通訊及控制系統

通訊及控制系統把控制信號送至系統前端，並把系統前端送來的資料寫入儲存體。通訊及控制系統自通訊組的電子郵箱或電腦的檔案伺服器中（當使用區域網路或大區域網路時）取得資料。電話自動通知系統亦可建入這個系統內，緊急狀況一經證實，自動電知系統即可同時呼叫各相關的緊急事件反應單位。

3.2.2 Communication and Control System

Communication and control system sends control signals toward and reads data onto the storage media from the front end. This system can retrieve data either from the electronic mailbox of the communication package or from the sensor computer's file server (when using a Local Area Network or Wide Area Network access method). This system may include an Automatic Telephone Notification (ATN) protocol to place simultaneous calls to alert the response team once an emergency is verified .

3.2.3 分析系統

分析系統執行即時資料

3.2.3 Analysis System

Analysis system performs real time

或現存資料之計算，此系統包含一資料庫，資料庫將每個感應器的資料錄入一筆資料記錄內，資料記錄包含了相關感應器的位置、它的現時讀數和往昔讀數。環境分析系統還應該包括化物蒸汽擴散模擬程式，與緊急狀況反應人員及裝備相關的資料庫，此資料庫應錄有人員及裝備的所在位置和現存量。

calculations or calculates data captured on disk. The analysis system also includes a database with one data record for each sensor being monitored. The data record consists of information about a sensor's location and its current and historical readings. In addition, an environmental analysis system should include contamination plume models.This system should also include inventory databases for response related equipment showing locations and quantities available. A database management capability for emergency response personnel is also necessary.

3.2.4 展示系統

展示系統顯示電子地圖、圖表和表示測量和計算結果的曲線圖解，一個漸漸通俗的方法是使用以圖符代表具體的元件的程式，這個系統在特定的時間間隔內更新螢幕顯示，並提示使用者哪些事項尚待完成。

3.2.4 Presentation System

Presentation system display maps, graphs, and charts of measurement and calculation results. An increasingly popular method is to use a program in which icons represent real world elements. This system also updates the display at specified intervals and helps the user visualize what has still to be accomplished. It is easy to learn yet powerful and flexible.

4. 工作中的系統

系統使用感應器組收集環境品質資料來分析，感應器所集得之資料經傳輸至一集散點，集散點依次將資料傳到資料處理站，此資料處理站組織資料並清理掉錯誤的資料，處理過之資料送到區域電腦網路去編輯、顯示、分析、和儲存。

最後，區域電腦網路將處理好的感應器資料傳入環境控制中心之中央電腦網路（此網路亦於同時監視社區內的環境品質），感應器資料在送到中央網路之前由區域電腦網路先處理好以避免資料的重複分析，亦避免過量資料被送到主網絡上。

操作員可發出自行測試指令以檢定感應器是否無誤，亦能自功能表中找出測試的指導原則來進行特種測試。

4. System at Work

The system uses an array of sensors to collect environmental quality data. The collected data are then transmitted to a node collector via radio frequency, telephone line, cable, and/or, most economically, Internet. The collector in turn transmits the data via telecommunication trunkline to a node processing station. This station organizes and cleans up erroneous data. The validated data are then sent via trunkline to a regional computer network for compilation, display, analysis, and storage. Finally, the computer network transmits the compiled data to the central computer network within an environmental control center (this network simultaneously monitors the community for environmental quality). The data are compiled at each regional network before transmission to the main network to avoid reanalysis of the raw data and to cut down on the volume of data sent to the central network. Users may check the integrity of the sensor by issuing a self-test command to it. The operator can pull down a menu and follow the guidelines to perform a particular test.

　　舉例來說，操作員可能需要就某感應器做特定氣體的月平均濃度分析，指導程式能指示使用者選擇該感應器、分析的時間和任何其他與測試相關的因素，然後程式會在磁碟中搜尋出正確的資訊，並將之以容易了解的圖形來顯示，樣品濃度若超過預設值程式就會警示使用者。此時使用者可就該感應器查證所獲得之資料，在確認有緊急狀況發生後，電話自動通知系統會警示有關單位來處理此環境問題。其他的決策支援功能應包括化物蒸汽擴散模擬程式、反應人員和裝備之配送、疏散廣播、反應進程之簡報和公共關條等。

For example, the operator may want to do a monthly analysis of the concentration of a certain gas at a given sensor. A guidance program can help users choose the sensor, the time of the analysis, and any other factors pertinent to the test. The program then search the mass data storage media for the correct information and display it in easy-to-understand graphics.Some of the samples may exceed the standard and pose a potential environmental hazard. Identification of samples exceeding the standard will prompt the software to alert users. The users will then verify the data on that sensor. Once the emergency is verified, the ATN system can alert the appropriate authorities correct the environmental probleMs. Other decision support such as plume simulation, response personnel and equipment dispatching, evacuation broadcasting, response progress briefing, and public relations can also be accomplished within this system.

以一個有保全、火警和化物蒸汽等感應器顯示幕的工廠為例，圖符在入口處若穩定則表示此入口是關閉的，電子警告聲「一號入口敞開」若響起，再加上圖符閃動，則表示此入口敞開，然後該處之錄影機就被打開，操作員即能開始監視該處之活動。

綠色的圖符代表未被發動的火警感應器，電子警報聲再加上閃動的紅色圖符顯示在國符位置上發生火警。防火設備的詳細位置和既定撤退路徑之標示會隨即在螢幕上閃動以利緊急應變。

上述的顯示方式亦可用於化物蒸汽外洩之狀況。在電子地圖的適當位置上也可開顯示天氣情況之視窗以利化物蒸汽擴散模擬之用。系統也能顯示感應器讀數的文字資訊。

Envisioning an industrial facility that has a display of security sensors, fire alarms, and chemical vapor sensors, one would note that: Steady icons on entrance locations would indicate that they are secured, while an electronic warning voice prompt (such as: "Entrance No. 1 is open") in addition to a flashing icon would report that the entrance in the icon location is open. A video camera would then be switched on so that the operator could monitor the activities in that area. Green icons would represent fire sensors that are not activated, while an electronic alarm in addition to a blinking red icon would indicate a fire alarm in the icon location. Details on fire fighting equipment locations and a pre-planned evacuation route would flash on screen to facilitate the emergency response.

The above two display protocols can be applied to chemical vapor alarms (a steady icon when nothing is detected and a flashing one when vapor level exceeds the warning threshold). Also, a window in the appropriate location of the map displays updated weather conditions to facilitate the plume modeling. The system can also display textual information for a sensor reading value.

　　舉例來說：當雨量感應器讀數超過一公釐且溫度感應器讀數低於攝氏零度時，室外感應器可能顯示結冰的情況，系統程式能在電子地圖上室外感應器的位置處標出「結冰」字樣。

For example, a field sensor may indicate icy conditions when the rain sensor reading is greater than 1 mm and the temperature sensor is less than 0oC. The program can interpret these readings and write the word "ICY" on the map at the exact location of the field sensor giving the rain and temperature readings. Every operator in the computer network can obtain part or all of this information anytime.

　　電腦網絡上的每個操作員都能隨時取得以上這些資訊的全部或任何一部分。

　　這些資訊能在環境監控室的螢幕（單螢幕或多螢幕之螢幕牆上）上出現，也能同時在緊急狀況控制中心或消防隊的螢幕出現。舉例來說，消防隊就能監視全工業區的防火警鈴，並將狀況及時報告給緊急應變隊的成員。

All these displays can appear on a screen (or multiple screens on a screen wall) in the environmental division's office. An identical display can appear in an emergency control or fire department. Each user on the computer network could retrieve all or any one of these displays any time.

8.2 管理類文

本章提綱

　　原文：Beyond Knowledge Management: Lesson from Japan
　　譯文：超越知識管理：日本的經驗

　　一九九○年代中期以後，新興的學門－知識管理－開始崛起，經過十餘年的發展，如今坊間探討知識管理的書籍已經極為豐富，本章所選譯的原文[1]是節錄自一位日本管理學者的「知識管理」方面的文章。

　　該文作者雖是日人，但是文章上只列出英文的作者姓名，譯者第一個負責任的做法，就是找出該作者的日文原名——竹內弘高。

Beyond Knowledge Management—超越知識管理
Lesson from Japan—日本的經驗

原文	中譯
Lewis Platt, the CEO[2] of Hewlett-Packard, contends that successful companies of the 21st century will be those that do the best job of capturing, storing and leveraging what their employees know. He is using the phrase, "Knowledge is our currency", as a	惠普的執行長 Lewis Platt 認為 21 世紀的成功企業將是那些很能獲取，儲存並利用員工知識的公司。Platt 用「知識就是金錢」做惠普的口號。

---

[1] 摘自 Hirotaka Takeuchi, "Beyond Knowledge Management: Lessons from Japan," http://www.sveiby.com/articles/LessonsJapan.htm, 1998/6.

[2] CEO = Chief Executive Officer。

mantra to spread his message across Hewlett-Packard's worldwide Organization.

The focus in the West has been on (1) explicit knowledge, (2) measuring and managing existing knowledge, and (3) the selected few carrying out knowledge management initiatives. This bias reinforces the view of the Organization simply as a machine for information processing.

What Western companies need to do is to "unlearn" their existing view of knowledge and pay more attention to (1) tacit knowledge, (2) creating new know-ledge, and (3) having everyone in the Organization be involved. Only then can the Organization be viewed as a living organism capable of creating continuous innovation in a selforganizing manner.

Why Knowledge?

Why are managers in the West so enthralled with knowledge? Several fundamental shifts are working to fuel the knowledge movement. They include 1) a shift to knowledge as the basic resource, 2) a shift to

西方知識管理的重點在於 1.顯性知識，2.評估及管理現有知識，3.僅有少數的代表在推動知識管理。

這徒然加強了「把組織當做資訊處理機器」的觀點。

西方公司真正需要做的是解除現有的知識體系，將重點放在：1.隱性知識，2.創造新知識，3.讓每人都參與知識管理。

只有這樣，組織才能被視為能以自我組織的形式持續知識創新的活體。

知識用來做什麼？

有幾個基本的轉型在促進知識管理的發展，即 1) 知識漸漸被當成基本資源；2) 產業結構漸漸轉向知識型；3) 企業成長漸漸成為管

knowledge-based industries, and 3) a shift to growth as the top managerial priority. We will examine each below.

理的最要點。

Shift to Knowledge as theBasic Resource

知識漸漸被當成基本資源

Peter Drucker contends that knowledge has become the resource, rather than a resource. Knowledge has sidelined capital and labour to become the sole factor of production:

"The central wealth-creating activities will be neither the allocation of capital to productive uses nor "labour"... Value is now created by "productivity" and "innovation", both applications of knowledge to work."

The productivity of knowledge is going to be the determining factor in the competitive position of a company, an industry, an entire country. No country, industry, or company has any "natural" advantage or disadvantage. The only advantage it can possess is the ability to exploit universally available knowledge.

Knowledge workers, who now constitute 35% to 40% of the workforce, will become

Peter Drucker 認為知識就是資源，它取代資本與勞動力成為生產的唯一要素。創造財富的活動將不是資本朝生產力分配，也不是勞動力。價值將由知識的創新及知識的生產力開創。知識生產力將成為公司，行業，國家競爭力的決定因素。而沒有任何國家，行業，公司擁有天生的優勢。它們唯一擁有的優勢是運用知識的能力。由於這樣的轉型，現今佔了勞動力 35%-40% 的知識工作者將成為社會的主體，他們將擁有生產資財與生產工具。他們有資金，成為真正的業主，知識這個生產工具又永不離身。

the leading social group as a result of this shift. According to Drucker, "They will own both the 'means of production' and the 'tools of production'...the former through their pension funds, which are rapidly emerging in all developed countries as the only real owners; the latter because knowledge workers own their knowledge and can take it with them wherever they go."

Shift to Knowledge-based Industries

Knowledge-based industries are becoming the leading industries in today's economy. To quote Drucker again:

"The industries that have moved into the centre of the economy in the last forty years have as their business the production and distribution of knowledge and information, rather than the production and distribution of things. The actual product of the pharmaceutical industry is knowledge,- pill and prescription ointment are no more than packaging for knowledge. There are the telecommunications industries and the industries, which produce information-processing tools

產業結構漸漸轉向知識型

知識行業已經成為當今經濟的主導產業。Drucker 談到那些過去 40 年中成為經濟核心的產業都是以知識與資訊（而不是以實的物資）的生產與傳播為核心業務，比如說，製藥行業的實際產品是知識，藥片及處方只不過是知識的包裝。電信業和生產資訊處理工具及設備（如電腦，半導體，軟體等）的產業也是這樣。此外還有資訊製造及分銷行業：電影，電視，影帶。在以開

and equipment, such as computers, semiconductors, and software. There are the information producers and distributors: movies, television shows, videocassettes. The "non-businesses" which produce and apply knowledge - education and health care - have in all developed countries grown much faster than even knowledge-based industries."

Knowledge-based industries include both the service sector and the manufacturing sector. The service sector includes industries where knowledge is effectively the product (such as management consulting or training) as well as industries where the product is based on the application of knowledge (such as architecture). The manufacturing sector includes industries, which produce products with high-knowledge intensity (such as packaged software), as well as those which produce products based on the application of knowledge (such as pharmaceuticals).

發國家中，生產及運用知識的行業（如教育事業與醫療保健業等）甚至比知識行業發展還快。知識行業包括服務及製造業。服務業包括那些把知識作為產品（如管理顧問及培訓）及運用知識的行業（如建築）。製造業包括那些生產高知識產品（軟體）及利用知識生產產品的行業（如製藥業）。

Shift to Growth as theTop Managerial Priority

In the last five to seven years, Western managers focused their attention on cutting costs to the bone through downsizing and

企業成長漸漸成為管理的
最要點

在過去的五至七年間，西方經理用裁員和再造工程

re-engineering. Recently, however, they discovered that the removal of all slack from a worker's day runs counter to creativity and innovation, which are the engines of growth. Nonaka and Takeuchi argue that Japanese companies have advanced their position in international competition because of their skills and expertise at organizational knowledge creation, which is the key to the distinctive way that Japanese companies innovate.

Organizational knowledge creation is defined as the capability of a company as a whole to create new knowledge, disseminate it through the Organization, and embody it in products, services and systems. Japanese companies, which have shunned downsizing and re-engineering for the most part, even during the recent recession, are especially good at utilising this process to bring about innovation continuously and incrementally.

Japanese companies' reluctance to accept knowledge management reflects Ikujiro Nonaka's influence. Nonaka's thoughts about knowledge are different from the popular

為手段來降低成本。然而晚進，他們發現壓榨工人是與企業創新和成長相違背的。野中和竹內認為日本公司正是因為在組織知識創造方面的技能和專長使得他們能不斷創新，才得以提高國際競爭力。

組織知識創造指的是一個公司整體創造和傳播新知識，並將它結合到產品、服務及系統中的能力。日本公司在過去的經濟衰退中，一般都不精簡人員或重組，即使在最近一次經濟蕭條期間，他們都善於利用過程來持續推進創新。

日本公司對於知識管理不願採納反映出是受到野中的思想影響，野中有關知識的思想有兩個方面與西方觀

Western view in two respects according to The Economist:

"The first is his relative lack of interest in information technology. Many American companies equate "knowledge creation" with setting up computer databases. Professor Nonaka argues that much of a company's knowledge bank has nothing to do with data, but is based on informal "on-the-job" knowledge - everything from the name of a customer's secretary to the best way to deal with a truculent supplier. Many of these tidbits are stored in the brains of middle managers -- exactly the people whom re- engineering replaced with computers.

The second thing that makes Professor Nonaka stand out is his insistence that companies need plenty of slack to remain creative.

Nonaka seems to be posing two fundamental questions about knowledge management in the above quote. Can you measure the tidbits of knowledge stored in the brains of managers? Can you really create new knowledge by trying to micro-manage it?

點不同。

　　第一是他對資訊技術缺乏興趣。許多美國公司將知識創造等同於電腦資料庫的建立。而野中教授認為一個公司的知識庫大都非關資料，而是植基於非正式的工作知識，例如顧客秘書的姓名、以及與頑固的供應商打交道的方法。這些瑣碎的東西一般都儲存在中層經理人的腦袋裡，而中層經理人正是再造工程用電腦取代的對象。

　　第二是他強調公司不該太緊繃才能保持創造性。

　　依上面的說法，野中似乎提出了兩個知識管理的基本問題：人腦中的瑣碎知識可不可以衡量？巨細靡遺的知識管理是否真能有助於創新？

Nonaka draws a clear distinction between knowledge management and knowledge creation, as illustrated by the following episode. In naming the first chaired professorship dedicated to the study of knowledge and its impact on business, the Haas School of Business at the University of California, Berkeley, initially recommended the title "Xerox Distinguished Professorship of Knowledge Management." Nonaka inquired if the title could be changed to Xerox Distinguished Professorship of Knowledge Creation." As a compromise, they agreed to call it "Xerox Distinguished Professorship in Knowledge".

The Japanese approach to knowledge differs from the West in a number of ways. We will highlight three fundamental differences here: 1) how knowledge is viewed, 2) what companies do with knowledge, and 3) who the key players are. To repeat, in Japan, knowledge is not viewed simply as data or information that can be stored in the computer; it also involves emotions, values, and

野中畫清了知識管理與知識創造之間的界限。它可由以下事例說明。在提名首位研究知識管理的首席教授時，加州大學柏克萊校區 Haas 商學院提出「全錄傑出知識管理教授」這一稱號，而野中卻問到可否將該稱號改為「全錄傑出知識創造教授」。後來妥協結果，將稱號改為「全錄傑出知識教授」。

日本人對於知識的觀念在有些方面不同於西方，這裡指出三個基本差異：1)知識是如何被看待的？2)公司運用知識來做什麼？3)誰是知識的參與者？

在日本，知識不只是能被儲存在電腦裡的數據或資訊，它也包括了情緒，價值和直覺。公司不只在管理知識，也在創造知識。組織中的每個人都在創建組織知

hunches;companies do not merely "manage" knowledge, but "create" it as well; andevery-one in the Organization is involved in creat-ing organizational knowledge,with middle managers serving as key knowledge engi-neers.	識，中層經理則是主要的知識工程師。
There is a long philosophical tradition in the West of valuing precise, conceptual knowledge and systematic sciences, which can be traced back to Descartes. In contrast, the Japanese intellectual tradition values the embodiment of direct, personal experience. It is these distinct traditions that account for the difference in the importance attached to explicit and tacit knowledge.	溯自笛卡爾時代，西方就有重視精確的概念知識及系統科學的哲學傳統，相反的，日本的智慧傳統則重視直接的個人體驗，正是這種顯著的區別說明了兩者對於顯性與隱性知識的不同重視程度。
Knowledge Creation, Not Knowledge Management The distinction between explicit knowl-edge and tacit knowledge is the key to un-derstanding the differences between the Western approach to knowledge (knowledge management) and the Japanese approach to knowledge (knowledge creation). The West has placed a strong emphasis on explicit	知識創造而非知識管理 顯與隱之分是理解西方知識管理與日本知識創造之間差異的關鍵，西方一般重視顯性知識，而日本一般重視隱性知識。 顯性知識通常可用電腦處理，用電子方式傳輸，用資料庫儲存。而隱性知識的

knowledge and Japan on tacit knowledge.

Explicit knowledge can easily be "processed" by a computer, transmitted electronically, or stored in databases.

But the subjective and intuitive nature of tacit knowledge makes it difficult to process or transmit the acquired knowledge in any systematic or logical manner. For tacit knowledge to be communicated and shared within the organization, it has to be converted into words or numbers that anyone can understand. It is precisely during the time this conversion takes place - that is, from tacit to explicit - that organizational knowledge is created.

主觀和直關特色卻使它難以用系統化或邏輯性的方式處理或傳輸。要想隱性知識能在組織中共享，就得將其轉化為人們能懂的文字或數據形式，隱性知識變為顯性知識的同時，組織知識就創造出來了。

The reason why Western managers tend not to address the issue of organizational knowledge creation can be traced to the view of knowledge as necessarily explicit. They take for granted a view of the Organization as a playing field for "scientific managements and a machine for "information processing".

西方經理避過組織知識創造這個大提的原由是因為他們一般都將知識看為顯性的，理所當然地把組織作為科學管理場所和資訊處理的機器，這種觀點從泰勒[3]到西蒙斯[4]時代都深深地植入

---

3 管理界稱其為科學管理之父。

4 1978 年諾貝爾經濟獎得主。

This view is deeply ingrained in the traditions of Western management, from Frederick Taylor to Herbert Simon.

Frederick Taylor prescribed "scientific" methods for the workplace, the most important being time-and-motion studies. Time-and-motion studies encourage "a preoccupation with allocating resources, ...monitoring and measuring performance, and manipulating organizational structures to set lines of authority. Taylor developed "an arsenal of tools to promote efficiency and consistency by controlling individuals' behaviour and compelling employees to comply with management dictates. Scientific management had little to do with encouraging the active cooperation of workers. As Kim and Mauborgne point out, "Creating and sharing knowledge are intangible activities that can neither be supervised nor forced out of people. They happen only when people cooperate voluntarily.

The Japanese emphasis on the cognitive dimension of knowledge gives rise to

西方的管理界。

泰勒為工作場的運行制定了科學方法，其中著名的為時間動作分析，該方法使用各種方式（如考績、監控、打卡等）來約束員工遵守管理制度，從而提高管理效率。這種的「科學化」的管理方法根本無法使工人積極合作。正如 Kim 和 Mauborgne 指出「知識創造和共享是一種無形的活動，無從監督也無法強迫。只有靠人們自願合作才能發生。

日本人強調的知識認知方向造成了一種完全不同的

a wholly different view of the Or-ganization - not as a machine for infor-mation process-ing but as a "living or-ganism". Within this context, sharing an understanding of what the company stands for, where it is going, what kind of a world it wants to live in, and how to make that world a reality, becomes much more crucial than processing objective information. Highly subjective, per-sonal and emotional dimensions of knowledge have virtually no chance for survival within a machine, but have am-ple opportunity to grow within a living organism. Once the im-portance of tacit knowledge is realised, one begins to think about innovation in a wholly new way. It is not just about putting together diverse bits of data information. The personal commitment of the employees and their identifying with the company and its mission become crucial. Unlike information, knowl-edge is about com-mitment and beliefs; it is a function of a particular stance, perspective or inten-tion. In this respect, it is as much about ideals as it is about ideas; and that fact fuels innovation. Similarly, unlike in-formation,

組織觀念—組織是個活體而不是資訊處理的機器，在這種前題下，了解公司的現況和助其實現前景比處理資訊更重要，高度主觀性、個性化和情感化的知識體系只有在這種活體裡才能發展，在機器裡是沒有生機的。

一旦了解了隱性知識的重要性，人就開始以新的方式思考創新，這與收集資料是不同的，員工對於公司使命的認同感也變得更加重要。，知識與資訊不同，是承諾與信念，也是見解與目標，是理想也是夢想。同時，知識也是行動，個人所擁有的資訊只有在行動下才能創造成為知識，這種自願的行為也能促進創新。

knowledge is about action; it is always knowledge "to some end." The unique information an individual pos-sesses must be acted upon for new knowledge to be created. This voluntary action also fuels innovation.

Although we have made a clear distinction bet explicit and tacit knowledge, they are not totally separate. They are mutually complementary. They interact with each other in the creative activities of human beings. Nonaka and Takeu-chi's theory of knowledge creation is anchored to a critical assumption that human knowledge is created and ex-panded through social interaction be-tween tacit knowledge and explicit knowledge. This interaction gives rise to four modes of "knowledge conver-sion": 1) from tacit to tacit, which is called socialisation, 2) from tacit to ex-plicit, or externalisation, 3) from explicit to explicit, or combination, and 4) from explicit to tacit, or internalisation.

雖然我們已經辨明清了隱與顯，而這兩者也並非完全分離，它們是互補的，在人的創造性活動下相互影響。野中和竹內的知識創造理論奠基於這個前提：人類知識乃是經由顯性與隱性知識的交互作用而創造與發展，這種交互作用產生了四種模式的知識轉化：1) 從隱性到隱性的社會化過程，2) 顯性到顯性的外化過程，3) 從隱性到顯性的結合過程，4) 從顯性到隱性的內化過程。

Knowledge conversion is a "social" process between individuals as well as between individuals and an Organization. But in a

知識轉化是個人與個人間以及個人與組織間的社會過程，但嚴格說來，知識只

strict sense, knowledge is created only by individuals. An Organization cannot create knowledge by itself. What the Organization can do is to support creative individuals or provide the con-texts for them to create knowledge. Organizational knowledge creation, therefore, should be understood as a process that "organizationally" amplifies the knowledge created by individuals and crystallizes it as part of the knowledge network of the Organization.

The infatuation in the West with knowledge management reflects the bias towards explicit knowledge, which is the easier of the two kinds of knowledge to measure, control and process. Explicit knowledge can be much more easily put into a computer, stored into a database, and transmitted online than the highly subjective, personal and cognitive tacit knowledge. Knowledge management deals primarily with existing knowledge. But in order to create new knowledge, we need the two kinds of knowledge to in-teract with each other through the actions of individuals within the Organization.

能由人來創造，組織自己並不能創造知識。只能用支持的態度或建立一個好的創造環境助人創造，因此，「組織知識的創造」應被視為一個過程，這個過程放大了個人所創造的知識，並將該知識聚入組織知識網。

西方對於知識管理的迷情反映出對於顯性知識的偏頗，顯性知識較隱性者易于衡量，控制和處理，而且很容易放入電腦、存入資料庫和在線上傳輸。知識管理也主要是與顯性知識打交道。但為了創造新知識，我們需要組織內個人的行動來使兩種知識交互作用。

第九章
法規合約的翻譯

本章提綱

9.1　法規名稱及條文結構

9.2　產品或服務授權書

在所有翻譯工作中，以法律類文書的翻譯最刻板、自由度最小，因為法律語言必須極為嚴密，以免顯出有機可乘的漏洞。本地的翻譯社兼民間公證人可以代譯法律證件，但其間良莠不齊，法律效力也可能有問題。在美國，沒有律師執照者不准代理與法律有關的事務，律師多按小時收取費用，除非是包辦式的案子，他們花在讀信、尋找、影印、及郵寄文件的時間，都會記錄下來，向你收取費用，他們的費率不便宜，每小時常高達數百美元，請他們翻譯法律文件所費不貲，自己事先譯好再請律師過目，可以省下不少銀子。

9.1 法規名稱及條文結構

以下所列的法規、行政規則、法規結構、及法條結構之標準英譯[1]應該對法律類文字的翻譯有幫助。

---

[1]　取材自行政院 2003/7/3 院台規字第 0920086471 號函核定之「法規名稱英譯統一標準」。

憲法

法規名稱	標準英譯
憲法	The Constitution
憲法增修條文	The Amendment of the Constitution

經立法院通過、總統公布之「法律」名稱

法規名稱	標準英譯
法[2]	1) Act[3], 2) Code[4]
律[5]	Act
條例[6]	Act
通則[7]	Act

---

[2] 屬於全國性、一般性或長期性事項之規定。

[3] *Act* 在英美係指須由國會經立法程序通過之成文法，而 *Law* 則係較廣義之概念，包括「法理、法律原則、判例、習慣法」等，不僅指立法機關通過之成文法而已。依我憲法及中央法規標準法規定之法律位階，係指經立法院（國會）通過之「法」。施行法，則譯成 *Enforcement Act of...*。

[4] 用於編纂成法典型態或規範為基本法性質之法律，例如：現行之民法、刑法、民事訴訟法、刑事訴訟法、行政訴訟法及其他類似性質之基本法均屬 *Code*。

[5] 屬於戰時軍事機關特殊事項之規定。戰時軍律今已廢止，現行法中已無名為「律」者，惟日後若有法律以「律」為名者，其英譯均應為 *Act*。

[6] 屬於地區性、專門性、特殊性或臨時性事項之規定。條例之英譯採用 *Act* 可表明其係屬國會通過之位階。

[7] 屬於同一類事項共通適用之原則或組織之規定。「通則」多見於章節，少見於法律名稱。為簡化名詞之翻譯並明確界定法律位階，如使用「通則」為法律名稱，其英譯為 *Act*。

法律授權之「法規命令」名稱

法規名稱	標準英譯[8]
規程[9]	Regulations
規則[10]	Regulations
細則[11]	1) Enforcement Rules, 2) Regulations[12]
辦法[13]	Regulations
綱要[14]	Regulations
標準[15]	Standards
準則[16]	Regulations

機關內部規範之「行政規則」名稱

行政規則名稱	標準英譯
各種行政規則[17]	Directions

8　*Regulations* 一詞在美國係指由行政機關制頒之法規（*issued by executive authority of government ,*
　　e.g. by federal ad-ministrative agency），與我中央法規標準法第三條所定由各機關發布之命令類
　　同，惟美國不像我中央標準法中區分機關訂定命令之種類，以規程、規則、細則、辦法、綱要、
　　準則等為法規之名稱，故英文中並無較精準之對應名詞，英譯名稱統一為 *Regulations*；中央法規
　　標準法命令名稱中之「標準」，依使用原則，可對應英文名詞中之 *Standard*，此名稱英譯名稱可
　　使用 *Standards*。

9　規定機關組織、處務準據

10　規定應行遵守或應行照辦之事項。

11　規定法規之施行事項或就法規另行補充解釋。

12　*Enforcement Rules* 為施行細則；*Regulations* 為細則。

13　規定事務辦理之方法、時限或權責。

14　規定一定原則或要項。

15　規定一定程度、規格或條件。

16　規定作為之準據、範式或程序。

17　非法律授權訂定而無對外效力之法規命令，由行政機關訂定以規範內部行為之行政規則均屬之。

法規結構及法規條文結構名稱

法規結構	標準化英譯	法條結構	標準英譯[18]
編	Part	條	Article
章	Chapter	項	Paragraph
節	Section	款	Subparagraph
款	Subsection	目	Item
目	Item	之一	-1
總則	General Principles		
通則	General Provisions		
罰則	Penal Provisions		
附則	Supplementary Provisions[19]		

　　也許很少有人會有翻譯法律文件的機會或需要，但是，由於一般人在安裝電腦軟體時，對授權事項常常略過不讀，那不妨趁這機會機細讀一下軟體授權書裡寫的到底是些什麼，以備不時之需。

　　以下選擇一分電腦軟體授權書做為翻譯的範例，讓讀者體驗個中文字的運用與其他類別的文字有何不同。

---

[18] 見第 9.2 節「產品或服務授權書」範例內「條、項、款」之翻譯。

[19] ***Supplementary Provisions*** 用在不可獨立之附件及法律條文章節中之附則，為法律之一部分，無法獨立分割立法。

9.2 產品或服務授權書

原文	英譯
使用者（即被授權人，個人或單一法人團體）請注意： 　　本授權書所稱之產品為＿＿＿＿公司（即授權人）所自行開發之軟體＿＿＿＿（下稱本產品）。請務於安裝產品前仔細閱讀下列內容。如您進行安裝，即表示同意接受本授權書全部條款。	Dear User (the licensee, individual or entity): 　　The product referred to herein shall mean the software ＿＿＿＿ ™ (Hereinafter called The Product) independently developed by ＿＿＿＿ Inc. (the licensor). Please read carefully the following articles before installation. If you install The Product, it shall be deemed that you agree with all the articles hereof.
第一條　授權範圍 **第一項**　使用授權範圍 **第 1 款**　授權人同意就本產品提供被授權人有限制、非專屬、不可移轉的使用授權。除另有約定書面外，被授權人僅得將本產品安裝於壹台電腦設備，並可備份本產品及其相關文件一套，此備份不得安裝或使用於任何電腦，被授權人不得轉讓此備份之權利。	**Article 1.** Scope of License **Paragraph 1.** Scope of licensed use **Subparagraph 1.** The licensor hereby grants a limited, nonexclusive and nontransferable right to use The Product to the licensee. The license shall install The Product in only one (1) computer and may make one (1) copy of The Product and the related documents, which shall not be installed or used in any other computer or transferred to any other person.

第 2 款　本產品之僅限於本授權書之被授權人單獨使用，被授權人尚應以其產品使用手冊、產品維護手冊及光碟為規範。

第 3 款　本產品若為教育版（請參照產品之光碟或外盒說明），被授權人之身分僅限於教育部及縣、市政府認可之各級公、私立學校（國民小學及以上）之行政、教學部門。

第 4 款　本產品所含之第三方軟體，其使用規範應遵守並參照第三方軟體之使用授權規定條款。

第 5 款　惟本產品之可被解讀軟體程式碼（原始碼），並不因本授權合約而產生從屬授權。

第二項　使用限制除雙方另有約定外，被授權人不得為下列行為：

第 1 款　將本產品為上開第一項所述範圍以外之使用。

Subparagraph 2. The use of The Product shall be limited to only the licensee, who shall refer to the users manual, product instructions and the disc of The Product.

Subparagraph 3. If The Product is made for educational purposes (see the disc or outer packing of The Product for details), the licensee shall be limited to the administrative and teaching department of public or private schools at all levels (national primary school or above) approved by the governments of cities, counties or the Ministry of Education.

Subparagraph 4. Any third party software contained in The Product shall be used in accordance with the articles of license thereof.

Subparagraph 5. However, the decodable code (source code) of The Product is not licensed by reason of this license.

Paragraph 2. Restrictions Unless otherwise agreed, the licensee shall not:

Subparagraph 1. Use The Product beyond the scope stipulated in Article 1.1 herein above.

第 2 款　對本產品為修改、轉譯或衍生相關創作之行為；或為解譯、反向組譯工程以企圖獲得本產品之原始碼。

第 3 款　出租、出借、發表、揭露或以任何方式提供本產品及其相關資料。

第 4 款　未經授權人事前書面之同意將本授權書所授予之權利義務再授權、轉讓或以其他任何方式移轉予第三人。

第 5 款　擅自移除本產品上宣示授權人所有權之標籤、圖示或字樣。

第二條　授權人權利聲明

關於本產品（包括未來修正、更新及升級版本等）的結構、組織、程式碼及其相關文件之一切權利（包括但不限於著作權、專利權、商標權、營業秘密及被授權人依本授權書所製作之複本等）皆屬授權人所有。授權人係依被授權人需求及本授權書，提供本產品及其相關資料之使用權予被授權人，並未移轉授予本產

Subparagraph 2. Revise, translate, adapt The Product or commit the related act, or obtain the source code of The Product by means of decoding or reverse engineering.

Subparagraph 3. Lease, lend, publicly display or disclose or provide howsoever The Product and related documents.

Subparagraph 4. Sublicense, transfer or assign in any other manner the rights and obligations contained herein to any third party without the prior written consent of the licensor.

Subparagraph 5. Remove without authorization the label, logo or words on The Product identifying the licensor.

Article 2. Ownership

All the rights to the structure, organization, code and the related documents of The Product (including the versions to be revised, updated or upgraded), including but not limited to copyrights, patent, trademark, trade secrets and the copies thereof made by the licensee in accordance herewith, shall be owned

品前述相關權利。

by the licensor. The licensor grants the right of use of The Product and related documents to the licensee in light of the needs of the latter and in accordance with this license and does not transfer the aforesaid rights thereto.

第三條　保證聲明及責任限制
第一項　授權人保證
第 1 款　授權人保證本產品在適當安裝及使用時，可執行其程式指示，自購買日起一年內，倘被授權人發現不符前述保證，授權人將針對無法執行其程式指示之軟體媒體進行更換。針對本產品之可能瑕疵，授權人將不定期提供修復檔案，但授權人保留決定提供與否之權利。
第 2 款　但前述之瑕疵修復不適用於下列因素所導致者：a 不適當的維修或校準。b 使用非授權人所提供之軟、硬體規格建議來安裝本產品。c 未經授權之修改或誤用。d 未於產品指定的環境條件下運作。e 於不適當的場所進行準備或維修。

Article 3. Warranties and Limitation of Liabilities
Paragraph 1. Warranty of the Licensor
Subparagraph 1. The licensor warrants that The Product may be executed with commands when properly installed or used and in case of any nonconformity found within one (1) year from the date of purchase, The Product may be replaced in respect of the software media nonexecutable. The licensor may, at its own discretion, decide to offer patches in respect of any possible defects of The Product on a non-periodical basis.
Subparagraph 2. Notwithstanding the foregoing, the defects caused by the following acts shall not be warranted:(a) improper maintenance or adjustment. (b) installation of The Product in accor-

第二項　保證之排除

第 1 款　授權人不擔保被授權人將本產品可獨立執行之元件與本產品分離安裝並單獨執行之效能，及本產品因意外、不當使用或誤用所導致之故障。

第 2 款　於相關法律允許之最大範圍內，以上保證聲明為被授權人之獨有權利。除上述載明指定以外，授權人對其他一切明示、默示或法定之擔保不予負責，亦即授權人針對資料遺失，或直接、特定、偶發、重大（包含利益或資料遺失），或其他損壞，概不負責。授權人就授權人指定或介紹之第三人賣方、開發者或顧問提供之任何服務或產品，均不承擔責任。

dance with the instructions for software and hardware not offered by the licensor. (c) unauthorized revision or misapplication. (d) operation not in the specified environment for The Product. (e) Preparation or maintenance at an inappropriate place.

Paragraph 2. Exclusion

Subparagraph 1. The warranty provided by the licensor shall not cover the independent execution of the components of The Product that should have been combined therewith and the failures caused by accidents, improper use or misuse.

Subparagraph 2. The above warranty is the exclusive right of the licensee to the extent permitted by applicable laws. Except as stated above, the licensor shall not be responsible for any other express, implied or statutory warranties, i.e. the licensor shall not be liable for direct, specific, incidental, material loss (including benefits or documents) or any other loss. The licensor shall not be responsible for any service or product

第三項　責任限制授權人或其供應商在任何情況下，皆不對被授權人負責任何損害、求償、或費用，或任何必然、間接、附帶的損害，或利潤、結餘的損失，即使授權人已預先獲悉可能發生此等損失、損害、求償或費用或任何第三當事人的求償，授權人仍無責任。授權人僅就本合約所述之不保證事項、保證及責任之限制等事宜代表供應商，但不就任何其他事宜或其他目的代表供應商。

第四條　授權起始及終止

第一項　本授權書所訂之產品授權期間，自安裝本產品起算。

第二項　立即終止

第 1 款　被授權人如有違反第一條所列事項之情形，本授權將立即自動終止。

provided by any third party seller, developer or consultant appointed or referred to thereby.

Paragraph 3. Limitations of liabilitiesIn no event will the licensor be liable to the licensee for special, incidental or consequential loss or damage, or loss of profit or balance, even if the licensor has been advised of the possibility of such loss or damages, claims or expenses or the claims of any third party. The licensor will represent suppliers only in respect of any warranty, exclusion and limitation herein instead of any other matters or for any other purposes.

Article 4. Period of License

Paragraph 1. Commencement of licenseThe period of license to The Product shall commence from the date of installation thereof.

Paragraph 2. Immediate termination

Subparagraph 1. In case of any violations of Article 1 hereof by the licensee, this license shall be automatically terminated immediately.

第 2 款　被授權人一旦取得本產品升級版本之合法使用授權，則本產品之使用授權許可屆時立即失效。

第三項　終止效力本授權一經終止，本授權書所列授權之事項即失其效力，被授權人應立即將本產品自被授權人之系統設備中移除並銷毀，且應同時銷毀本產品及其相關資料之所有備份。被授權人並應於授權終止後七日內開具書面證明予授權人，以確認其銷毀之事實。

第五條　其他事項

第一項　一部無效如本授權書之條款有違法、無效或無法執行之情形，其餘條款仍保有完整效力。

第二項　本授權書若有修訂之情形，應以書面進行並經授權人簽名始具效力。

第三項　本產品之所有權利皆受各國法律保護，包括但不限於：台灣、美國與其他國家的著作權法，並受國際條約保護。除非本

Subparagraph 2. If the licensee has obtained the license to the upgraded version of The Product, this license shall be invalidated immediately.

Paragraph 3. Effect of termination Upon termination, all the matters contemplated herein shall be invalidated, the licensee shall remove The Product from its system and destroy the same and meanwhile destroy all the copies thereof and of related documents. The licensee shall, within seven (7) days after the termination of the license, submit a written certificate proving the act of destruction.

Article 5. Miscellaneous

Paragraph 1. Part invalidationIn case some of the articles hereof is found to be illegal, invalidated or unenforceable, the remaining articles shall be kept in full force and effect.

Paragraph 2. The modifications of this license shall not be valid unless in writing and signed by the licensor.

Paragraph 3. All the rights to The Product are protected by every country,

合約明文規定，否則本合約不授予被授權人本軟體任何智慧財產權，所有未明文授予的權利均為授權人予以保留。

第四項 準據法及合意管轄本授權書之解釋、效力、履行及其他未盡事宜，悉依台灣法律。如因本授權事項爭執而涉訟，以台灣台北地方法院為第一審之管轄法院。

including but not limited to the copyright law of Taiwan, the US and the international treaties. Unless expressly stipulated herein, this agreement does not grant any intellectual property right to the licensee and all the rights not expressly stipulated shall be owned by the licensor.

Paragraph 4. Applicable Law and Consensual JurisdictionThe interpretation, effect, performance hereof and other unspecified matters shall be governed by the laws of the Taiwan. In case of any action arising from or related to matters of license, Taiwan Taipei District Court shall be adopted as the competent court of the first instance.

第十章
企畫類文的翻譯

本章提綱

10.1 活動計劃

原文	英譯
節能示範巡迴宣導及太陽能車設計製作體驗營計畫書	**Energy-saving Demonstration Tour and Hands-on Solar Car Design Camp**
緣起 　　在面臨溫室效應全球暖化、能源短缺與環境惡化下，「節能減碳」成為本世紀各國需要面對與解決的重要課題。隨著＿＿＿國留台學生遽增，歷年返台之＿＿＿國僑生已超過＿＿＿人，本計畫特選定＿＿＿國為本次活動地點。	**Introduction** 　　The global warming caused by the greenhouse effect along with the energy shortage and the environmental deterioration have made energy conservation and carbon reduction the international issues of the century. Over the years, ＿＿＿ overseas students in Taiwan have dramatically increased to over ＿＿＿. As a result, ＿＿＿ is

	chosen by the planning committee to-host this event.
目的 　　本宣導與競賽活動為增進＿＿國中學生對「能源與環境」之重視，＿＿＿＿大學藉由曾協助中華中學建置＿＿＿＿國第一所「永續能源示範校園」之經驗，提供宣導以及實作課程，藉此活動來使＿國中學生對再生能源太陽能有更深入的體會與實際上的應用，期許學生們能夠從參與中學習及自我提升節能減碳知能。	**Purpose** 　　This contest aims to promote the consensus of the energy and environment conservation among high school students in ＿＿＿. As an institute that has assisted ＿＿＿ Chinese School in building ＿＿＿'s first sustainable energy demonstration campus, ＿＿ University will use the know-how and the experience to offer energy and environment awareness courses and lab exercises to educate the young students about renewable energy applications through their participation this activity..
‧指導單位： ‧主辦單位： ‧協辦單位： ‧籌備委員： ‧總幹事： ‧秘書處： ‧新聞組： ‧庶務組：	‧Advising Committee: ‧Organizing Committee: ‧Sponsoring Committee: ‧Preparatory Committee: ‧Program Director: ‧Secretariat: ‧Newsgroup:s ‧General Affairs Group:

· 接待組： · 參加對象：	· Public Relations: · Participants:
· 活動時間：＿＿＿年＿月＿日 　至＿＿＿年＿月＿日（日程表 　如附件一） · 活動地點：＿＿＿＿＿＿＿＿ · 報名時間：即日起至＿＿＿年 　＿月＿日（報名表如附件二） · 報名費用：每人＿＿＿元（三 　人一組，含含太陽電池車材 　料、活動紀念品、研習活動證 　明） · 請填妥報名表，寄至： 　abcde@gmail.com	· When:＿＿＿/ /＿＿ ~ ＿＿＿/ /＿＿ 　(See Attachment 1 for schedule) · Where:＿＿＿＿＿＿＿＿＿＿ · Registration Deadline:＿＿＿/ /＿＿ 　(See Attachment 2 for registration 　form) · Registration fee: $＿＿＿ per person 　(including souvenir, certificate, and 　materials for a team of three partici- 　pants) · Please email your registration to: 　Mr. ＿＿＿ (abcde@gmail.com),
競賽獎項： · 冠軍 獎狀獎牌及美金 500 元 · 亞軍 獎狀獎牌及美金 300 元 · 季軍 獎狀獎牌及美金 200 元 · 佳作 5 名頒獎狀及獎品 備註：參賽者參與全程活動，可 獲得參賽證明。	**Awards:** · The winner will be awarded with a 　winning certificate, a plaque, and 　U$500; · The first runner up will be awarded 　with a winning certificate, a plaque, 　and U$300, · The Second runner up will be 　awarded with a winning certificate, a 　plaque, and U$200,

	· Certificates and prizes will be award-ed to participants finish in the 4th through 8th places. Note: The participants who have attend-ed the entire event will be awarded with a certificate of participation.

10.2 活動表格

報名表

編號（No）： 由本主辦單位填寫 To be filled by the Registra-tion Office	節能示範巡迴宣導及太陽能模型車設計製作體驗營 Energy-saving Demo Tour and Model Solar Car Design Camp			
參加者隊伍組員資料（每組成員 3 人） Team Member Info. (3 in each team)	隊名（Name of Team）			
成員（Team Members）：				
主要聯絡人 （Point of Contact）		性別 （Sex）	□男（M） □女（F）	
地址（Address）	（　　　　　）			
聯絡電話／手機 （Home Phone/Cellular）				
所屬單位（Affiliation）				
家長姓名／電話（Phone and Name of Parents）				

切結書	Affidavit
本人參加「節能示範巡迴宣導及太陽能車設計製作體驗營」，將完全遵守活動之規定，如有違反，視同放棄。 　　　　參加人：　　　（簽章） 　　　　　年　　月　　日	I hereby agree to follow the rules and regulations of Energy-saving Demo Tour and Hands-on Solar Car Design Camp. I understand that any breaching of the agreement can result in my disqualification. 　　　　　　　Signature: _____ 　　　　　　　Date: _____

活動日程表

活動時程 Event Check Point	日期 Date	事項說明 Description	備註 Remark
公佈比賽辦法 Announcement of the activity	___/ /	敬邀各界參加 The activity is opened to all participants.	請依參與之競賽項目至競賽網站線上報名。 Please register on line.
活動報名 Registration	___/ __/ __ ~ __/ __/ __	線上報名 Online registration	如有任何疑問請電：01-2345-6789 __小姐 Please call Ms. ____ at 01-2345-6789 for nfo,

繳交構想書 Submitting the proposal	____／___／ __～____／ ／__	上傳 PDF 格式構想書，單檔請勿超過10MB。 Upload your proposal in pdf format. Please limit the file to 10 MB.	如有特殊情況可透過官網聯繫。 Access official web for special needs.
第一階段審查 Preliminary evaluation	____／／___	初審委員會審查參賽隊伍之構想書，決定入選隊伍。 The committee will conduct preliminary evaluation	
初審公告 Announcing the result of the pre-liminary evalua-tion	____／／___	官網公佈初賽入圍名單 The result of the pre-liminary evaluation will be posted online.	入圍者將公佈於網站並以 Email 通知 The qualified partici-pants will be notified via email.
活動開始 Starting the event	____／／___	通過初審隊伍進行海報／實作展示及 PPT 報告 The qualified teams will demonstrate their designs via posters and powerpoint.	評審委員會依評審標準決定名次，現場公佈決賽結果 The referee commit-tee will announce the outcome on site.

活動時間表

日期 Date	時間 Time	活動 Activity
＿＿／＿／＿	11:00am - 12:30pm	報到（手冊、衣服、名卡）Check In (handbook, uniform, and name tag)
	12:30pm - 01:00pm	午餐／休息 Lunch
	01:00pm - 02:00pm	開幕禮 Opening Ceremony
	02:00pm - 06:00pm	太陽能應用展 Solar Energy Exhibition
	06:00pm - 07:00pm	晚餐 Dinner
	07:00pm - 09:00pm	環保講座 Environmental Protection Lecture
	09:00pm - 10:00pm	宵夜 Snack Time
	10:00pm - 00:00pm	休息 Bed Time
＿＿／＿／＿	07:00am - 08:00am	早操／早餐 Morning Exercise/Breakfast
	08:00am - 11:00am	參觀工廠（包含午餐）Tour And Lunch
	11:00am - 02:00pm	賽事 Racing Event
	02:00pm - 06:30pm	旅遊 Tour
	06:30pm - 09:00pm	團康活動 Group Activity
	09:00pm - 10:00pm	宵夜 Snack
	10:00pm - 00:00pm	休息 Bed Time

	07:00am - 08:00am	早操 / 早餐 Morning Exercise/Breakfast
___ / ___ / ___	08:00am - 11:00am	模擬練習賽 Racing Rehearsal
	11:00am - 12:00pm	交車 / 檢查 / 午餐 Model Inspection And Lunch
	12:00pm - 03:00pm	正式比賽 Racing Event
	03:00pm - 04:00pm	閉幕及頒獎禮 Closing Cermony

活動議程表

日期 Date	時間 Time	項目 Activity	地點 Location
___ / ___ / ___	08:00-09:00	報到 Sign In	大廳 Auditorium
	09:00-10:00	專題講座 Special topic: 主講人 Speaker:	講堂 Lecture Room
	10:00-10:10	茶點 Tea time	食堂 Dining Hall
	10:10-12:00	太陽能模型車創意造型 Solar car model design	實習室 Laboratory
___ / ___	08:00-08:10	報到 Sign in	大廳 Auditorium

	08:10-10:00	太陽能模型車製作課程與實作 Solar car model assembly	實習室 Laboratory
	10:00-10:10	茶點 Tea time	食堂 Dining Hall
	10:10-12:00	測試模擬試跑 Test runs	賽場 Racing Ground
	12:00-13:00	正式比賽 Game time	賽場 Racing Ground
	13:00-13:30	閉幕式 Closing ceremony	講堂 Lecture Room

10.3. 活動規則

競賽規則與車輛製作	Contest rules and model car preparation
A. 一般規定 1. 太陽能車車體、車輪及齒輪結構等，可自行設計。完成品不超過 $10 \times 14cm^2$（車輛不可小於 $7 \times 7cm^2$，包含導輪），軌道寬度 $11cm^2$。（注意車體彎道部分適應性）	**A. General Guidelines** 1. The partipants may design the body, structure, and all moving parts of their solar model car at will. However, to adapt the curve of the 11 cm track, the dimension of the model car should not be smaller than 7 x 7 cm^2 or larger than 10 x 14 cm^2

2. 在平面軌道中，3 秒內需能行駛 1.5 公尺。	2. The model car should be able to cruise 1.5 m in 3 seconds.
3. 各隊需在所參賽的車輛上顯著位置標示其學校校名及隊名，比賽中不得掉落或修改。	3. The model car should carry the title sign of the team and its affiliation. The sign should not be dropped or changed during the race.
4. 所有車輛在車檢通過後，由大會集中保管放置車輛保管區。	4. All model cars should be placed in an area designated by the organizer.
5. 主辦單位所提供的馬達不得以任何方式進行改裝，並且太陽能車不得加裝太陽電池外任何形式的電池，違者得以取消其參賽資格。	5. The motor provided by the organizer should not be altered in any way. The model car should not be quipped with any form of battery other than solar cells. The violator will be disqualified.
B. 比賽規則	**B. Rule of Competition**
1. 比賽當天必須有 3 人到達會場。	1. At least three members of the team should present at the game event.
2. 每輛車子必須通過車檢。	2. All model cars must pass the inspection.
3. 參加隊伍於報名截止後，抽籤決定出賽次序。	3. The race order is determined via lot drawing.
4. 比賽當日，隊伍未報到者，視同棄權論。	4. The team fails to sign in at the event day shall be disqualified.
5. 初賽暫定分 32 組，每組 2 隊，分組方式采樹狀圖，實際分組以比賽報名隊伍數量為準則，以比賽時間快慢直線競速淘汰賽，分	5. The 64 teams will be grouped in 32 pairs. The preliminary is to qual-

別由勝出的 32 隊進入復賽。

6. 復賽暫定分 16 組，每組 2 隊，分組方式采樹狀圖，實際分組以比賽報名隊伍數量為準則，以比賽時間快慢直線競速速淘汰賽，分別由勝出的 16 隊進入准決賽。

7. 准決賽分 8 組，每組 2 隊，分組方式采樹狀圖，實際分組以比賽報名隊伍數量為準則，以比賽時間快慢單圈環競淘汰賽，分別由勝出的 8 隊進入決賽。

8. 決賽以比賽時間障礙路線比賽，決賽最快的三隊分別為冠、亞、季軍及佳作 10 名。

9. 比賽采競賽計時方式，每次二隊模型車下場比賽繞行一圈，時間最短者為勝。倘若兩隊皆未在規定時間完成賽程，則由大會依時間計算方式計算之，時間短者為勝。倘若兩隊的時間經計算後相同，則以兩車中較接近終點的為勝隊。

ify 32 teams for the quarter-final through the straight line acceleration.

6. The 32 qualified teams will be grouped in 16 pairs. The quarter-final is to qualify 16 teams for the semi-final through the straight line acceleration.

7. The 16 qualified teams will be grouped in 8 pairs. The semi-final is to qualify 8 teams for the final through a one lap circle.

8. The 8 finalists will be grouped in 4 pairs. The final is to determine the winner along with the 1st and the 2nd runner-ups through an obstacle course challenge.

9. In each racing session, the model cars from two racing team will race in the track for one lap. The team that finishes first wins the race. On the occasion when both cars fail to reach the end, the one that is closer to the end wins the race.

10. 比賽時由裁判以口令或哨聲作為模型車啓動的訊號，模型車需在啓動訊號下達前依裁判指示將模型車擺放於大會所設之靜止線前。參賽人員在擺放好車輛之後，不得再以手碰觸車輛，一但碰觸則以一次行走失敗論處。模型車必須依循軌道行走。

11. 比賽進行時，不得再對模型車所有元件進行調整或置換（例車體、車輪、齒輪等），亦不得要求暫停。

12. 如行走失敗，操作者應將模型車調整後在原地重新啓動。假如行走失敗達二次時即須退場，不得再比賽。所謂行走失敗系指：
· 模型車滑出軌道。
· 停止不動超過 5 秒
· 比賽開始後參賽者以手觸碰模型車

13. 模型車及參賽人員不得破壞比賽場地，若裁判發現模型車有此項行為，得宣告該模型車退場，喪失比賽權。

10. The model car should be set on its mark before the referee's go signal. The participant is not allowed to touch his/her model car by hand as soon as the car is on the mark.

11. No part adjustment or replacement are allowed upon the start of the race.

12. On the occasion of failure, the participant should re-enter the race at the spot where the model car fails. Two failures should result in disqualification. The following conditions are consider failures:
· When a model car is off the track.
· When a model car fails to move for over 5 seconds
· When the participant touches his/her model car by hand after the race starts.

13. Any damage of the racing track by the participants or the model car are punishable by disqualification.

14. 依據大會規則裁判可視軌道及其他突發狀況終止該場次比賽，重新競賽。

15. 比賽開始或進行當中參賽隊員嚴禁以手推車，違者將予以取消資格論處。

16. 競賽時間為 3 分鐘，超過競賽時間未完成賽事（跑完一圈），則以車輛所在位置進行加秒（6 秒）處罰。

14. The referee has the authority to stop the race as per the racing guidelines.

15. Any hand-on maneuver of the model car is not allowed upon the start of the race. Violation of this results in disqualification.

16. The total racing time is 3 minutes. The model car that fails to complete the cycle should be penalized by adding 6 second to its time.

C. 違規及懲罰：

若車隊在賽事期間違規，主辦單位會按以下情況分別施罰。

1. 未完成賽程

· 所有賽道以區段為單位分為若干區。競賽時間平均分配在各區段，則為未完成賽程的區段予以加秒（例如：大會規定競賽時間為 10 分鐘，則每段未完成區段加 6 秒）。

· 若未完成者為上坡路段，則除依上項加秒外，每段另加罰 10 秒。

C. Violation and Penalty

Violation will be subject to the following penalty accordingly.

1. Penalty for unfinished sections:

· All racing tracks are divided in sections. A 6-second penalty will be imposed for each unfinished section.

· Additional 10-second penalty will be imposed for each uphill section.

2. 一般碰撞及輕微犯規

以下違規每次加罰 5 秒：

- 太陽能模型車撞到其他物件（包括其他參賽隊伍）。
- 比賽進行期間，如有任何裝飾品或物品，從太陽能模型車上掉落及遺留在賽道上。
- 參賽隊伍在開賽前，刻意除下任何裝置或裝飾部分，每隊會加 5 秒時間作為懲罰。

3. 嚴重犯規

以下違規每次加罰 10 秒：

- 在賽事進行期間，除技術支援人員一人外，其他隊員在未經大會工作人員許可的情況下進入賽區。
- 參賽太陽能模型車在賽道上以反方向行駛。
- 故意損毀或碰撞其他參賽車輛之任何部份。
- 完成賽事後並未儘快在指定出口駛離賽道。

2. A 5-second penalty will be imposed for each of the following violations:

- Causing collisions (include colliding with other model car,
- Dropping any object from the model car during the race, or
- Rremoving any object or decoration from the model car deliberately.

3. A 10-second penalty will be imposed for each of the following violations:

- Any unauthorized entry to the racing area (only one technical support staff per team is allowed in the racing area),
- Model car moving on the wrong way,
- Damaging or colliding the model car of any other participant deliberately,
- Exiting the track through the non-designated exit, or
- Endangering any participant (including self) or impeding the prog ress of the event.

4. 取消資格

以下情況，主辦單位得即時取消該隊參賽資格：

- 危害車手自身和他人安全或阻礙賽事順利進行之任何舉動。太陽能模型車過分裝飾或改裝過度，以致對比賽構成危險。
- 太陽能模型車裝有危險物品或設計，危害該車隊本身或其他隊伍的安全。
- 在未經大會批准下，擅自做任何維修或改裝，因而未能通過的車子安全檢查程式。車輛安裝電池或進行不當改裝以致影響比賽公平性。
- 參賽隊伍發生多次碰撞，並影響賽事的進行。
- 參賽隊伍重複犯規，莫視警告。
- 以手推車，意圖改變比賽成績。
- 破壞比賽場地軌道。

D. 競賽關卡：

1. 初賽直線加速賽，篩選 32 隊。
2. 復賽直線加速賽，篩選 16 隊。

4. The following violations are punishable by immediate disqualification:

- Endangering the participants (including self) or affecting the fairness of the race,
- Over decoration or alteration of the model car,
- Dangerous design or carrying hazardous object,
- Unauthorized model car maintenance or alteration,
- Repetitive collision that may impede the progress of the race,
- Repetitive violations and disregard of the warning issued by the referee,
- Pushing the model car with intention to change the result of the race, or
- Vandalizing the racing track.

D. Level of Game:

1. 32 teams will be screened via preliminary straight line acceleration.
2. 16 teams will be screened via quarter-final straight line acceleration.

3. 准決賽單圈環加速賽，篩選 8 隊。	3. 8 teams will be screened via semi-final lap racing.
4. 決賽綜合挑戰障礙路線。（包含 S 型彎曲挑戰、坡度挑戰及地形變化挑戰）。	4. The remaining teams will participate the final game that includes slope, s-curve, and topographical challenges.

第十一章
本篇習作

本章提綱

11.1 致詞類文翻譯習作

　　你如果應邀為致詞者口譯，可以要求提供講稿，以減少因忙亂造成的錯譯和不必要的誤會。下例的開幕致詞，難度不高，請不妨試譯。

Ladies and Gentlemen,

　　Welcome and thank you for coming. I am Professor _____ from Department of Material Engineering at _____ University. I am delighted to have you here in the International _____ Workshop sponsored by the _____.

　　It is my honor to chair this session. The fact that many of you travel a long way get join us reminds me how important our work is.

　　We are honored to have Ms. _____ and Dr.. _____ with us today. They are the esteemed specialists in their respective field. They will be hosting a speciall topic session this morning. Please prepare yourself to be challenged, excited and inspired.

　　Before I hand my microphone over to Ms. _____, our host for the morning section, let me say once more on behalf of this year's International _____ Workshop organizing committee, welcome. It's a pleasure to see so many of you here.

11.2 心靈類文翻譯習作

　　請先讀讀原文，然後針對其暫譯文發表看法與評論，如有需要，亦可重新翻譯。

原文	暫譯
You may be feeling a change in the energy of the planet. All of you reading this are pioneers, for you would not be attracted to this information if you were not ahead of your time.　　Sometimes the hardest thing of all is saying "no" to someone in need. If you constantly pay attention to people in crisis, you affirm that the way for them to get your attention is by creating crisis. If you want people in your life to respect and	你可能感到地球上的能量正在發生變化。你們所有閱讀本文的都是先鋒，因為你若非領先於你的時代便不會受這訊息吸引。有時候最難的事莫過於對一些有所求的人說「不」。如果你一直注意那些處於危機中的人，你就肯定了他們製造危機以博你注意的辦法。如果你想讓生活中的人尊重和珍惜你的時間，當他們這

honor your time, teach them by rewarding them when they do so.

The world is going through a change, things are speeding up. You may already be feeling it. Those who are not focused on their higher vision and self will experience even more problems. Some of the people around you may be speaking of this as the greatest, most joyful time of their lives, while others are speaking of it as the most difficult. If you are experiencing this as the most joyful time in your life, look around at others. Rather than judging or feeling separate from those who are having difficulties, simply send them light, and let go.

麼做時,用獎勵他們的辦法來教會他們。你可能已經感覺到世界正在經歷一場變遷,事物正不斷加速。那些不關注自己更高理想和更高自我的人會遇到更多的難題。你周圍有些人可能說這是他們一生中最偉大、最快樂的時光,而另一些人則說是最艱難的。如果在你覺得這是你一生中所經歷的最快樂的時光,再環顧你四周的人。勿去評判那些有困難的人,也不要感到與他們有隔閡,只需意想將光明發送他們,隨它去吧。

11.3 學術類文翻譯習作

下文摘自一科技類論文,其文字比一般的論文簡明易讀,所有的專門名詞都已用英文標出,請嘗試予以連同其圖說一起英譯。

凸透鏡具有集光效果,如果要聚集大面積的光於一小點上,就需加大凸透鏡的面積,這樣一來,透鏡中間也就需要加厚,增加的厚度不但會造成透鏡的重量加大,而且透光率也會

減低。Fresnel 透鏡為 1822 年法國科學家 Fresnel 所發明的一種
集光透鏡，真正折射光線的，並不是透鏡的厚度，而是透鏡的
曲度，因此，Fresnel 的想法是，如果把凸透鏡中央的材料移
除，使得透鏡只剩下薄薄的一層（如圖一所示）必然仍有集光
效果，結果他的想法正確，依他的構想所發明的透鏡，使稱為
Fresnel 透鏡。

　　Fresnel 透鏡上排列了許多小小的稜鏡，每一個稜鏡的角
度都經過設計，使得所有的稜鏡都能把平行入射的光線折向鏡
後的某一個小小的範圍（姑且稱之為焦點），達成與凸透鏡同
樣的效果，只是它不能像凸透鏡那樣聚出精確的影像，故不能
用在照相機和其他精密光學器材上。但是，由於其目的不在成
像而在集光，因此只要能把透過每一稜鏡的光儘量折向同一點
就成了，無需講究成像的精確度，因此又稱之為非成像式透鏡
（non-imaging lens），此鏡具有輕薄的特性，可以用在對精密
度要求不高的、非精密影像用的投影機、舞台燈光和探照燈的
集光上。

圖一：Fresnel 透鏡示意圖，虛線部分為原凸透鏡面，黑色部分為透鏡材料部份
　　　移除後之情形

11.4 文藝類文翻譯習作

　　以下這則英譯乃是譯自第 7.2 節的同一篇鬼故事，請比較兩譯並發表
看法與評論。

Ji Ru'ai from Jiaohe and Zhang Wenfu from County Qing were two old scholars who were both teaching in Xian. One night they took a walk under the moon between the south village and the north village, and found themselves in a place that was a bit far from their boarding house. The place was deserted, hushed and shadowy with exuberant vegetation. Zhang was scared and wanted to go back. He said: "There are often ghosts in a graveyard, and we'd better leave here as soon as possible." Presently an old man appeared before them, a stick in his hand. He bowed with collapsed hands to invite the two to sit down, and said: "How can there be any ghosts in the world? Haven't you ever heard of the theory of Ruan Zhan? You two are both learned scholars, and how come you accept the nonsense of Buddhism about ghosts?" Then he expounded the theory of Cheng Yi and Zhu Xi about the ebbing and flowing of the two energies. He was erudite and eloquent. The two nodded and exclaimed over the penetrating views of the scholars in the Song Dynasty. They chatted with the old man and actually forgot to ask his name.

Presently several wagons loomed up in the distance, the bells on the necks of the oxen clanking resonantly. Wiping his clothes hastily and rising to his feet, the old man said: "As a deceased man under the grave, I had been suffering from loneliness for too long. If I hadn't made use of the theory that ghosts do not exist in this world, I could not have detained you two for such an enjoyable and long talk. Now that we are bidding farewell, I tell you the truth. Please don't accuse me of making fun of you." In a moment he disappeared.

There were rarely any men of letters in the place, and only the tomb of Mr. Dong Kongru is nearby. Maybe it was his ghost?[1]

11.5 科技類文翻譯習作

下面這兩段文字是本章的範例中所漏錄和漏譯的，請把第一段譯成中文，第二段譯成英文，完成後請比較你自己的翻譯風格與本章範例的異同，並發表一些評論和感想。

英翻中

Gaining an understanding of potential risks is the beginning of any emergency management planning. Thus, the assessment of risk from hazards has become a critical requirement of effective emergency management. However, a snapshot hazard assessment is not sufficient to provide true safety in a rapidly changing environment. Fortunately, microprocessors have stimulated the construction of a completely new inventory of data acquisition schema in recent years. The implementation of a real-time data acquisition strategy can transform the one time assessment of hazards into a continuous monitoring of potential risks in an industrial community. The introduction of user-friendly software, combined with hardware that is easy to install and use, has even more greatly increased the number of those who can benefit from data acquisition systems. A real-time

---

[1] 摘自 http://www.wangqian.com.cn/ancient/3.htm, 2011/9/30。

environmental monitoring system can facilitate better planning of emergency prevention by continuously monitoring industrial pollutant outputs that may exceed standards and checking vital points for chemical incidents that can cause environmental emergencies. Such a system will uninterruptedly display up-to-date data, compile the data for long-term analysis, and notify users of unusual events through a graphical user interface (GUI).

中翻英

感應器把電子信號送入資料擷取硬體，每個感應器都與電腦連結，電腦將感應器送來的資訊存在磁碟、磁帶或光碟上，儲存下來的資訊可能包括了所有感應器的紀錄，或只包括那些已經感應到特殊狀況之感應器的紀錄。

11.6 管理類文翻譯習作

下面這段文章的中譯並不完整，請仔細對照原文與譯文，把不完整的部分補譯出來，並檢驗你自己的翻譯風格，看它與原譯有何異同。

Knowledge management in Japan

原文	暫譯
As evident from the above, the boom that has hit the West like lightning is not about knowledge per se, but about knowledge	這場風行西方的現象非關知識本身，而是知識管理。目前，歐洲似乎在

management. Europe appears to have an edge on measuring knowledge and the US on managing it.

To repeat, knowledge management is about capturing knowledge gained by individuals and spreading it to others in the Organization. Where does Japan stand with respect to knowledge management? "Nowhere" is probably the most accurate answer.

Visible signs of the boom we saw in the West are nowhere to be found in Japan ... no onrush of new books and journals on knowledge management being published, no conferences being organised, no new databases being formed, and no new corporate titles being created. Neither are Japanese companies sending their managers in droves to Scandinavia to learn how knowledge is being measured, nor to the US to observe how knowledge initiatives are being managed at Hewlett-Packard, GE or 3M, as they have typically done with other new management ideas.

Why are Japanese companies not jumping

評估知識方面具有優勢，美國則在管理知識方面有優勢。那麼日本在知識管理方面又處於什麼地位呢？

雖然日本過去對於各種管理思想非常感興趣，但這一次日本並沒有出現像西方的知識管理熱潮，並沒有出版的書籍雜誌，並沒有知識管理的研討會，並沒有建立知識庫，並沒有新的知識管理職稱，日本公司也沒有送他們的經理西方取知識管理經。

為什麼日本公司不熱衷知識管理呢？這並不是因為他們未認識到知識管理對創新的重要性。他們只是懷疑僅以機械性和系統性的方法來評估與管理知識是否真的能促進創新。

on the bandwagon with respect to knowledge management? It is not because they do not fully recognise the importance of knowledge as the resource and as the key source of innovation. They do, as Nonaka and Takeuchi pointed out in The Knowledge-Creating Company: How Japanese Companies Create the Dynamics of innovation. What they are not convinced about is the value of simply measuring and managing existing knowledge in a mechanical and systematic manner. They doubt if that alone will enhance innovation.

11.7 表格文件翻譯習作

　　一般表格中所列的，多是單字、單詞或簡短的句子，因此表格類的文件翻譯起來較為省事，有時為了求快速，我們會直接用翻譯程式來翻譯表格。其實，網路上的優良語言翻譯器所真正能為人分憂解勞的部份，也只有表格類文件的翻譯了，因為，表格內容的文字少了複雜文法和不同句型的干擾，電腦比較能夠應付得過去，因此翻譯的結果可能不會太離譜，可以湊合著使用，當然事後的人工修改潤飾是絕對必要的。

　　以下有中英表格各一，請分別譯成英文及中文。有心的話，你可以先完成習作，然後將之與翻譯器翻出的結果比對一下，看看差別如何。

　　至於本書中所引用的所有其他類型文字，若想偷懶而用翻譯器來代勞，那自然是上不了檯面的。

中翻英

太陽能產業學程			
學程名稱	太陽能產業學程	實施期程	___/ / ___ ~ ___/ / ___
地區		學校名稱	
學制		申請科系	
整合科系			
地址			
主持人姓名			
身分證字號		性別	
職稱		電話	
E-MAIL		傳真	
參訓學生甄選條件			
電子、電機、資訊或辦理該學程的該系或輔系之大學部二年級以上的學生。			
預期修習本學程後未來可從事之行業或擔任職務			
能源產業 太陽能產業 節能產業之工程師 能源設計師 節能管理師			
預期指標			
一、就業率：____% 二、就業穩定度：____% 三、就業關聯性：____%			
內容規劃摘要			

英翻中

Price	$499.99 list price	$275.00 at Amazon
Software	Operating System	webOS 3.0
	App Store	HP webOS App Catalog
	Adobe flash	Yes
Computing Power	Processor	Dual-CPU 1.2GHz
	Ram	1 GB
	Storage	16 GB or 32 GB
	Storage expansion	No
Display	Display size	9.7 inches (246.4 mm)
	Display resolution	1024 x 768
	Multi-Touch	Capacitive Multi-touch
Size	Height	9.45 inches (240.0 mm)
	Width	7.48 inches (190.0 mm)
	Depth	0.54 inches (13.7 mm)
Input & Output	Speakers	Yes
	Microphone	Yes
	Headphone jack	Yes
	Computer connector	Charger/microUSB connector
	USB Input	microUSB
Wireless Radios	Wi-Fi	802.11 b/g/n
	Bluetooth	Bluetooth 2.1 with EDR
	3G / 4G Data	3G and 4G Optional
	GPS	A-GPS (3G models only)
Cameras	Rear-facing Camera	No

	Front-facing Camera	1.3 Megapixel
	Video recording	HD Camcorder
	Video conferencing	Yes
	Camera flash	No
Sensors	Accelerometer	Yes
	Gyroscope	Yes
	Ambient light sensor	Yes
	Compass	Yes
Battery	Battery type	Rechargeable 6300 mAh
	Battery life	Unknown
	Removeable Battery	No
Availability	15	

　　語言是活的，時時刻刻都可能有外來的新種生出來，豈是任何人窮究所能及。

　　其實，只要試題委員別太過時髦地出些令人傻眼的火星文，我們不懂一些新興的俚語，也不會有啥傷害。而且，那些出火星文的試題委員業已有人追打，可見大家不用對非正統的東西太花心力。

　　這是個我在美國與同事一起上餐館的舊事。

　　同事們一起出差到了異地，晚上多會結伴到餐館裡用餐和打發時間，某些美式餐館裡酒類繁多，很有些同事點起酒來，竟然如數家珍，而且能夠為我這個土包子介紹得滔滔不絕，酒名夾些法文或義大利文，我聽得甚是吃力，多半的時候只有在旁維維諾諾的份，暗想，怎麼這些美國佬一個個對酒這玩意兒這麼熟悉，輪到我的時候，我只能 red wine, white wine 地敷衍過去，一時慚愧起來，整個人氣勢大減，暗暗盤算，回去後一定要把那些名堂好好研究一下。

　　有一次大家一起到中國餐館，點茶的時候，我想，機會來了，這下可得讓這些老美見識見識我點茶的功力，可是那個看來高級的餐館裡，竟然只有 green tea, brown tea，其他什麼烏龍、普洱、鐵觀音，武夷、香片、鐵羅漢，龍井、包種、碧螺春等的名目全然沒有，大大煞了我的銳氣，我只好咕噥了一些聽來怪怪的茶名譯音，什麼 Oolong, Long Ging, Wuyee……等等，自下台階，不了了之。

　　本篇介紹一些英文贅詞的真正涵義、以及現成可循的英翻中漢中翻英範例，讓翻譯者少流些汗。至於那些冷僻或新穎的，自有專書去深究。

第十二章
英文俗常用贅詞的簡化

本章提綱

　　不論中西的寫作者，都可能在敘述事情時使用過多贅文，以致文字過長，這固然可能是寫作者的個人風格所致，也可能表示其人懶得花心思精簡文字。本章列出近兩百條書信、報告或其他應用文中寫法累贅的例子，這些例子若要依原文逐字翻譯，實在頭痛，不如先把它們簡化之後，再行譯出，較爲省時省力。但是話説回來，如果在文藝創作（如小説）中，作者爲了要塑造角色拖泥帶水的風格而代擬的文字，則不應予以更動，宜乎原樣照譯。

原句	原文涵義	譯意
a decreased amount of	less	減低
a decreased number of	fewer	減少
absolutely essential	essential	必要的
accounted for by the fact	because	因為
Additional work will be required before understanding	It is not yet understood	目前尚不了解
adjacent to	near	接近
after which time	then	然後
along the lines of	like	類似
an adequate amount of	enough	足夠的
an example of this is that	for example	例如
an order of magnitude faster	ten times faster	十倍速

are of the same opinion	agree	意見一致
as a consequence of	because	因為
as a matter of fact	in fact	事實上
as a result of	because	因為
as is the case	as happens	同樣發生
as of this date	today	今天
as per your letter of ＿＿／／ at hand... your letter of recent date...	in your mail on ＿＿／／	你＿日的信上
at a later date	later	日後
at a rapid rate	rapidly	立即
at an earlier date	previously	以前
at an early date	soon	盡快
at no time	never	從未
at some future time	later	以後
at the conclusion of	after	在…之後
at the present time at this point in time	now	現在
at your earliest convenience	soon	盡快
Attached hereto is	Here is	附上
based on the fact that	because	因為
because of the fact that	because	因為
by means of	by, with	以…方法
causal factor	cause	導致
cognizant of	aware of	察覺
completely full	full	充滿
consensus of opinion	consensus	一致

Contents duly noted	It is noted	收悉
contingent upon	dependent on	依…而定
definitely proved	proved	證明
despite the fact that	although	雖然
determination is performed	is determined	決定
Do not hesitate to	Please	請勿遲疑
due to the fact that	because	因為
Due to the fact that	Because	由於
due to the fact that	since	因為
during the course of... during the time that...	during, while	在…期間
enclosed herewith	enclosed	隨…附上
Enclosed herewith and attached hereto... Enclosed please find	Here areEnclosed are	附上
end result	result	結果
entirely eliminate	eliminate	消除
fatal outcome	death	死亡
fewer in number	fewer	較少的
First and foremost	First	首先
first of all	first	第一
for the purpose of	for	為了
for the reason that	because	因為
For your perusal	Please read	請你詳閱
forthwith now	at once	立即
from the point of view of	for	依…之見
future plans	plans	計劃

give an account of	describe	描述
give rise to	cause	導致
has engaged in a study of	has studied	研究
has the capability of	can	能
have the appearance of	look like	似乎
having regard to	about	關於
Hereafter and henceforth	From now on	此後
I have insufficient knowledge	I don't know	我不知道
implement	start	開始
important essentials	essentials	必要的
in a number of cases	some	有些
in a position to	can, may	可以
in a satisfactory manner	satisfactorily	令人滿意
in a situation in which	when	在…時
in a very real sense	in a sense（或略）	就…來說
in accordance with your kind wishes	as you requested	據您要求
in accordance with your request	as you requested	據您要求
in case	if	假如
in close proximity to	close, near	接近
in connection with	about,	關於
In due course of time	In time	即時
in light of the fact that	because	因為
in many cases	often	時常
in order to	to	為了
in relation to	toward, to	相關於
in respect to	about	關於

in some cases	sometimes	有時
in terms of	about	關於
in the absence of	without	沒有
in the amount of	for	量、面值
in the event that	if	假如
in the not-too-distant future	soon	不久
in the possession of	has, have	擁有
in the very near foreseeable future	soon	盡快
in this day and age	today	今天
in view of the fact that	because	因為
inasmuch as	for, as	鑑於
incline to the view	think	認為
is defined as	is	是
is desirous of	wants	想要
It is apparent that	Apparently	顯然
It is clear that	Clearly	清楚
It is crucial that	Must	必須
It is doubtful that	Possibly	可能的
It is evident that a produced b	A produced b	A產生b
It is generally believed	Many think	一般認為
It is of interest to note that	Please note that	重點在
It is often the case that	Often	時常
It is worth pointing that	Note that	注意到…
It may, however, be noted that	But	但是
join together	join	結合

Kindly advise the undersigned... Kindly command me...	Please tell me (let me know)	請告知
lacked the ability to	couldn't	不能
large in size	large	大的
make reference to	refer to	提到
met with	met	符合
militate against	prohibit	禁止
more often than not	sometimes	有時
new initiatives	initiatives	倡議
no later than	by	在…之前
of great practical importance	useful	有用的
of long standing	old	長久以來
of the opinion that	think that	認為
on a daily basis	daily	每日的
on account of	because	因為
on behalf of	for	代表
on no occasion	never	從未
on the basis of	by	基於…
on the ground that	because	因為
on the occasions in which	when	在…時
on the part of	by, for	就…而言
owing to the fact that	because	因為
place a major emphasis on	stress	強調
pooled together	pooled	集中
presents a picture similar to	resembles	類似、像
previous to; prior to	before	在…之前

pursuant to your recent request	as you requested	據您要求
pursuing a policy of	according to	根據
red in color	red	紅色
referred to as	called	稱做
regardless of the fact that	even though	即使
relative to	about	關於
resultant effect	result	產生
reverse side	other side	反面
root cause	cause	原因
should it prove the case that	if	如果
smaller in size	smaller	較小的
so as to	to	以便
subject matter	subject	主題
subsequent to	after	在…之後
take into consideration	consider	考慮
the question as to whether	whether	是否
the reason is because	because	因為
the result seem to indicate	the result shows	結果表示
through the use of	by, with	以…方法
to my attention	to me	給我
to the fullest possible extent	fully	完全
unanimity of opinion	agreement	一致同意
under separate cover	Separately...	分別寄出
until such time	until	到…為止
was of the opinion that	believed	相信
ways and means	ways（或means）	辦法

We are contemplating	We are thinking	我們正想
We are herewith changing your address	We've changed your address	我們已更正貴址
We are this day in receipt of... We are today in receipt of...	Today we receive	今天我們收到
trust this will meet with your approval	hope you will approve	相信你會同意
We wish to thank	We thank...	我們感謝
We would like to thank you for	Thank you for	謝謝你
what is the explanation of	why	為何
with a possible exception of	except	除…之外
with a view to	to	為了
with reference to	about	關於
with regard to	about	關於
with respect to	about	關於
with the result that	so that	結果
With your kind permission	Please	請准予
within the possibility	possible	可能的
Would you be good enough to	Please	敬請
Would you kindly be good enough to send me	Would you please send me	請寄下
Your check in the amount of $____	Your $____ check	你的$__支票
Your esteemed communication	Your letter	你的來信

第十三章
英文俗常用詞的中譯

本章提綱

　　經過長久的西學東漸，許多英文的俗語、片語都已經有了約定俗成的中譯，有些固然譯得極為貼切，有些則還是免不了因文化的差異而只表達得差強人意，本書選擇了近千條目，分別細閱修訂之後，臚列於本章，讓翻譯工作者少絞些腦汁。

原文	中譯
A bad penny always comes back.	惡有惡報
A bad thing never dies.	禍害遺千年
A bad workman always blames his tools.	人笨埋怨刀鈍
A baited cat may grow as fierce as a lion.	人急懸樑狗急跳牆
a bear hug	緊緊擁抱
A bird in hand is worth two in the bush.	一鳥在手勝於二鳥在林
A bully is always a coward.	惡人膽小
A burnt child dreads the fire.	一朝被蛇咬，三年怕井繩
A cat has nine lives.	貓有九條命
A cat may look at a king.	小人物也有些權利
A clear conscience can bear any trouble.	不虧心，不驚心
A constant guest is never welcome.	客久生厭
A contented mind is a perpetual feast.	知足常樂
A cook is bold on his own dunghill.	狗仗人勢
A couldn't hold a candle to B.	A區不如B

A cracked bell can never sound well.	狗嘴裏長不出象牙
A crooked stick will have a crooked shadow.	上樑不正下樑歪
A deceitful peace is more hurtful than an open war.	明槍易躲暗箭難防
A door must be either shut or open.	門非關即開；兩擇其一
A drowning man will catch at a straw.	病急亂投醫
A dwarf on a giant's shoulders sees the farther of the two.[1]	引他人經驗為己用
A fault confessed is half redressed.	知錯能改善莫大焉
A fool and his money are soon parted.	笨人難聚財
A fool's mouth is his destruction.	禍從口出
A forced kindness deserves no thanks.	勉強為善不值回報
A fox may grow grey but never good.	江山易改本性難移
A friend in need is a friend indeed.	患難見真情
A full purse never lacks friend.	有錢有酒必有朋友
A golden key opens every door.	錢能通神
A good husband makes a good wife.	夫善則妻賢
A good medicine tastes bitter.	良藥苦口
A good name is sooner lost than won.	好名易失難求
A good tale is none the worse for being told twice.	好故事不厭多說
A hedge between keeps friendship green.	保持距離友誼長存
A honey tongue, a heart of gall.	嘴甜如蜜心黑如漆
A house divided against itself cannot stand.	分裂就會瓦解
A house divided against itself cannot stand.	不和之家難長存
A Jack of all trades is a master of none.	樣樣通樣樣鬆

---

1 巨人肩上的侏儒看得比巨人遠也。

A journey of a thousand miles begins with a single step.	萬丈高樓平地起
A lazy youth, a lousy age.	少壯不努力老大徒傷悲
A leopard cannot change his spots.	本性難移
A liar is not believed when he tells the truth.	騙子就說真話也沒人信
A lion may come to be beholden to a mouse.	強者亦有求於弱者時
A little fire burns up a great deal of corn.	星星之火可以燎原
A little gall spoils a great deal of honey.	一粒屎壞了一鍋粥
A little leak will sink a great ship.	牽一髮而動全身
A little learning is a dangerous thing.	一知半解最危險
A little neglect may breed great mischief.	小疏失可出大麻煩
A little pot is soon hot.	小人易怒
a little too far	太過分了
A man apt to promise is apt to forget.	輕諾者，信必寡
A man cannot spin and reel at the same time.	一心不可二用
A man without a smiling face must not open a shop.	和氣生財
a millstone around one's neck	一大累贅
A miss is as good as a mile.	失之毫釐謬之千里
A near neighbor is better than a distant cousin.	遠親不如近鄰
a pain in the neck	令人討厭的人或物
a pat on the back	鼓勵或贊美的話
a penny for your thoughts	告訴我你在想什麼
A penny saved is a penny earned.	省一文賺一文
a piece of lemon	劣品（尤指汽車或機械類）
A promise is a promise.	答應了就不反悔
A rolling stone gathers no moss.	滾石不生苔

A slow fire makes sweet malt.	慢工出細活
A sound mind in a sound body.	健全心智來自健全身體
A still tongue makes a wise head.	寡言為智
A stitch in time saves nine.	防微杜漸
A thing of beauty is a joy for ever.	美是永恆的喜悅
A watched pot never boils.	候水不沸，急不得
A word is enough to the wise.	聰明人一點就通
A word spoken is past recalling.	一言既出駟馬難追
A young idler, an old beggar.	少壯不努力，老大徒傷悲
Able men are always busy.	能者多勞
Absence makes the heart grow founder.	小別勝新婚
Accidents will happen in the best-regulated families.[2]	百密難免一疏
According to your purse govern your mouth.	量入為出
Achieve two goals with one action.	一舉兩得
Actions speak louder than words.	行動勝過空談
A-day-old puppy doesn't know to be afraid of the tiger.	初生之犢不畏虎
Advice when most needed is least heeded.	忠言逆耳
After a storm comes a calm.	雨過天晴否極泰來
After dinner sit a while, after supper walk a mile.	大餐後坐一坐 晚飯後走一走
after you	你先請
All are not thieves that dogs bark at.	狗吠者未必皆為賊
All cats are grey in the dark.[3]	貓在暗中皆為灰色

2　家規再嚴也難免會出問題也。

3　有「關了燈什麼都一樣」的意思。

All good things come to an end.	好事總會告終
All is vanity.	人生如夢
All lay loads on a willing horse.	馬善被人騎
All roads lead to Rome.	條條大路通羅馬
All Sales Are Final.	貨物售出概不退還
All that glitters is not gold.	閃爍者未必是金
All the winning is in the first buying.	先下手為強
All things are difficult before they are easy.	凡事必先難而後易
All things are easy that are done willingly.	天下無難事，只怕有心人
All things in their being are good for something.	天生我才必有用
All work and no play makes Jack a dull boy.	只工作不玩樂讓人變鈍
All's fair in love and war.	情場如戰場，不擇手段
All's fish that comes to the net.	進網的都算魚
All's well that ends well.	結局圓滿就算好
An early bird gets the worm.	捷足先登
An empty sack cannot stand upright.	空口袋站不直
An eye for an eye, and a tooth for a tooth.	以眼還眼以牙還牙
An old man's sayings are seldom untrue.	不聽老人言，吃虧在眼前
Another day, another dollar	又幹了一天活啦
Any port is a good port in a storm.	暴風雨中不要擇港
Anybody can make mistakes.	人熟能無過
Anything you said	隨你怎麼說
Appearances are deceptive.	人不可貌相
Apples on the other side of the wall are the sweetest.	東西是人家的好
Are you kidding me?	你在開我玩笑嗎？
Are you telling me?	用得著你說嗎？

Art is long, life is short.	生命短暫藝術恆常
As well be hanged for a sheep as a lamb.[4]	一不做二不休
As you brew, so you must drink.	自作自受
As you make your bed, so you must lie on it.	自己做事自己當
As you sow, so shall you reap.	種瓜得瓜種豆得豆
As you wish (= up to you)	隨你便
Ask no questions and be told no lies.	不問就聽不到假話
at the outside	至多、充其量
Avoid a questioner, for he is also a tattler.	好探人私者亦喜搬弄是非
Bad news travels fast.	壞事傳千里
Barking dogs seldom bite.	會叫的狗不咬人
be all ears	凝神傾聽
be all legs	又高又瘦
Be my guest.	請便
be there.	要準時到
beat one's brains out.	想破腦袋；打破頭
Beats me.	我搞不懂
Beauty is but skin deep.	美祇不過是外表
Beauty is in the eye of the beholder.	情人眼裏出西施
Beauty is only skin deep.	美只是表面的
Beggars must not be choosers.[5]	飢者勿擇食
Behave (yourself) = Mind your P's and Q's	放規矩點！
Believe it or not.	信不信由你
Best is cheapest.	最好的即最划算

---

4 偷小羊不如偷大羊，因為都一樣要問吊。
5 乞丐無挑選的權利，有求於人則無權挑剔。

Better an egg today than a hen tomorrow.[6]	把握現有的
Better be a fool than a knave.	寧為傻瓜不做無賴
Better be sure than sorry.	防患未然謀定後動
Better be the head of a dog than the tail of a lion.	寧為雞首不為牛後
Better bend than break.	能屈能伸
Better late than never	寧遲勿缺
Better master one than engage with ten.	多不如精
Better one eye witness than two hearsay witnesses.	耳聞不如目見
Better the devil you know than the devil you don't.	明槍易躲暗箭難防
Better to ask the way than go astray.	問道勝如迷途
Between two stools you fall to the ground.	劈腿早晚會穿幫
Birds in their little nests agree.	同巢之鳥以和為貴
Birds of a feather flock together.	物以類聚人以朋分
bite one's head off	向某人惡言相向
Blessed is he who expects nothing, for he shall never be disappointed.	無求則無患
Blood is thicker than water.	血濃於水
blowing one's top/cap = to go mad	氣瘋了
Bon voyage	一路平安
Books and friends should be few but good.	書與友貴精不貴多
Boys will be boys.	男孩終究是男孩
Bread is the staff of life.	民以食為天
bread-and-butter letter	感謝函
break even	盈虧平衡勝負各半
break off	驟然結束

6　今天有個蛋勝過明天有隻雞。

break up	分手；結束
Brevity is the soul of wit.	言尚簡捷
bright and early	一大清早
Burn not your house to fright the mouse away.[7]	勿因小失大
Burn the midnight oil.	挑燈夜戰
Business is business.	公事公辦
busy on another line	在另一條線上
Butter him up a little.	奉承他幾句
Call a spade a spade.	實話實說
Call no man happy till he is dead.	蓋棺才能論定
calling the turn	預測比賽的結果
can eat a horse.	餓極了。
Can we charge it?	可以賒賬嗎？
Can you give me a lift?	可以搭便車嗎？
can't help it	忍不住；已盡力了
can't hold a candle to	不能與之相比
can't see the forest for the trees	見樹不見林
can't tell (= I don't know)	不知道
captain of the head	船上管理廁所者
Care killed a cat.[8]	憂能傷神
carrot and stick	威脅利誘兼施
carry coals to Newcastle	多此一舉、白費事
carte blanche	全權委任

7　莫為滅鼠而焚屋也。

8　貓有九命而煩惱能殺之。

Cast never a clout till May is out.[9]	勿操之過急
Cast not the first stone.[10]	責人之前先自省
Catch not at the shadow and lose the substance.	勿捨本逐末
catch one's breath	嚇了一跳；喘口氣
catch you later	待會兒見
Catch your bear before you sell its skin.[11]	凡事宜按部就班
Charity begins at home.	仁愛始於自家
chewing the fat	閒聊
Children should be seen and not heard.	小孩子少說話
Christmas comes but once a year.[12]	好日子不是天天有
Circumstances alter cases.	此一時彼一時
clear the air	澄清
Clothes do not make the man.	勿以衣冠取人
come down in buckets/sheets	傾盆大雨
Come on	算了吧！來吧！
Coming events cast their shadows before.	即來之事必有先兆
Comparisons are odious.	人比人氣死人
Conscience does make cowards of us all.	良心令人不敢妄為
Constant dripping wears away the stone.	滴水穿石
cooking one's goose	殺人
Could be.	有此可能
Count me in.	算我一份，我也來
Courtesy costs nothing.	禮多人不怪

---

9 五月結束前莫收冬衣也。
10 莫做第一個丟石頭的人。
11 要先捉到熊才賣熊皮。
12 畢竟耶誕節一年才一度。

crashing a party (or the gate)	不速之客
Cross the stream where it is shallowest.	渡溪當擇淺處
Custom makes all things easy.	熟能生巧
Custom reconciles us to everything.	習慣成自然
Cut it out. = Stop it.	夠了！可以停了
Cut it short!	長話短說
cut someone dead	不理睬
Cut your coat according to your cloth.	量入為出
day in and day out	每日不停
Dead men tell no tales.	死人不洩密
Dear John letter	絕情書，分手信
Death is the great leveler.	死亡使一切平等
Deeds, not words.	行動勝於空談
Desires are nourished by delays.	拖越久就越渴望
Desperate diseases must have desperate remedies.	惡疾需要猛藥醫
Diamond cuts diamond.	勢均力敵
digging out	趕快離開
Discontent is the first step in progress.	不滿足是進步之始
Discretion is the better part of valor.	有勇貴乎有謀
Distance lends enchantment to the view.	距離讓景色增色
Do as I say, not as I do.	照我說的做 別管我怎麼做
Do as most men do, then most men will speak well of you.	凡事隨順，眾人稱頌
Do as you would be done by.	己之所欲施之於人
Do in Rome as the Romans do.	入境隨俗

Do not cast your pearls before swine.	莫對牛彈琴
Do not halloo till you are out of the wood.	未脫險前先別高興
Do not kick against the pricks.	勿以卵擊石
Do not put new wine into old bottles.	莫用舊瓶裝新酒
Do not quarrel with your bread and butter.	別找自己飯碗麻煩
Do not wear out your welcome.[13]	作客不久留
Do something, please. = Don't just stand there.	快想點法子！
Does it matter?	有關係嗎?
Dog does not eat dog.	同類不相殘
dog-eat-dog world	互相殘殺的世界
Don't be silly.	別傻了！
Don't be so fussy.	別太吹毛求疵了
Don't be so sure.	別太自信了！
Don't blow it= Don't goof	別搞砸了
Don't boss me around.	別老支使我
Don't brush me off.	別敷衍我！
Don't change horses in mid-stream.	臨陣莫換將
Don't count your chickens before they are hatched.[14]	別盡打如意算盤
Don't cross a bridge till you come to it.	勿杞人憂天
Don't cry before you are hurt.	莫沒受傷就先叫痛
Don't cut off your nose to spite your face.	別拆自己的台
Don't cut the bough you are standing on.	勿自斷生路
Don't empty the baby out with the bath water.[15]	勿莽撞，別輕心

[13] 不要使人厭倦對你的歡迎。

[14] 小雞還沒孵出來，別盡忙著數。

[15] 不要把嬰兒和洗澡水一起給倒了。

Don't get me wrong.	別誤會我的意思
Don't have too many irons in the fire.	勿操之過急
Don't look a gift horse in the mouth.	莫挑禮物的缺點
Don't make a mountain out of a molehill.	勿小題大作
Don't make a rod for your own back.	勿自討苦吃
Don't make a scene.	別出醜了、別鬧了
Don't make yourself a mouse, or the cat will eat you.	勿自貶身價；自辱者人辱之
Don't meet trouble half-way.	別自找麻煩
Don't pull my leg.	別扯我腿！別搗蛋
Don't push me.	別逼人太甚
Don't put all your eggs in one basket.[16]	勿孤注一擲
Don't put the cart before the horse.	勿本末倒置
Don't ride the high horse.	莫趾高氣揚
Don't speak ill of others behind their backs.	莫在背後說人壞話
Don't take it so hard.	別太難過！看開點
Don't take your harp to the party.	別老談舊調
Don't teach your grandmother to suck eggs.	勿班門弄斧
Don't tease me.	不要戲弄我了
Don't tell a soul.	不要對人說
Don't tell tales out of school.	莫搬弄是非
Don't wash your dirty linen in public.	家醜不可外揚
down in the dumps	沮喪
down to earth	親切和藹的
drive someone up the wall	把人逼上牆了

---

16 不要把蛋全放在一個籃子裏。

drunk as a fish	爛醉如泥
Dying is as natural as living.	生死由命富貴在天
dying to/for	渴望
Early birds catch the worm	早鳥得其蟲
Easier said than done	說來容易做來難
Easier said than done.	說易行難
East and west, home is best	在家千日好
Easy come, easy go.	來得容易去得快
eating (crying, talking) one's head off	吃（哭、說）得厲害
Empty vessels make the most sound.[17]	空罐子最響
Enough is as good as a feast.	知所節制適可而止
Even a worm will turn.	人急懸樑狗急跳牆
Every ass likes to hear himself bray.[18]	自鳴得意
Every bullet has its billet.	生死有命富貴在天
Every cloud has a silver lining	天無絕人之路
Every dog has his day.	風水輪流轉
Every family has a skeleton in the cupboard.	家家有本難念的經
Every flow must have its ebb.	潮起潮落人生變幻
Every horse thinks its own pack heaviest.	人皆自認負擔最重
Every law has a loophole.	法律皆有漏洞
Every man for himself, and the devil take the hindmost.	人不為己天誅地滅
Every man has his ill day.	人無千日好
Every man has his price.	每個人都有個價錢

---

17 喻沒肚裡沒料卻會吹牛。

18 驢喜聽自己鳴。

Every man has his taste.	人各有所好
Every man has the defects of his own virtues.	美中皆有不足之處
Every man is his own worst enemy.	人之大敵乃是自己
Every medal has two sides.	凡事皆有兩面
Every minute seems like a thousand.	度日如年
Every oak must be an acorn.	高樓從地起
Every why has a wherefore.	事出必有因
Everybody's business is nobody's business[19]	眾人之事無人管
Everyone to his taste.	各有所好
Everything comes to him who waits.	耐心等待必能如願
Everything must have a beginning	事有本末
Evil be to him who evil thinks.	邪念致邪
Example is better than precept.	言教不如身教
Expectation is better than realization.	期待總比現實美
Experience is the mother of wisdom	經驗為智慧之母
Extremes meet.	相對的事常可互通
face off	針鋒相對
facing someone down	壓伏某人
Facts speak louder than words.	事實勝於雄辯
Faint heart never won fair lady.	懦夫難得美人心
False friends are worse than open enemies.	損友比敵人還糟
Familiarity brings contempt.	近則狎，熟能生不敬
feeding off other people's troubles	幸災樂禍
feel it in one's bone	惡預感
Fine feathers make fine birds.	人要衣裝佛要金裝

---

19 三個和尚沒水喝，大家的事沒人做。

First come, first served	先來先得捷足先登
First impressions are most lasting.	第一印象令人難忘
First thrive and then wive.	先立業，後成家
Fling dirt enough and some will attack.	積非成是
Fling dirt enough and some will stick.	眾口鑠金人言可畏
food for thought	思考之事
fooling around = horsing around;	鬼混
Fools rush in where angels fear to tread.	愚者趨之賢者避之
for the pot	為了餬口
Forbidden fruit is sweetest.	禁果最甜
Force can never destroy right.	強權不敵公義
Forewarned is forearmed	有備無患
Forgive and forget.	有容乃大既往不咎
Fortune favors the bold.[20]	勇者行好運
Fortune knocks at least once at every man's gate.	人總有走運之時
From saving comes having.	儉能致富
From the sublime to the ridiculous is but a step.	偉大與可笑間祇差一步
Full of courtesy, full of craft.	禮多必詐
Gather ye rosebuds while ye may	有花堪折直須折
get cold feet	怯場，害怕，緊張
get down to business = get on business	言歸正傳吧
getting stood up	對方爽約
getting to somebody	攏絡某人
getting/having the last laugh on someone	得到最後勝利
Give a dog a bad name and hang him.	欲加之罪何患無辭

20 幸運總是眷雇有勇氣嘗試的人。

Give a lie twenty-four hours' start, and you can never overtake it.[21]	三人市虎；謊言說久了就成真
Give a thief enough rope and he'll hang himself	多行不義必自斃
Give and take.	施受之間或多或少
Give credit where credit is due.[22]	歸功於有功者
Give him an inch and he will take a yard.	得寸進尺
give someone cold shoulders	對某人冷淡
Give the devil his due.	應得之罪
Gluttony kills more than the sword.	暴食傷身
go against the grain.	違反原則
go ahead	請便、就這麼做吧
go bananas	發狂
go downhill	走下坡
go Dutch	各付各的
go in one ear and out the other	左耳進右耳出
Go on[23]	說下去；去你的
go out on the town; go paint the town red	我們去瘋一瘋吧
go to one's head	神氣活現
God helps those who help themselves.	自助者天助
God never shuts one door without opening another.	天無絕人之路
God tempers the wind to the shorn lamb.	天道扶弱濟傾
God's mill grinds slow but sure	天網恢恢疏而不漏
going to one's head	沖昏了頭、酒醉

---

21 不及時遏止的謊言會以訛傳訛，終致讓人信以為真。

22 要有雅量承認他人的優點。

23 此語有雙重含意，其一是一般的請人繼續說之意，另一則有內心喜愛，但表面裝討厭的意味

Good advice is harsh to the ear.	忠言逆耳
Good company on the road is the shortest cut.	佳伴同行不覺路遠
Good fences make good neighbors.	好友間必有分寸
Good show = Nice doing = Nice going	幹得好
Good wine needs no bush.	好酒無須吹噓
got nothing to hide.	沒什麼好隱瞞的
Grasp all, lose all.	貪多必失
Great minds think alike.	英雄所見略同
Great oaks from little acorns grow.[24]	凡事由基礎始
Greed has no limits.	人心不足蛇吞象
grin from ear to ear	咧嘴大笑
grow on someone	逐漸愛上某人物
Half a loaf is better than no bread.	有勝於無
Handsome is as handsome does.	內心美才是真美
Handsome is that handsome does.	做得好才是真好
Harp not for ever on the same string.	莫舊調重彈
Haste makes waste.	欲速則不達
Haste trips over its own heels.	忙中有錯
have a close call	好險
have a crow to pluck with someone	對某人有煩言
have a sweet tooth	喜愛甜食
have a waking dream	作白日夢
have another fish to fry	另有要事
have money to burn	錢多得花不完
have the (acting) bug	熱衷於（演戲）

---

24 參天橡樹長自小小橡實。

having a crush on someone	迷戀某人
having a sweet tooth	喜歡甜食
He cannot speak well that cannot hold his tongue.	言多必失
He gives twice who gives quickly.	及時幫助效益大
He is rich that has few wants.	寡慾即富
He laughs best who laughs last	最後的才是勝利者
He puts one over on me.	他耍我花槍（噱頭）
He see things, not people.	他論事不論人
He that cannot obey cannot command	不受命即不能發令
He that commits a fault thinks everyone speaks of it.	作賊心虛
He that fights and runs away may live to fight another day.	跑得了和尚跑不了廟
He that has a great nose thinks everybody is speaking of it.[25]	心虛者多疑
He that touches the pitch shall be defiled.	近朱者赤近墨者黑
He travels the fastest who travels alone.	獨行者走得最快
He wants some prestige.	他想要姿態
He who begins many thing, finishes but few	事多力分
He who denies all confesses all.	欲蓋彌彰
He who excuses himself accuses himself	原諒自己即為難自己
He who gives fair words feeds you with an empty spoon.	美言者如灌迷湯
He who has a mind to beat his dog will easily find his stick.	欲加之罪何患無辭
He who hesitates is lost	遲疑者必失

---

25 大鼻子的人總懷疑別人在談論他的鼻子。

He who makes no mistakes makes nothing	不錯者無成
He who rides a tiger is afraid to dismount.	騎虎難下
He who says what he likes shall hear what he does like	暢言者必聽逆言
He who would climb the ladder must begin at the bottom	登高必自卑
Health is better than wealth.	健康勝於財富
Heaven helps those who help themselves.	天助自助者
high and low	到處
History repeats itself.	歷史會重演
hitting the jackpot	走運
Hoist your sail when the wind is fair.	見風使帆見機行事
Hold it = Just a moment	等一下、慢著
hold one's breath	焦急地等待某事
Hold your horses.	稍安勿躁
Honesty is the best policy.	誠實乃是上策
Hope for the best and prepare for the worst.	抱最好的希望，作最壞的打算
Hot dog	好極了
How come?	1. 怎麼會這樣呢？ 2. 怎麼一回事？
How do you figure that?	1. 你怎會有這種想法？ 2. 你怎麼想出來的？
How's that?	怎麼樣？
Hunger is the best sauce.	飢餓是最好的佐料
I am stuffed.	我很飽了

I made it.	成功了
I mean what I said	我這可是說真的
I said no.	不行就是不行
I think, therefore I am.	我思故我在
Idle folk have the least leisure	懶人不得閒
If a man deceives me once, shame on him; if he deceives me twice, shame on me.	受欺一次羞之在人，受欺兩次羞之在己
If a thing is worth doing it is worth doing well.	值得做的事就要好好做
If at first you don't succeed, try, try, try again	一次不成就再試，再試，再試
If each would sweep before his own door, we should have a clean city.[26]	人人能獨善則天下兼善
If I had my way	要是我做主的話
If it were not for hope, the heart would break.	若無希望吾心碎矣
If one sheep leaps over the ditch, all the rest will follow.	一人領頭，眾人隨之
If the blind lead the blind, both shall fall into the ditch.	一盲引眾盲，相將入火坑
If two men ride on a horse, one must ride behind.[27]	要有個先後次序
If you cannot bite never show your teeth.	不能咬就別亮牙
If you have no hand, you cannot make a fist.	無手難為拳
If you run after two hares you will catch neither.[28]	三心二意一事無成

---

[26] 若人人皆能保持自家門前的清潔，便能擁有一個乾淨的城市

[27] 兩人共乘一馬必有一人在後也。

[28] 同時追兩兔兩頭都落空。

If you want a thing well done, do it yourself.	想做得好就自己做
If you want peace, prepare for war.	要和平，先備戰
I'll be the judge of that.	我自己心裡有數
I'll go only so far.	我只能答應這麼多； 我只能說到這裡
I'll say.	那可不，就是說嘛
I'm flattered = You are just being polite	我受寵若驚
I'm green on this job.	我對這工作還不熟
I'm not a saint.	我又不是聖人
I'm not a Wall Street banker.	我又不是錢太多
I'm only teasing.	只是鬧著玩的
I'm quite a stranger here.	我對這兒很陌生
I'm serious.	我說真的。
I'm sick and tired of you.	我對你很厭煩
I'm through (I'm finished).[29]	我做完（或完蛋）了
I'm together.	我沒問題
Imitation is the sincerest form of flattery.	模仿是最好的恭維
In a calm sea every man is a pilot.	無事無法見真章
In for a penny, in for a pound.	一不做二不休；橫豎都是做
In the country of the blind, the one-eyed man is king.	山中無老虎，猴子作大王
In wine there is truth.	酒後吐真言
Is that so?	真的嗎？
It breaks my heart but...[30]	非常不好意思，但我不能…

---

29 這兩句話都有「做完了」和「完蛋了」的雙重意思，應依前號後文而定，但是I'm through較偏於前者，I'm finsihed則較偏於後者。

30 用於婉拒的場合。

It depends.	不一定，看情形
It doesn't sit well (or right) with me.	我看不順眼
It is a sad house where the hen crows louder than the cock	牝雞司晨大不妙
It is as well to know which way the wind blows.	識時務者為俊傑
It is better to give than to take.	施比受更有福
It is better to wear out than to rust out.	用壞比廢掉好
It is easier to pull down than to build.	破壞易於建設
It is easy to be wise after the event.	馬後炮容易放
It is good fishing in troubled waters.	混水好摸魚
It is love that makes the world go round.	愛使世界生生不息
It is never too late to learn.	活到老，學到老
It is never too late to mend.	亡羊補牢猶未晚
It is no use crying over spilt milk.	覆水難收
It is the unexpected that always happens.	世事難料
It isn't like you.	這不像你的作風
It makes sense.	有道理
It served her right.	她活該，自作自受
It stands to reason.	道理顯而易見
It takes all sorts to make a world.	一種米養百種人
It takes two to make a quarrel.	一個巴掌拍不響
It won't do anything good.	沒有用；於事無補
It won't do.	這樣不行
It's a cinch.[31]	那簡單
It's all Greek to me.	我完全不懂

---

[31] 又作 *It's a piece of cake; It's as easy as pie; It's a walk in the park* 等等。

It's no picnic.	不好玩、不輕鬆
It's not my cup of tea.	非我所愛
It's a bargain.	很划算、合算
It's a deal = It's done	一言為定
It's a long lane that has no turning.	時來運轉
It's a long story.	說來話長
It's a lousy choice of words.	口不擇言出言不遜
It's a matter of degree.	程度問題
It's a problem of face.	面子問題
It's a tall order.	這事不容易辦
It's an ill wind that blows nobody any good.	邪風不帶好事來
It's dogged that does it.	有毅力者能成事
It's no use crying over spilt milk.	覆水難收
It's not only immoral; it's illegal.	不僅不道德還犯法
It's out of my line.	這我外行、我不懂
It's your turn.	輪到你了
I've got a problem of mine.	我有自己的事要管
Judge not, that you may not be judged.	不批評就不會受批
Just leave it.	算了，別管它了！
Just look at you.	瞧你那副德性
Just one thing	還有一個問題。
keep someone posted	隨時告知
Keep something for a rainy day.	未雨綢繆
Keep your eyes peeled.	小心、照子放亮點
keeping one's fingers crossed	祈禱好運
kick the bucket	翹辮子、死了

kidding around	兜圈子、裝蒜
Kill not the goose that lays the golden eggs.	勿殺雞取卵
Kill two birds with one stone.	一石二鳥
knit one's brows	皺眉深思
knock it off; cut it out; stop it	停、別這樣
Know your own faults before blaming others for theirs.	責人之前先責己
knowing (something) like the back of one's hand	對事瞭如指掌
Knowledge is power.	知識就是力量
Laugh and grow fat.	心寬則體胖
laugh one's head off	大笑、狂笑
Learn to walk before you run.[32]	由淺入深循序漸進
Least said, soonest mended	慎言可避禍
Leave it to me.	交給我來辦
Leave me alone.[33]	別管我；別惹我
Let bygones be bygones.	過去的就讓它過去
Let not the sun go down on your wrath.	勿留宿怨
let one's hair down	放輕鬆、隨和
Let sleeping dogs lie.	勿惹事生非
Let's have a round of applause.	鼓掌
Let's call it a day.	今天到此為止
Let's get it straight.	坦白說吧
Let's make a deal.	來談個條件吧

---

32 學跑之前先學走。

33 此語有雙重含意，其一有「別來煩我」的抗議意味，另一則有「讓我獨自靜一靜」的意思，視說話的語氣而定。

Let's take a vote.	我們表決一下吧
Liars should have good memories.[34]	說謊者要有好記性
Life is not all beer and skittles.	人生並非只是吃喝
Life is short and time is swift.	人生苦短光陰易逝
Life is sweet.	生命是美好的
like a bull in a china shop	情況失控
Like father, like son.	有其父必有其子
Like will to like.	物以類聚
lion's share	最大或最好的一份
Little by little and bit by bit.	積少成多
Little money, few friends.	錢少朋友少
Little pitchers have ears.	別讓小孩聽到
Live and learn = It is never too late to learn	活到老學到老
Live and let live.	自己活也讓別人活
Live not to eat, but eat to live.	活著不是為了吃，而吃是為了活著
Look before you leap.	三思後行
Look here = Listen, please	你聽我說
Lookers-on see most of the game.	旁觀者清
lose one's shirt	身無分文輸得精光
Love is blind.	愛是盲目的
Love me, love my family.	愛屋及烏
Love will find a way.	真情所至金石為開
made a slip of tongue.	說溜了嘴
make a mountain out of a molehill	小題大作

---

34 免得穿梆也。

Make haste slowly.	欲速則不達
Make hay while the sun shines.	把握良機
making the fur fly	引起騷動
Man proposes, God disposes.	謀事在人成事在天
manage to keep one's head above water	餓不死、過得去
Many hands make light work.	人多好辦事
Marriage is a lottery.	婚姻靠運氣
Marriages are made in heaven.	姻緣天註定
Men are blind in their own cause.	當局者迷
Men are known by the company they keep.	觀其友而知其人
Might is right.	強權即公理
Mind your own business.	少管閒事
Misfortunes never come singly.	禍不單行
Moderation in all things.	凡事中庸而行
Money begets money.	財能生財
Money doesn't grow on trees.	錢不是樹上長的
Money talks.	有錢的最大
More haste, less speed.	欲速則不達
More than enough is too much.	凡事宜適可而止
Murder will out.	要人不知除非莫為
my cup of tea	我最喜愛（熟）的事
My feet are killing me.	我的腳痛死了
My pleasure = My honor	樂意之至！
my treat	我請客
nailing somebody	盯牢某人
Name it.	你（要什麼就）說吧

Necessity is the mother of invention.	需要是發明之母
Necessity knows no law.	急需之下難雇法律
need an extra pair of hands	需要幫手
Never ask pardon before you are accused.	不要不打自招
Never better	再好不過了！
Never do things by halves.	不可半途而廢
Never judge by appearances.	不可以貌取人
Never make threats you cannot carry out.	莫虛張聲勢
Never put off till tomorrow what may be done today.	今日事，今日畢
Never say die.	永不氣餒
No chance	沒辦法，行不通
No comment	無可奉告，沒意見
No Credit, Cash Only	現金交易恕不　欠
No cross, no crown.	不吃苦焉得福
No dice	徒然無功、不行
No gain without pain.	天下事無不勞而獲
No kidding	不是開玩笑！
No man can serve two masters.	一僕難侍二主
No man is an island.	人不可離群索居
No man is content with his lot.	人皆難知足
No man is infallible.	天下無完人
No news is good news.	沒消息就是好消息
No pains, no gains	不勞即無獲
No point = No use	不管用
No rule without an exception.	凡事都有例外

No sweat	沒問題，不麻煩
No sweet without some sweat.	有捨才有得
No way	不行！不可以！
None of your business	少管閒事
Not necessarily = Not always	不盡然
Not necessary	不必要。
Not precisely	不盡然
Not that I know	這我就不知道了
Nothing going	不行，沒啥動靜
Nothing is as good as it seems beforehand.	世事不如預料的好
Nothing serious	沒啥嚴重
Nothing venture, nothing gain	不入虎穴焉得虎子
Nothing works	真是一籌莫展！
Now, you're talking.	這才像話。
Of two evils choose the lesser.	兩害相權取其輕
off the cob	舊式的、鄉野的
Oh yeah?!	真的嗎？是哦
on a diet	正在節食中
on one's toes	保持警覺
on the button	正好
On the double	快一點
on the fritz	不能用、壞了
on the go	忙個不停
on the heels	緊追
on the house	免費，店家請客
on the phone	正在聽電話

on top of the world	得意洋洋興高采烈
Once bitten, twice shy.	一朝被蛇咬，三年怕井繩
One cannot put back the clock.	時光不倒流
One day you'll make it.	有一天你會成功的
one G (Grand)	一千元
One good turn deserves another.	以德報德；以恩報恩
One is never too old to learn.	活到老，學到老
One lie makes many.	說一謊需百謊圓
One man's meat is another man's poison.	人各有所好
One swallow does not make a summer.	獨燕不成夏；一葉豈可知秋
Only the wearer knows where the shoe pinches.	局內人方知其苦
Opportunity seldom knocks twice.	機會難再逢
Or else what	不然你要怎樣
out of breath	喘不過氣
Out of sight, out of mind.	久別情疏；眼不見心不煩
out of sorts	惱怒
out of the blue	晴天霹靂
out of the frying pan into the fire	剛出油鍋又上刀山
over the hill	已過黃金時期
Paddle your own canoe.	自力更生
parachute candidate	空降候選人[35]
passing the buck	推諉責任
Patience is a virtue.	忍耐是美德
Pay somebody back in his own coin.	以其人之道還諸其人
pebble on the beach	芸芸眾生中的一個

---

[35] 外來候選人（在非居住地競選者）。

Period = That's it = That's final	就這樣了
picking someone off	射殺某人
pie in the sky	畫餅、渺茫的事
pin something on somebody	歸咎於某人
Play it by ear.	見機行事
Pleasant hours fly fast.	歡樂時光總易逝
Poverty is the mother of crime.	貧窮為罪惡之母
Practice makes perfect.	熟能生巧
Prevention is better than cure.	預防勝於治療
Pride goes before fall.	驕兵必敗
pull strings	拉關係
Put all one's eggs in one basket.	孤注一擲
put one's foot into one's mouth.	說錯話、弄糟
put one's foot down	堅拒
Put some beef into it.	加把勁
Put someone in his place.	挫其銳氣
Put your cards on the table.	坦白說吧
putting one on to	要某人留意某事
Quite so	是啊、可不是嗎
rack one's brains	絞盡腦汁
raining cats and dogs	傾盆大雨
raise the roof	大聲喧嘩
ready money	現款
Rome was not built in a day.	羅馬非一天造成的
sack time = to sack out	睡覺時間
save one's breath	勿白費口舌

Say it with flowers.	說些好話吧
Saying is one thing and doing is another.	說是一回事，做又是一回事
Says you.	胡扯
Searching for a needle in a haystack.	大海撈針
Second thoughts are best.	退一步想最穩當
See I told you so.	你總算相信了吧 我不是早跟你說過
Seeing is believing.	眼見為真
Self-praise is no recommendation.	自己說好不算好
setting someone up[36]	設計某人
She asked for it.	她活該！
She is always nagging.	她總是嘮叨不停
Silence gives consent.	沉默表示同意
Silence is golden.	沉默是金
Sing the same song.	志同道合
skeleton in the closet	家醜
sleep like a log	睡得很熟
Slow and steady wins the race.	穩紮穩打必致勝
smell a rat	覺得可疑
smoothing out	大事化小
So far so good	到目前大致上還好
so help me God.	我對天發誓
So that's how it's done.	原來是這麼回事
So what	是又怎樣？
Some other time	改天吧。

---

36 此語有雙重含意，其一有「設計陷害」之意，另一則有「玉成、撮合」的味道。

Some people cannot see the wood for the trees.	捨本逐末
Spare me.	饒了我吧！
Spare the rod and spoil the child.	不打不成器
Speak for yourself.[37]	替你自己講講話吧
stacking the deck	設局行騙
Start off with a bang and end with a whimper.	虎頭蛇尾
Stay put.	稍安勿躁，別亂跑
Steak my foot[38]	什麼鬼牛排
Steal the whole show.	搶盡風頭
step into the breach	填補空缺
Still waters run deep.	水深流靜；大智若愚
Stop bothering me.	別煩我
Strike while the iron is hot.	打鐵趁熱
Take a break.	休息一下吧！
Take a deep breath.	深呼吸一下
Take a rain check.	改期
take a shine to…	愛上
Take care of the check.	付帳
Take it easy.	別太衝動、慢慢來
Take it or leave it.	要不要隨你
Take my word for it.	相信我
take someone to the cleaners	詐人錢財
take someone's breath (away)	使人驚訝（或驚喜）

---

37 此語有雙重含意，其一有「那是你說的，我可沒說」的意味，另一則是「替自己講話」的意思，但通常以前者較為常用。

38 …my foot 有不滿之意，可譯成「……個鬼」，例如：Five-star hotel my foot 可譯「五星級飯店個鬼」。

take something up with someone	向某人提出某事
Take the rough with the smooth.	逆來順受
Take things as they come.	隨遇而安
Take your time	慢慢來，不急
taking leave of one's senses	發瘋
Talk of the devil and he's sure to appear.	說鬼鬼到
talk one's ear off	喋喋不休
talk through one's hat	瞎說
talk turkey	說正經的
Tall trees catch much wind.	樹大招風
That I can't say.	這我不敢肯定
That is so = So that is	原來如此
That takes time.	這要花時間的
That's great! That's just great!³⁹	真棒；這下可好
That's swell.	好極了、漂亮極了
That'll do.	這就行了
That's a bargain.	真划算
That's it.	這就對了！
That's more like it.	這還差不多。
That's more than I can say.	恕我無可奉告
That's my line.	那是該我說的
That's news to me.	真新鮮、我沒聽說
That's not fair.	差勁、不公平
That's not for you to say.	這不是你該說的

---

39 此語有正反兩用，其一是一般的「真好、真棒」之意，另一則有「這下不妙」的味道，要依說話
時的情境而定。

That's the ticket.	正符所需
the apple of one's eye	掌上明珠
The apples on the other side of the wall are the sweetest.	別人的東西總比自己的好
The bait hides the hook	口蜜腹劍
The bait hides the hook.	餌中藏鈎
The beaten road is the safest.	人多的路最安全
The best fish swims in the bottom.	好魚遊溪底
The best mirror is an old friend.	老友是最好的鏡子
The best of friends must part.	友聚必有散
The biter is sometimes bitten.	捕蛇難免被咬
The bull must be taken by the horns.	捉牛須先捉牛角；抓准竅門
The case is over.	別再提了
The cat is out of the bag.	不小心洩密
The child is father of the man.	三歲看老由小見大
The course of true love never did run mooth	好事多磨
The course of true love never did run smooth.	愛情之路多坎坷
The darkest hour is that before the dawn.	黎明前是最黑暗的
The devil can cite Scripture for his purpose.	魔鬼也會引用聖經
The devil finds work for idle hands to do	閒人心中易生邪
The early bird catches the worm.	早起的鳥有蟲吃
The end justifies the means.	為達目地不擇手段
The exception proves the rule.	例外因規則而存在
The fairest rose is at last withered	好花不常開
The first blow is half the battle.	先下手為強
The gods send nuts to those who have no teeth.	事與願違造化弄人

The grapes are sour.	酸葡萄作用
The greatest talkers are the least doers.	多言者少做事
The hand that rocks the cradle rules the world.	推動搖籃的手可支配世界
The highest branch is not the safest roost.	高處非安
The last straw breaks the camel's back.	凡事有個極限
The longest day must have an end.	長日漫漫終須盡
The love of money is the root of all evil.	貪財是萬惡之源
The mills of God grind slowly.	天網恢恢疏而不漏
The more you have, the more you want.	擁有越多求得越多
The pen is mightier than the sword.	文勝於武
The pot calls the kettle black.	五十步笑百步
The sale is on.	又在大減價了
The spirit is willing but the flesh is weak.	心有餘而力不足
The tailor makes the man.	人靠衣裝佛靠金裝
the third degree	拷問
The tongue is not steel, yet it cuts.	舌頭雖軟但能傷人
The truth will out.	真相終將大白
The world is much the same everywhere.	天下烏鴉一般黑
There are plenty of fish in the sea.	天涯何處無芳草
There are tricks in every trade.	每一行皆有其竅門
There are two sides to every question.	事情不只一面
There is a black sheep in every flock.	群中總有害群之馬
There is a witness everywhere.	要人不知除非莫為
There is honour among thieves.	盜亦有道
There is no disputing about tastes.	人各有所好
There is no rose without a thorn.	玫瑰皆有刺

There is no royal road to learning.	求學無捷徑
There is no satiety in study.	學無止境
There is no smoke without fire.[40]	煙因火起
There is nothing new under the sun.	太陽底下無新事
There is nothing permanent except change.	世事無常
There is nothing that costs less than civility.	謙恭價最廉；禮多人不怪
There is safety in numbers.	人多則無患
There you go again.	又來了
There's a black sheep in every flock.	害群之馬
There's no place like home.	在家千日好
They brag most who can do least.	吹噓最多的人能做到的事最少
Things are seldom what they seem.	事物極少如其外表
Think not on what you lack as much as on what you have.[41]	知足常樂
thinking the world of somebody	很喜歡某人
Those who live in glass houses should not throw stones.	投鼠忌器
Those whom the gods love die young.	好人不長壽
Throw out a minnow to catch a whale.	以小博大
Time and tide wait for no man.	歲月不饒人
Time flies.	時光飛逝
Time is money.	時間就是金錢
Time is the great healer.	時間是好的治療者

40 有「無風不起浪」之意。
41 少想你所缺乏的，多想你所有的。

Times change.	時代在變
Time's up.	時間到！
to be all for it	完全贊同
to be at one's throat	攻擊某人
to be on the needle	上了毒癮
to be pink-slipped	被解雇
to be spoiling for a fight	一心想打一場
to buy = to accept or believe	相信
To err is human.	人孰無過
to go far	成功
to go for	接受、贊許、爭取
to haul up short	突然停下
to hold out	隱藏
to hold up	搶劫；暫避風頭
to lay out	呈現
to make do	勉強應付
to pop the question	求婚
to pull off	完成
to put stock in	相信
to stand pat	堅守立場、不換牌
to take (get) forty winks	打盹兒
to unwind	輕鬆一下
to write home about	值得大書特書
Tomorrow is another day.	明天又是新的開始
Too many cooks spoil the broth.	人多壞事
tough nut to crack	難以捉摸

True gold fears not the fire.	真金不怕火
turn a new leaf	改過自新
Turn a stumbling block into a stepping stone	化絆腳石為墊腳石
twisting one's arm = to compel	強迫某人
two bits	兩毛五分錢
Two blacks do not make a white.[42]	兩黑不能成一白
Two dogs fight for a bone, and a third runs away with it.	鷸蚌相爭漁翁得利
Two halves make a whole.	兩個一半成為整個
Two heads are better than one.	集思廣益
Two of a trade never agree.	同行相嫉
Two wrongs do not make a right.	積非不能成是
under the weather	生病；不舒服
United we stand, divided we fall.	合則存，分則廢
up to one's ear	忙得不可開交
Variety is the spice of life.	變化是生活的情趣
Virtue is its own reward.	為善最樂
Wake not a sleeping lion.	別自找麻煩
Walls have ears.	隔牆有耳
Waste not, want not.	不浪費，不愁缺
waste one's breath	白費口舌
Water far off will not quench a fire near at hand.	遠水救不了近火
We can't take any chances.	千萬別出錯
We have a deal.	我們講好在先
Well begun is half done.	好的開始是成功的一半

---

42 有「兩非不能成一是」之意。

We'll say = We'll see	到時再說吧
Well, I never	啊，真想不到！
We're even now.	這下我們扯平了。
We're here on business.	我們是來談正事的
What a coincidence.	可真巧！
What a line.	多麼中聽的話！
What a pity = It's a pity = It's too bad	多可憐！真遺憾！
What did you say = I beg your pardon	請再說一遍。
What do you say?	你怎麼說？
What does that have to do with the price of tea in China?[43]	八竿子打不著
What is one man's meat is another man's poison.	人各有所好
What line is yours?	你是搞那一行的
What must be must be.	事實就是事實
What's the story here?	怎麼回事
Whatever you say = You are the boss	悉聽尊便！
What's cooking?	有什麼大消息
What's done cannot be undone.	覆水難收
What's going on (what's up? what's it all about)?	怎麼回事？
What's on your mind.	你有什麼打算？
What's the difference?	這有啥關係？
When the cat is away, the mice will play.	貓不在老鼠就作怪
When the chips are down.	緊要關頭
Where there's a will there's a way.	有志者事竟成

Where was I?	說到哪裡了
Where's the John?	廁所在哪裡？
While there is life there is hope.[44]	留得青山在，不怕沒柴燒
Whom are you kidding?	你在開啥玩笑？
Who keeps company with the wolf will learn to howl.	近朱者赤近墨者黑
Who knows = God only knows	天曉得！
Why don't you have a go in business?	你不妨做做生意吧？
Will you behave or not?	你守不守規矩？
Wise men learn by other men's mistakes; fools by their own.	智者學自他人錯誤，愚者則必自蹈錯誤
Words cut more than swords.	舌劍利於刀劍
Work while you work, play while you play.	工作時工作，遊戲時遊戲
working over somebody	修理某人
You are calling the shots (tune).	由你指揮、支配。
You are seeing things.	你見鬼（胡思亂想）
You bet.	當然！
You can't have your cake and eat it, too.	你不能兩面得利
You can't teach an old dog new tricks.	老狗學不會新把戲
You cannot burn the candle at both ends.	不要蠟燭兩頭燒
You cannot catch old birds with chaff.[45]	老手難欺
You cannot have it both ways.	你不可能兩面討好
You cannot make an omelet without breaking eggs.	要煎蛋就得先把蛋打破

---

44 只要活著就有希望。

45 別想用穀殼捕到老鳥。

You cannot make bricks without straw.	巧婦難為無米炊
You can't be serious.	你不會是認真的吧？
You do all the talking.	由你出面交涉
You don't look your age.	你看來沒那麼老
You don't say so.	此話當真？
You got me.	你把我難住了
You have my blessing.	我祝福你
You know something?	你可知道？
You may know by a handful the whole sack.[46]	見微知著
You never know what you can do till you try.	試了才知道
You never know.	這可說不定
You've got me.	你可把我問住了
You'll be sorry for this.	你會後悔的！
You'll pay for it.	你會付出代價的
You're all wet.	你完全誤會了
You're going to get it.	你要挨打了 會有報應的
You're not just saying.	你當真嗎？
You're so fussy.	你真是難搞
You're telling me.	這還用你說

46 見一把就知整袋也。

第十四章
中文成語及俗常用詞英譯

本章提綱

　　長期的中西交流，也讓中文成語有了英譯的必要，但是中文成語的英譯比較少有約定俗成者，其中還有些是中英成語的互相套用，一部分固然極為貼切，但多數還是無法天衣無縫；還有，還有一些源自英文的中譯用辭，如「分期付款、泡沫經濟、知識經濟、自然保護區」等等，我們早已耳熟能詳，但是對其原文卻不甚熟悉；另外，一些本土發展出來的名詞如「粉領族、檳榔西施、一國兩制、公正公平公開」等等，也因國際化的關係而廣為人知，但中文人士卻仍對其英文譯名了無所聞。本書收集了600餘項類此種種的詞，加以細閱修訂之後列於本章，給翻譯工作者帶來一些方便。

中文	英譯
寸陰寸金	An inch of time is an inch of gold. Time is money.
一切皆空	All is vanity.
一心一意	with all one's heart
一毛不拔	as close as a clam
一丘之貉	birds of a feather
一帆風順	smooth sailing
一年之計在於春， 一日之計在於晨	Plan your year in spring and your day at dawn.
一死百了	Death pays all scores.

一見鍾情	fall in love at the first sight
一言以蔽之	in a nutchell; to make along story short
言出必行	A promise is a promise. A real man never goes back on his words.
一言為定	That's a deal.
一知半解	half knowledge
一笑置之	laugh off
一國兩制	one country, two systems
一貧如洗	as poor as a church mouse
一報還一報	tit for tit; an eye for an eye, a tooth for a tooth
一絲不掛	in one's birthday suit; not a stitch on
一視同仁	treat all men alike
一意孤行	have one's own way
一模一樣	as like as two peas
一線員工	worker at the production line
一舉兩得	kill two birds with one stone
一籌莫展	at one's wits' end
九牛一毛	a drop in the bucket
九死一生	have a narrow escape
二胎貸款	re-lending; subloan
人口負增長	negative population growth
人山人海	a sea of faces
人才流失	brain drain
人不可貌相	Appearances are often deceptive. Men are not to be judged by their appearance
人生如夢	life is but a dream

人生自古誰無死	Man is mortal.
人各有偶	Every Jadk has his Jill
人地相宜	the right man in the right place.
人行天橋	foot bridge
人定勝天	Man can conquer Nature
人海浮沈	ups and downs
人海戰術	huge-crowd strategy
人孰無過	to err is human
人情債	debt of gratitude
人笨埋怨刀鈍	a bad workman quarrels with his tools
人間地獄	a hell of a life
人際交往	human communication
人機互動	human-computer interaction
人類免疫缺陷病毒	Human Immunodeficiency Virus (HIV)
入不敷出	unable to make both ends meet
十人十心	many men, many minds
十有九次	nine cases out of ten, nine times out of ten
三十而立	A man should be independent at the age of thirty.
三三兩兩	by twos and threes
三心兩意	neither off nor on
三句不離本行	talk shop
三更燈火五更雞	burn the midnight oil
三角戀愛	love triangle
三思而行	look before you leap
三番五次	over and over again
三維動畫	three-dimensional (3D) animation

三維電影	three-dimensional (3D) movie
下游行業	downstream industry
上網	to get on the Internet
千方百計	leave no stone unturned
口是心非	play a double game
口惠而實不至	give lip service
土地沙漠化	desertification of land; desert encroachment
夕陽產業	sunset industry
大事化小小事化了	Make an error sound less serious, then reduce it to nil
大開眼界	open one's eyes; broaden one's horizon; be an eye-opener
大飽眼福	feast one's eye on
子肖其父	like father, like son
小時正經老來怪	young saints, old devils
小康	a comfortable level of living; a better-off life; moderate prosperity
小康之家	well-off family; comfortably-off family
小題大作	Make a mountain out of a molehill.
山珍海味	dainties of every kind
山窮水盡	at one's wits' end
己所不欲勿施於人	Do not do to others what you do not want others to do to you.
不毛之地	barren land
不可再生資源	non-renewable resources
不打不成器	spare the rod and spoil the child
不打不相識	No discord, no concord

不正之風	bad (harmful) practice; unhealthy tendency
不共戴天之仇	mortal or sworn enemy
不名一文	dead broke
不合時宜	behind the times
不告而別	take French leave
不良貸款	non-performing loan
不夜城	sleepless city, ever-bright city
不治之症	fatal disease
不知所措	at a loss
不省人事	unconscious
不倫不類	neither fish, flesh nor fowl
不速之客	unexpected visitor
不勝枚舉	too numerous to mention
不義之財	ill-gotten gains
不擇手段	by fair means or foul
中看未必中用	All that glitters is not gold.
中庸之道	golden mean
中飽私囊	feather one's nest
中輟生	dropouts
互動廣告	interactive advertisement
仁者不憂	A virtuous man is free from anxieties.
見仁見智	So many men, so many opinions
元宵節	Lantern Festival
內耗	in-fighting
公正公平公開	just, fair, and open
公益彩券	welfare lotteries

公費醫療	medical services at state expense
公開招標	public bidding
分內之事	one's bounden duty
分崩離析	to fall asunder
分期付款	installment payment
切入點	point of penetration; breakthrough point
化干戈為玉帛	to bury the tomahawk
化為烏有	to be burnt to ashes
匹夫之勇	brute courage / courage without discipline
反敗為勝	bring about a complete turnabout, pull out of the fire
反覆無常	to blow hot and cold / to play fast and loose
天下烏鴉一般黑	Crows are black all over the world.
天下無難事 只怕有心人	Nothing is difficult to a man who wills.
天之驕子	the child of fortune
天涯海角	the ends of the earth
天壤之別	It's all Lombard Street to a China orange
天網恢恢	Justice has long arms.
孔子面前賣文章	to teach one's grand-mother to suck eggs
少年老成	to have an old head on young shoulders
少壯不努力 老大徒傷悲	A lazy youth, a lousy age.
少說為妙	Least said soonest mended.
少說廢話	Less of your nonsense!
心不在焉	absence of mind
心有餘力不足	The spirit is willing but the flesh is weak.

心神不寧	to have a bee in one's bonnet
心理素質	psychological quality
心廣體胖	Laugh and grow fat.
戶口名簿	residence booklet
戶口管理制度	domicile system, residence registration system
戶主	head of household
手忙腳亂	to act with confusion
手段高明	to play one's cards well
支吾其詞	to hum and haw
文過飾非	to gloss over one's faults
文韜武略	military expertise; military strategy
日趨滅亡	to be on the highroad to ruin
比上不足，比下有餘	to fall short of the best, but be better than the worst
水中撈月	to fish in the air
水乳交融	to be hand and glove with each other/to be hand in glove with each other
水深火熱	in deep water
水落石出	Truth will come to light.
水墨畫	Chinese brush drawing; ink and wash painting
火上加油	to add fuel to the fire (= flame)
火中取栗	to pull the chestnut out of the fire
王儲；王太子	Crown Prince
世世代代	from generation to generation
主要市場	primary market
以人為本	people oriented; people foremost
以子之矛，攻子之盾	to turn a person's battery against himself

以小博大	to throw (out) a minnow to catch a whale
以己度人	to measure another's corn by one's own bushel to measure other people's corn by one's own bushel
以夷制夷	to play both ends anainst the middle
以身作則	to practise what one preaches
以其人之道，還治其人之身	to pay one (back) in one's won coin
以怨報德	to bitte the band that feeds one
以毒攻毒	to set a thief to catch a thief
以寡敵衆	to fight against (onlger) odds
以德報怨	to render good for evil ／ to return good for evil
付之一炬	to commit a thing to the flames
仔仔細細	at full length
代人受過	to be made the scapegoat for a person
代理職務	function in an acting capacity
出口傷人	to sepeak daggers
出口轉內銷	domestic sales of good orginally produced for exports
出言不遜	to use offensive language
出身行伍	to rise from the ranks
出身微賤	to be of mean birth (= of bumble origin, of obscure origin)
出風頭	show off; in the limelight
出爾反爾	to play fast and loose (with)
加工出口區	export processing zones
加班	work extra shifts
加密	encrypt

加權平均值	weighted average
包工包料	contract for labor and materials
半斤八兩	It is six of one and half-a-dozen of the other.
半信半疑	half in doubt
去者日以疏	Long absent, soon forgotten
古往今來	in all ages
司儀	master of ceremonies
四面八方	in all directions
四面楚歌	to have the world against one
海內皆兄弟	All are brothers withing the four seas.
外柔內剛	an iron hand in a velvet glove
失戀	be disappointed in love; be jilted
左右為難	to be in a dilemma
市場疲軟	sluggish market
市場導向	market-oriented
平平安安	in peace
平均主義	equalitarianism
平面設計師	graphic designer
必恭必敬	with all due submission
打破僵局	break the deadlock
打草驚蛇	to wake a sleeping dog (wolf)
打開天窗說亮話	to put all cards on the table
打落水狗	to hit a person when he's down (= who is down)
打錯算盤	to bring one's pigs to a pretty market
本末倒置	to put the cart before the horse
未觀其人，先觀其友	We judge people by their friends

正式照會	formal note
民族凝聚力	national cohesion
民進黨	Democratic Progressive Party
永續發展	sustainable development
生態農業	environmental-friendly agriculture
白手起家	starting from scratch
白馬王子	Prince Charming
白雪公主	Snow White
白璧微瑕	a fly in the ointment
目標管理	management by objectives
立體農業	three-dimensional agriculture
企業文化	corporate culture
全人教育	education for all-around development
全天候飛機	all-weatehr aircraft
全方位外交	multi-faceted diplomacy
全能冠軍	all-around winner
全球定位系統	global positioning system (GPS)
劣等品	shoddy goods; substandard goods; lemon
劣質商品賠償法	lemon law
吉祥物	mascot
同等學力	have the same educational level as the regular graduate
同鄉會	an association of fellow provincials/townsmen
吊銷執照	revoke license
各就位	On your marks!
各盡所能	let each person do his best; from each according to his ability

向錢看	mammonism, put money above all
因材施教	teach students according to their aptitude
地方保護主義	regional protectionism
地區差異	regional disparity
地球村	global village
地熱資源	geothermal resources
好事不出門 惡事傳千里	Good news never goes beyond the gate, while bad news spread far and wide
尖端產品	highly sophisticated products
年夜飯	family reunion dinner
有勇無謀	use brawn rather than brain
有情人終成眷屬	Jack shall have Jill, all shall be well
此地無銀三百兩	consciously protesting one's innocence
陳腔濫調	cut and dried
老字號	an old and famous shop or enterprise
自由港	free-trade port, free port
自作自受	stew in one's own juice
自助式售票	self-service ticketing
自助銀行	self-help bank
自我保護意識	self-protection awareness
自律機制	the self-discipline system
自動櫃員機	automatic teller machine (ATM)
自然保護區	natural reserve; nature preservation zone
自營	self-run
業內的龍頭老大	leading enterprise; flagship of the industry

低調	low keyed (a metaphor for taking a cautious and slow approach)
免頭款	zero down (payment)
利基	niche
助跑	approach run, run-up
君子之交淡如水	the friendship between gentlemen is as pure as crystal; a hedge between keeps friendship green
吸收遊資	absorb idle fund
快訊	news flash; flash
戒急用忍	overcome impetuosity and exercise patience
戒毒所	drug rehabilitation center
抗稅	refusal to pay taxes
技術密集產品	technology-intensive product
扭轉局面	reverse the tide, turn the table
把握大局	grasp the overall situation
每逢佳節倍思親	One misses his dear most on the festival occasions
沙塵暴	sand storm; dust storm
男權主義思想	male chauvinism
育成企業	incubated enterprises (incubator)
良性迴圈	virtuous circle
言情小說	romantic fiction; sentimental novel
走私貨、水貨	smuggled goods
防洪工程	flood-prevention project
來電顯示電話	telephone with caller ID
來電顯示話機	caller ID telephone
函授大學	correspondence university

受災地區	disaster-affected area
往事如風	What in past, is past
房地產管理	real estate management
房貸	mortgage loan
拉關係	try to curry favor with
拒載	refuse to take passengers
招生就業指導室	enrolment and vocation guidance office
抬槓	argue for the sake of arguing; bicker
放下身段	to get off one's high horse; throw off one's airs
武俠小說	tales of roving knights; martial arts novel; kung fu novel
泥菩薩	hardly able to save oneself, like a clay Buddha fording the river
沾光	benefit from one's association
法制國家	a state with an adequate legal system
法治國家	a country under the rule of law
泡沫經濟	bubble economy
物業管理	estate management, property management
物價局	Price Bureau
狗仔隊	paparazzi (those who hunt for the news of celebrities)
直播	live broadcast, live telecast
知識產權	intellectual property rights
知識經濟	knowledge economy, knowledge-base economy
空服員	air hostess; air stewardess; flight attendants
空頭支票	accommodation note, lip service
虎父無犬子	A wise goose never lays a tame egg
表演賽	demonstration match

近水樓臺先得月	A water-front pavilion gets the moonlight first; advantage of being in a favored position
近海漁業	offshore fishery
金本位	gold standard
金無足赤，人無完人	Gold can't be pure and man can't be perfect.
金融電子化	computerize financial services
信用危機	credit crisis
信用緊縮	credit crunch
信用額度	line of credit
保值儲蓄	inflation-proof bank savings
保健食品	health-care food
冒牌銷售[1]	copycat packaging
削減戰略核武會談	strategic arms reduction talks (START)
城市規劃	city's landscaping plan; urban planning
封殺出局	force out
封閉式基金	close-ended fund
屋頂花園	roof garden
待業	job-waiting
拜年	pay New Year call
拜把兄弟	sworn brothers
挖東補西	rob Peter to pay Paul
拼圖	jigsaw puzzle
政治迫害	political prosecution; witch hunt
染指	reap undeserved profit from; encroach upon
毒梟	drug trafficker

---

1 將劣品包裝成像名牌產品出售。

流動人口	transient population
流動圖書館	travelling library; bookmobile
洗錢	money laundering
活到老學到老	One is never too old to learn.
派出所	local police station
皈依三寶	become a Buddhist
看守政府；看守內閣；過渡政府	caretaker cabinet
科教興國	rejuvenate the nation via science and education
紅包	gift money in red envelope, bribery, kickback
美食節	gourmet festival
耐用消費品	durable consumer items (goods)
致命要害	Achilles' heel
風險投資	venture capital; risk investment
首航	maiden voyage (of an aircraft or ship)
各人自掃門前雪莫管他人瓦上霜	hoe one's own potatoes
兼差收入	income from moonlighting
准博士	all but dissertation (ABD) [2]
家族企業	family firm
恭喜發財	May you be prosperous! Wish you all the best!
息事寧人	pour oil on troubled waters
時不我予	Time and tide wait for no man
消費信貸	consumer credit services
涉外事務	foreign-related business

[2]　ABD 有時有眨意，謂久年拿不下博士學位者。

浮動工資	floating wages; fluctuating wages
特技演員	stunt man
留學諮詢	consulting on the study abroad
留職停薪	retain the job but suspend the salary
真空包裝	vacuum packing
祝人一路順風	speed somebody on their way; speed the parting guest
粉領族	pink-collar tribe (female office workers, secretaries, models, airline hostesses, etc)
航空母艦	aircraft carrier
記者席	press box
財產公證	notarize the properties
逃票	to sneak through without a ticket
逃票者	ticket evader
逃漏稅	tax evasion
追平	produce the equalizer
配股	allotment of shares
配套政策	supporting policies
高空彈跳	bungee, bungee jumping
高度自治	high degree of autonomy
高架公路	elevated highway; overhead road
高清晰度	high definition
高層全方位對話	high-level and all-directional dialogue
偽君子	hypocrite; a wolf in sheep's clothing
假公濟私	abuse of power for personal gains
剪綵	cut the ribbon
商品條碼	bar code

商檢局	Commodity Inspection Bureau
啦啦隊	cheering squad
唱高調	mouth high-sounding words
問訊處	information office; inquiry desk
啤酒肚	beer belly
售後服務	after-sale services
圈外人士	people out of the loop
國防動員	the mobilization for national defense
國際換日線	International Date Line (IDL)
國際慣例	international common practice
基因工程	genetic engineering
基因改造食品	genetically modified food
基層民主	democracy at the grassroots level
基層組織	organizations at the grass-roots level
婚外情	extramarital love
婚姻介紹所	matrimonial agency
專門術語	buzzword; jargon
專案支持	project support
專案預算	project budget
專賣店	exclusive agency; franchised store
強化訓練班	intensive training class
情有獨鐘	have special preference (favor) to …
控股公司	holding company
採取高姿態	show magnanimity
教學法	pedagogy; teaching method
殺手	sudden thrust of the mace--one's trump or master card

液晶顯示幕	liquid crystal display (LCD)
清倉、特賣	clearance sale; be on sale
涮羊肉	instant-boiled mutton
現代企業制度	modern enterprise system; modern corporate system
產業升級	upgrading of industies
產銷聯營	directly link production with marketing
票房	box office
笨鳥先飛	A slow sparrow should make an early start
統一市場	single market
脫口秀	talk show
莫失良機	make hay while the sun shines
貨到付款	cash on delivery
貧富懸殊	polarization of rich and poor
通貨緊縮	deflation (of currency)
連帶責任	joint liability
造假帳	falsified accounts
野生動物園	wildlife park; safari park
釣金龜	find a sugar daddy; be a mistress for a rich man;
閉門羹	given cold-shoulder
創業精神	pioneering spirit
勞動合同制	labor contract system
喜憂參半	mingled hope and fear
惡性通貨膨脹	hyperinflation
惡性循環	vicious circle
普選制	general election system
景泰藍	cloisonne

智囊團、思想庫	the brain trust；think tank
替身演員	stand-in
無中生有	make/create something out of nothing
無形資產	intangible assets
無為而治	govern by non-interference
無稽之談	a mare's nest
短期債務	floating debt
策略夥伴關係	strategic partnership
善後工作	round-off work; wind-up work
虛設行號	bogus company
評頭論足	nit-pick
買一送一	two-for-one offer, buy one get one free
超高速電腦	giant ultra-high-speed computer
跑龍套	utility man, play a bit role, general handyman
進口滲透	import penetration
進出口商會	chamber of import and export trade
進修班	class for further studies
開工典禮	commencement ceremony
開夜車	burn the midnight oil; work over night
開放式基金	open-ended fund
開後門	offer advantages to one's friends or relatives by under-hand means
開場報告	opening speech; opening report
集團婚禮	collective wedding ceremony
黃金時段	prime time
黑店	gangster inn

黑社會	Mafia-style organizations; gangland
傳銷	multi-level marketing
廉政建設	constructing a clean and honest administration
感謝款待的信	a bread and butter letter
愛滋病（後天免疫缺陷症候群）	AIDS (Acquired Immune Deficiency Syndrome)
搶跑	false start, beat the gun
搖錢樹	cash cow
搖頭丸	dancing outreach
敬業精神	professional dedication; professional ethics
新秀	up-and-coming star, rising star
新新人類	New Human Being；X Generation
新寵	new favorite
暗虧	hidden loss
暗戀	unrequited love; fall in love with someone secretly
滄海桑田	time brings great changes to the world
當成耳旁風	like water off a duck's back
當機	system halted
碰釘子	get snubbed
禁漁期	closed fishing seasons
經常性支出	running expenses
經常性貸款	commercial lending
經濟失調指數	misery index
經濟全球化	economic globalization; economic integration
經濟頭腦	commercially minded people; people with business sense

義氣之交	faithful pal; buddies; sworn friend
義務兵役	compulsory military service, conscription
義務教育	compulsory education
義演	benefit performmance
腳踏實地	be down-to-earth
腳踩兩隻船	sit on the fence
裙帶風	nepotism; petticoat influence
裙帶關係	networking through petticoat influence
補選	by-election
試用期	probationary period
資產保值增值	maintenance and appreciation of assets value
資源配置	the distribution (allocation) of resources
跨世紀工程	a trans-century project
路邊攤	sidewalk snack booth; large stall
跳蚤市場	flea market
農村剩餘勞動力	surplus rural labor
檳榔西施	betelnut girl / betelnut beauty
逼上梁山	Be driven to drastic alternatives
過度開墾	excess reclamation
過猶不及	going beyond is as wrong as falling short
過路費	road toll
電子商務認證	e-business certification
零配件	spare and accessory parts
預售屋	forward delivery housing
嘉賓	distinguished guest, honored guest
圖利他人	bend the law for the benefit of relatives or friends

奪金有望者	a gold medal hopeful
實話實說	speak the plain truth; call a spade a spade
實體經濟	the real economy
對…毫無顧忌	make no bones about
對外招商	attract foreign investment
敲竹槓	make somebody pay through the nose; rob by a trick
滿意度	degree of satisfaction
滲透、顛覆和分裂活動	infiltrative, subversive and splittist activities
狂牛症	mad cow disease; bovine spongiform enceohalopathy
睽度情勢	size up the situation
磁浮列車	Maglev train (magnetically levitated train)
有競爭力的產品	competitive products
綜合國力	comprehensive national strength
綠化	afforestation
綠地覆蓋率	forest coverage rate
綠色食品	green food
緊追	cling to, shadow, thunder on one's trail
緊箍咒	inhibiting magic phrase
網上交易平臺	online trading platform
網路出版	online publishing
網路經濟	cybereconomy
網路管理員	network administrator
網戀	online love affair
蒙古大夫	quack
蜜月結婚	have a honeymoon trip
豪賭	unrestrained gambling

遠程發展目標	long-term development targets
遠距會議	teleconference
遠端學習	distance learning
寬限期	grace period
寬頻網	broadband networks
寫真集	photo album
廣告代言人	image representative of a product or a brand
廣域網	wide area network (WAN)
彈性工資	flexible pay
彈性外交	elastic diplomacy
緝毒隊	narcotics squad
緣分	chemistry, predestination, be preordained to come together
論工計酬	achievements-related wages; wages based on benefits
論文答辯	oral defense
適者生存	survival of the fittest
養老金	pension
鬧情緒	be disgruntled; be in a fit of pique
學而優則仕	he who excels in study can follow an official career
學務處	students' affairs division
機場建設費	airport construction fee
激烈競爭	cut-throat competition
燒錄機	CD writer; disc-carving machine
積壓產品	overstocked commodities (inventories)
融資管道	financing channels

遵紀守法廉潔奉公	observe the relevant code of conduct and the law and honestly perform one's official duties
選舉人制	electoral system
選舉人票	electoral vote
選舉和被選舉權	the right to vote and the right to be elected
險勝	cliff-hanging win, narrow victory, nose out
駭客	hacker
優化組合	optimization grouping; optional regrouping
優化結構	optimize structure
壓軸戲	grand finale; last and best item on a theatrical program
環太平洋地區	Pacific Rim
績優股	blue chip
總統選舉團（由各州推選組成）	electoral college
聯合兼併	conglomeration and merger of enterprises
聯合國會費	the UN membership dues (fee)
舉報電話	informants' hot-line telephone
虧損企業	enterprises running in the red/under deficit
輿論監督	supervision by public opinion
輿論導向	direction of public opinion
隱形收入	invisible income; off-payroll income; side money
擺架子、擺譜兒	put on airs; show off; keep up appearances
斷交信	Dear John letter (from woman to man)
獵頭公司	head-hunting company
禮尚往來	Courtesy calls for reciprocity
繞圈子	beat around the bush

覆蓋率	coverage rate
轉業服務	re-employment service
醫療保險	medical insurance
雙刃劍	double-edged sword
藥物檢查	dope control, drug testing
證券交易所	stock exchange; security exchange
辭舊迎新	bid farewell to the old and usher in the new
邊際報酬	marginal return
關稅壁壘	customs barrier; tariff wall
難得糊塗	Where ignorance is bliss, it's folly to be wise
騙稅	tax fraud
籌備委員會	preparatory committee
鐵飯碗	job security
顧問公司	consultanting company
囊括	complete a sweep
攤牌	put/lay one's card on the table
變相漲價	disguised inflation

參考書目

1. Lin, Yutang, "Famous Chinese Short Stories," J. Day Co., 1952。（林語堂：《英譯重編傳奇小說》）

2. Roberts, Jane, "Seth Speaks: The Eternal Validity of the Soul," Reprint Edition, New World Library, June 1994.

3. 百度文庫，《六級長難句分析》，http://wenku.baidu.com/view/78cb49eae009581b6bd9eb88.html, 2011/8/15.

4. 余光中《創作與翻譯》演講詞，中國中央電視臺，http://www.cctv.com/special/131/61/73133.html，2006/9/15。

5. 紀曉嵐〔清〕（1980），《閱微草堂筆記》，台北：文光圖書公司。

6. 胡英音、王育盛合譯（1991），《時空之外》，台北：法爾出版社。（譯自 Seth Speaks: The Eternal Validity of the Soul）

7. 張振玉（1993），《翻譯散論》，東大。

8. 張振玉（1996），《英文翻譯與寫作》，華南。

9. 張振玉（2004），《實用漢英英漢翻譯基礎》，久鼎。

10. 張振玉（2005），《漢文英譯示例》，久鼎。

11. 梁實秋（2002），《雅舍精品》，台北：九歌出版社。

12. 黃文範（1989），《翻譯新語》，東大。

13. 黃文範（1993），《翻譯偶語》，東大。

14. 葉乃嘉（2002），《商用英文的溝通藝術》，文京。

15. 葉乃嘉（2005），《英文書信與履歷的藝術》，台北：五南。

16. 葉乃嘉（2009），《中英論文寫作綱要與體例》，南京大學。

17. 葉乃嘉（2009），《我的第一本應用英文書》，南京大學。

18. 劉宓慶（1993），《當代翻譯理論》，書林。

19. 劉宓慶（1995），《翻譯美學導論》，書林。

20. 劉宓慶（2000），《翻譯與語言哲學》，書林。

21. 魯迅（1930），〈且介亭雜文二集〉，《文學》月刊第五卷第一號。

22. 嚴復〔清〕（1995），《天演論》。上海：古籍出版社。

國家圖書館出版品預行編目資料

英漢雙向翻譯實務與習作：中英文讀、寫、
譯的新視野／葉乃嘉著. — 二版. — 臺北
市：五南，2012.10
　　　　面；　　公分.--（研究方法系列）
　　參考書目：面　含索引
　　ISBN 978-957-11-6747-3（平裝）
　1.翻譯

811.7　　　　　　　　　　101013939

1XX7　　研究與方法系列

英漢雙向翻譯實務與習作
中英文讀、寫、譯的新視野

作　　者 ― 葉乃嘉(323.2)

發 行 人 ― 楊榮川

總 編 輯 ― 王翠華

主　　編 ― 黃惠娟

責任編輯 ― 胡天如

出 版 者 ― 五南圖書出版股份有限公司

地　　址：106台北市大安區和平東路二段339號4樓

電　　話：(02)2705-5066　　傳　　真：(02)2706-6100

網　　址：http://www.wunan.com.tw

電子郵件：wunan@wunan.com.tw

劃撥帳號：01068953

戶　　名：五南圖書出版股份有限公司

台中市駐區辦公室/台中市中區中山路6號

電　　話：(04)2223-0891　　傳　　真：(04)2223-3549

高雄市駐區辦公室/高雄市新興區中山一路290號

電　　話：(07)2358-702　　傳　　真：(07)2350-236

法律顧問　元貞聯合法律事務所　張澤平律師

出版日期　2012年10月二版一刷

定　　價　新臺幣380元